"Where did you come up with the name for your business?"

Patrick was watching Lauren with genuine interest in his eyes.

"My mom was addicted to romance."

"What do you mean?" he asked. "She read lots of romance novels?"

If only. "No, I mean she loved to fall in love. When it was over, her first response was to start over someplace new."

"You could never settle down because you knew it wouldn't last."

"Yes." Lauren's eyes welled up. "When I was ten, our backyard butted up against a pasture with a couple of horses and a few cows grazing. To me, a farm sounded like heaven. To settle down in one place and stay there forever. So I made up stories about Now and Forever Farm, where I lived happily-ever-after."

She looked at him then, into deep blue eyes that seemed to see right into her...to understand her longing for a place to belong.

Dear Reader,

I'm excited to bring you the newest book in the Northern Lights series. This one involves a treasure hunt, goats and, of course, romance. I had a lot of fun writing it. What a great excuse to learn more about Alaskan history and to find cute goat photos on the internet. I even visited a goat yoga class!

One of the scenes in the book is based on an anecdote my father told me from when he was a boy. I don't want to give too much away, but when you get to that part, know that the car involved in the original incident was a ragtop Model T Ford.

I hope you enjoy the story. If you've read other books from the series, you might recognize a few characters that pop up. If you haven't, don't worry; each book stands alone.

I love to connect with readers. You can find my email, Facebook and Twitter contacts at bethcarpenterbooks.Blogspot.com. You can sign up for my newsletter there, too.

Happy reading!

Beth Carpenter

HEARTWARMING

Alaskan Dreams

—

Beth Carpenter

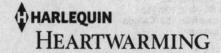

HARLEQUIN
HEARTWARMING

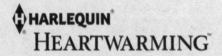

HARLEQUIN®
HEARTWARMING™

ISBN-13: 978-1-335-88972-0

Recycling programs
for this product may
not exist in your area.

Alaskan Dreams

For questions and comments about the quality of this book,
please contact us at CustomerService@Harlequin.com.

Harlequin Enterprises ULC
22 Adelaide St. West, 40th Floor
Toronto, Ontario M5H 4E3, Canada
www.Harlequin.com

Printed in U.S.A.

Beth Carpenter is thankful for good books, a good dog, a good man and a dream job creating happily-ever-afters. She and her husband now split their time between Alaska and Arizona, where she occasionally encounters a moose in the yard or a scorpion in the basement. She prefers the moose.

Books by Beth Carpenter

Harlequin Heartwarming

A Northern Lights Novel

The Alaskan Catch
A Gift for Santa
Alaskan Hideaway
An Alaskan Proposal
Sweet Home Alaska

Visit the Author Profile page at Harlequin.com.

In memory of my Dad, a voracious reader.

Thanks, Dad, for the stories, and for everything you taught me, by word and by example.

Also thanks to my agent, Barbara Rosenberg, and to my editor, Kathryn Lye, for their ideas, encouragement and support. And to all those people who take the time to post articles and share their knowledge and expertise about history, goats and all things Alaska.

CHAPTER ONE

THE INVENTOR OF the showerhead deserved a Nobel Prize. At least that was Lauren's opinion, as the muscle-melting, soul-cleansing water ran over her stiff shoulders and down her back, washing away the physical and emotional grime she'd collected. After six days on the road, sleeping in an ancient truck camper each night, a hot shower with adequate water pressure was bliss. Even if it was in a cracked concrete shower stall in the middle of a crowded campground.

Was that sound a bleat? Lauren leaned out from under the showerhead to listen. People and goats could sound remarkably alike, but these shouts and squeals clearly came from the human kids playing kickball outside. Besides, she'd double-checked the latch on the stock trailer before she came to the bathhouse. She squeezed out a dab of shampoo.

From the tree outside the bathhouse window, a chickadee serenaded her with a series of two-tone whistles. Lauren worked lather through her long hair. She wanted to look her best when she met Bonnie in person tomorrow. After all, tomorrow was the first day of her new life. The life she'd always wanted.

A sudden shriek pierced the happy sounds, followed by excited calling and nervous laughter. Lauren stopped moving and listened, trying to convince herself she'd imagined the goatlike quality of that last bellow. After all, her three goats were busy munching alfalfa. She'd already cleaned their soiled straw, taken them for a walk and let them browse on the edge of the forest. There was no reason they would have left their dinner to tramp through the campground, even if the gate wasn't latched, which it absolutely was.

A bleat and a fit of giggles convinced her. Lauren turned off the water, wrapped a towel around herself and peeked out the bathhouse door. Sure enough, a trio of black-and-white goats gamboled across the field like fuzzy pied pipers, leading the cluster of children on a merry chase. One dad called for the kids to stop and approached the goats. They let him get within two yards before kicking up their heels and scrambling out of reach.

Lauren pulled jeans over her still-damp legs, a sweatshirt over her head and thrust her feet into flip-flops. After a quick assessment of the area, she circled the field to try to head off the goats before they reached the edge of the woods.

They say you should never look a gift horse in the mouth, but maybe Lauren should have been a little more suspicious of a gift goat. She'd gone to buy the two Alpine dairy goats based on a local listing on the Goat People forum. Muffin and Biscotti were a little expensive, but they came from a well-respected line of dairy goats, so Lauren agreed to the price. When the owner had heard Lauren planned to start a new herd in Alaska, she'd offered to throw in Spritz for free. "She's a little older, but an excellent milker and she has some good years left in her." At the time, Lauren had been touched at the sweet gesture, but now she was beginning to wonder if generosity was the farmer's true motivation.

The first time she'd looked out the window of her camper to see the goats swiping the grapes she'd left on the picnic table, she thought she must have neglected to latch the gate. The second time, when Spritz showed up in the middle of a walk with Biscotti and Muffin, Lauren knew she'd latched it, but she hadn't bothered to fasten the safety hasp, and hadn't realized Spritz knew how to pull out a pin. Today, before she'd gone to the bathhouse, Lauren had latched the gate, sealed it with a cotter pin, and fastened the hasp that should have been impossible for anyone without opposable thumbs to operate. And yet here they were.

Once she'd positioned herself between the goats and the woods, Lauren approached them, slowly. Spritz spotted her and ambled in her direction. "That's a good girl," Lauren crooned. "Just come a little closer."

Spritz took another step toward her, a gleam in her eye. Lauren eased out a hand. The halter was almost within Lauren's reach but Spritz jerked back at the last second. Lauren dove toward her, caught her flip-flop on a rock, and landed face down on the grass. Spritz and the other goats pranced around her, their bleats sounding suspiciously like laughter.

"Miss, are those your goats?"

Lauren looked up to see the camp host staring down at her. He took off his trucker's cap, ran a hand through thinning gray hair and replaced the cap. Behind him, a crowd of children and several adults watched her. "Yes, they are," she admitted.

"Well, they can't run loose. We have a strict leash policy. You'll need to put them away."

Did the man not see that was exactly what she was trying to do? "I'm sorry my goats disturbed you." Lauren climbed to her feet and dusted grass from her clothes, pretending she didn't notice Spritz edging closer from the corner of her eye.

"Rules are rules. If I overlook your goats, everyone will think their pets should run loose."

"And the campground would erupt into anarchy," Lauren said with a straight face. A couple of the campers hid smiles. Lauren edged closer to Spritz.

"I'm glad you understand." The camp host turned and walked away, but the rest of the group stayed and watched expectantly. Lauren should really ask for a discount on her camping fee for providing free entertainment.

She took one more step and lunged toward Spritz. Her fingers brushed the goat's halter but Spritz ducked under her arm and ran several steps away. The children laughed.

Lauren surveyed the other goats. Lauren could probably coax Muffin close enough to grab her halter but Spritz was the leader. While she was putting Muffin away in the trailer, Spritz might lead Biscotti on a tour of the county. Did they have counties in Yukon? Lauren shook her head. Focus.

"Maybe we could make a circle around the goats," one of the moms suggested.

"Yeah, let's try that," a teenager seconded.

Lauren was game. At her direction the group formed a large circle and gradually stepped toward the center until they were close enough together to join hands, trapping the three goats in the middle. Lauren had the children on either side of her close the circle while she stepped inside with the goats.

Spritz eyed her from across the circle. Lauren could almost see the wheels turning in her head, as she calculated the weakest point to make her escape. "Does anyone happen to have any fruit?" Lauren asked. "Spritz loves apples."

"I have some raisins," a boy offered, digging a handful from a none-too-clean pocket.

The goats probably wouldn't mind a little lint. "Thank you." Lauren spread raisins on her open left hand. "Look, Spritz. Raisins."

Spritz gave a disdainful glance, but Biscotti showed interest. The younger goat took a few steps toward Lauren and reached for her hand, which prompted Spritz to push her aside and claim the rest of the raisins herself. She lipped the treat from Lauren's hand and allowed Lauren to grasp her halter as though that had been her plan all along.

"I've got her now. Thanks so much, everyone." Lauren smiled at the boy with the raisins. "Especially you."

"Can I pet her?" The boy asked.

"Sure." Spritz stood calmly and allowed the children to stroke her face and neck while Lauren held her halter. The other goats followed her example and allowed the children to approach and pet them. After a few minutes, Lauren thanked everyone again and led Spritz toward her camp spot, the other two goats following docilely behind.

Lauren found the cotter pin—the one she'd used to latch the gate—lying in the dirt, the half-circle safety hasp pulled up and away from the pin. How did Spritz undo it with her mouth?

The goats returned to their trailer without any fuss. Lauren reached up to brush a wet strand of hair out of her face, only to discover sandy suds on her hand. Oh yeah, she'd been in the middle of shampooing her hair when this all started.

This time, Lauren latched the gate and locked it shut with her bicycle lock before she went to rinse the dirt and shampoo out of her hair. When she returned, the goats were still in the trailer, but several children had surrounded it and were pushing raisins between the slats. Lauren had read that raisins weren't good for dogs, but she'd never heard anything like that for goats. She'd have to ask the people on the forum. Anyway, it looked like the kids had only a couple of small boxes between them, so it should be okay. Besides, the goats were happy and the children were happy, so why break up a good thing?

Happiness. That's all Lauren was looking for, really. A place to settle down and be happy. A place in the country, with space and green and sky, making a living raising animals. It was her lifelong dream. And it was being made possible by a woman she'd never met.

Lauren checked her itinerary. She was fifty miles ahead of where she'd projected to be, which meant she should arrive at Bonnie's house tomorrow evening. Last time they'd talked was a week ago before she'd started driving. She took out her phone to update Bonnie on her progress, but she hesitated, hearing that little voice of doubt in her mind. The one that said this was too good to be true, that nobody really wanted a stranger living in her house and running goats on her farm for only a small share of the profits.

Sure, they felt like friends on the Goat People forum, and they'd talked on the phone a few times since Bonnie made her offer, but they were still strangers. What if she called and Bonnie explained it was all a misunderstanding, that she'd never intended for Lauren to drive to Alaska with a trailer full of goats?

No. Lauren took a breath and blew out the doubt. Bonnie had been perfectly clear. She was getting older and wanted someone in the house with her. She'd never sounded the least bit confused or undecided. The little voice was just one of Lauren's insecurities, leftover from her childhood spent as the third wheel her mother dragged from romance to romance. This was different. Bonnie wanted her there.

Lauren dialed. "Hi, Bonnie. It's Lauren. I'm at Beaver Creek, so if all goes well at the border, I should be there tomorrow by the end of the day."

"Wonderful!" Bonnie's enthusiastic response drove away all Lauren's concerns. "So tomorrow we finally get to meet in person, God willin' and the creeks don't rise."

"What creeks? Are you expecting flooding?"

Bonnie laughed. "It's just an expression,

something my father used to say. It means if nothing unexpected happens to prevent it."

"Oh." Lauren grinned. "Then I'll hope the creeks stay where they are because I'm really looking forward to meeting you tomorrow."

"I can hardly wait."

A BUSY SIGNAL buzzed in Patrick's ear. His grandmother refused to allow call waiting on her landline. "First come, first served, I always say." At least if Gran was talking on the phone, that meant she was okay. Unless she'd fallen, knocked the phone off the hook, and was currently lying on the kitchen floor unable to summon help. Briefly he considered trying the cell phone he'd gotten her for Christmas, but even though his grandmother's farm was within three miles of Palmer, the topography made cell coverage poor to nonexistent. Besides, she seldom turned it on unless she was going to town. He dialed again, but the line was still busy. She was probably just chatting with one of her yoga buddies. He'd get dinner and try again later.

Patrick wasn't usually the type to conjure up imaginary emergencies, but Gran had him worried. He wasn't quite sure why. True, his grandmother had fallen and badly sprained her ankle, but before he'd left for his two-week slope rotation, he'd personally hired an aid to stay with her until she was back on her feet. This particular aid had an annoying habit of speaking to Gran as though she were a contrary two-year-old, but she had good references and it was for only a couple of weeks. Still, something Gran said—or maybe something she didn't say—on their last phone conversation left him suspicious that the aid wasn't working out the way he'd hoped.

Not a great time to be tapped to work an extra two days past his usual rotation. He'd considered turning down the overtime, but the pay was good, and they wanted the project finished, so he'd agreed. But when he got back to Anchorage in three days, he was driving directly to the farm in Palmer. He and Gran were going to have a serious conversation about Gran moving to town. She could cut the conversation short over the phone, but she couldn't run away from him in person. He chuckled to himself. Not on crutches, anyway.

Randy, a fellow electrician on Patrick's team, stopped him in the hallway and waved a rolled blueprint. "Hey, Pat, got a minute? I have questions about that installation tomorrow."

"Sure. I was on my way to the cafeteria, but—"

"No problem. We can talk while you eat. I wouldn't mind another ice cream bar myself."

Thirty minutes later, having answered Randy's inquiries and consumed his meatloaf and mashed potatoes, Patrick dropped his empty tray into the return window and made his way to the tiny dorm room that was his Prudhoe Bay home. His roommate wasn't there, probably still watching the game in the rec room, but would no doubt be returning soon. Working twelve-hour shifts meant early bedtimes. It was eight forty-five now. Gran wouldn't be asleep yet. He dialed, and this time the phone rang through.

"Hello?"

"Gran, it's Patrick."

"Ah, Paddy my boy." She was the only one in the world who could get away with calling him Paddy. "How are things up on the slope?"

"Good, although I'm staying another two days to finish the project, so I won't be back until Monday. How is your ankle? Is your aid working out okay?"

"Everything's fine. No worries at all." Which didn't directly answer his question.

"How's her cooking? Is she feeding you well?"

"No complaints." Again, not exactly an answer.

"May I speak to her?"

"Who?"

"The aid. Would you call her to the phone, please?"

Gran gave a dramatic sigh. "Patrick, I'm already in my pajamas, reading in bed. Do you really want me to get up and walk all the way down the hall on crutches just so that you can talk to—"

"Never mind. So, you're still using the crutches?"

"For the time being. Doc said not to rush it."

"I'm glad you're following the doctor's advice. Did you get that brochure I sent about the senior apartments in Palmer?"

"I don't need a brochure to tell me about the Easy Living Apartments. I have friends there. I probably know more than the person who wrote the brochure."

"That's great. So, wouldn't it be nice to live near your friends? I understand there's a bridge club and craft demonstrations. Maybe we can visit when I'm back in town on Mon—"

"If I want to play bridge at the senior apartments, I'm always welcome. I don't see any reason to leave my home here."

"Oh, you don't?"

"No."

"Really? Because I think if you look down at the brace on your foot, you'll find at least one good reason."

"Patrick Sean O'Shea, are you sassing me?"

"No, ma'am." Patrick decided to try another tactic. "I talked to Mom last week. She was asking about you." If there was one person on earth who Bonnie O'Shea feared, it was her ultraefficient daughter-in-law. "She said if you need her, she could be on a plane tomorrow. All it would take is a call from me."

"You wouldn't," Gran gasped.

"I will if I have to."

"You're bluffing. If she visits, she'll organize your life just as ruthlessly as she organizes mine."

"I'm willing to chance it. Are you?"

There was a short pause. "My goodness. Look at the time. You'd better get to sleep. I know you have an early morning."

"Gran—"

"It will all be fine. We'll talk more when you come home. Good night, Paddy. Sleep tight." She hung up the phone before he could comment further.

Patrick shook his head as he plugged his phone into the charger. Obviously, she'd sent the aid away, and just as obviously she wasn't going to let him do anything about it. Oh well, Gran had made it through eighty-two years of life; she'd most likely survive another three days. He wasn't really going to summon his mother from Japan. Not yet anyway. But eventually, something was going to have to change. Gran shouldn't be alone out there on the farm.

CHAPTER TWO

"Left at the barn with the Alaska flag painted on the side," Lauren recited aloud. She was almost at the end of the journey. At least she thought so, but since she didn't have a street address to put into her phone's GPS, she was going by the directions Bonnie had sent her by email.

What did the Alaska flag look like, anyway? Lauren tried to think back to Mrs. Simpson's fourth-grade geography class. The capitol of Alaska was Juneau, the state bird was a plump-looking partridge or pheasant or…ptarmigan, that was it. The flower was something blue, and the flag… Lauren just hoped she recognized it when she saw it.

A big red barn loomed up ahead, but Lauren saw no sign of any flags, Alaska or otherwise. What were the odds someone would have repainted the barn since the last time Bonnie passed it? Not too high, Lauren decided. Another half mile along, a jog in the road revealed another barn, this one painted dark blue with eight golden stars arranged in the shape of the Big Dipper and North Star. Yes, that was it.

Lauren made the left and peered down at the printed instructions. *In about a mile, you'll see a big rock shaped like a walrus. Turn in and follow the drive to the house.* Oh, come on. A walrus? And just how big was a big rock?

At nine-tenths of a mile, she spotted a rock about the size of a suitcase next to a driveway. She slowed down and squinted, but she couldn't get the rock to look like anything except a rock. She was never one of those people who saw shapes in clouds, though, at least not the same shapes as other people seemed to. She could come back if she didn't find anything more promising.

At one mile, she passed another drive. This one had a pile of cobbles at the base of a miniature totem pole. Surely if this were the place, Bonnie would have mentioned the pole and not the rocks. Around another jog, she spotted a boulder half the size of a Volkswagen. Okay, that was a big rock. It was rounded, with lines along the side like wrinkles, and a smaller round shape on the front, like a muzzle, below two dips in the rock forming eyes. Two rock shards protruded like tusks. It did look like a walrus.

The old pickup and trailer Lauren had traded her car for rattled along the unpaved driveway. She stopped in front of a white two-story farmhouse with deep blue shutters and a red door. A white picket fence enclosed a shaggy front lawn and an enormous lilac bush bloomed next to the front porch. A gentle breeze carried the sweet scent to Lauren as soon as she stepped out of the truck. As she drew closer, she realized a woman had been sitting in a rocking chair on the porch and was now struggling to her feet. A pair of crutches were propped against the porch railing.

The woman wore a Matanuska Feed cap on top of snow-white hair and a wide smile. "Lauren, I assume?"

Lauren smiled back. "And you must be Bonnie." Lauren looked at the brace on her ankle. "What happened?"

"Nothing serious. Just a sprain. You're a sight for sore eyes. Come here and give me a hug."

All of Lauren's worries about being unwanted evaporated. After a firm embrace, Bonnie released her and reached for the crutches. "Such a nuisance, but the doctor says I should use them another week or two. Let's go inside."

"I should let the goats out first. Where should I put them?"

"You brought goats with you?" A line appeared between Bonnie's eyebrows. "I thought you mentioned buying them here."

"I did, and I will, but I saw these Alpines on the Goat People forum, and I couldn't resist. They come from great stock. I can't wait to post pictures on the forum."

"Uh-huh." Bonnie didn't really seem to be listening. "Maybe we could rig up something in the barn temporarily."

"I thought you had pasture. Didn't you say this used to be an old-fashioned dairy farm with forage?"

"Yes, but I'm not sure about the condition of the fences. I haven't run cows since my husband died seven years ago."

"Oh. I thought…" Lauren summoned a bright smile. "Never mind. It doesn't matter. I've been walking them each day and putting them back in the trailer. I'll just do that for now."

"Let's go check out the barn." Bonnie hoisted her crutches and started for the porch steps.

The barn was at least a hundred yards

away. "No, not on your crutches. I'll check it out. You just stay here."

Bonnie looked ready to argue, but then she smiled. "All right. I'll get some supper together for us while you do that."

Lauren started to protest, but it was clear Bonnie wanted to do something, and the kitchen was probably the safest place. "I appreciate that. Thanks."

A gravel road connected the house and the barn. Weeds and saplings were growing in the roadbed, but the barn itself was in good shape, although a coat of paint wouldn't hurt. One end was open for storage, with a big hayloft up above. The other end was divided into milking stations and a few pens. Lauren opened the gate to the first pen, but it broke away from the rusted hinges. The structure seemed sound, though, and she found no broken boards, nails, or other dangers. This could work.

She returned to the trailer and snapped a lead onto Spritz's halter. The other two goats hopped down beside her. They seemed as happy as Lauren was to have arrived. Lauren led them to the barn and secured them in the pen, using baling wire to hold the gate in place. Once she'd given them hay and water, they seemed happy enough to be on solid ground.

Biscotti nudged Muffin and took off, running around the pen and urging her friend to chase her. Spritz looked on with a bemused expression for a moment, but then she joined in the chase. Lauren laughed. "You girls enjoy your dinner. I'm going for mine, now."

Back on the front porch, Lauren paused. Should she knock? Before she could decide, a window opened on the wall next to the porch. "Come on in, hon. I've got chicken and rice casserole on the table. You might want to come in the kitchen door on the side of the house and wash up."

The side door past the lilac bush led to a mudroom with a huge farmhouse sink, washer, dryer, and chest freezer, and a bench with a row of pegs above. Several coats and jackets of various thicknesses hung from the pegs. Lauren removed her shoes, washed her hands, and padded into the kitchen in her stocking feet.

"Good, you appreciate a clean floor. I don't know how many times I had to get on to my husband, Tim, before I got him trained to leave his rubber boots in the mudroom. I tell you, housebreaking a puppy is nothing compared to housebreaking a man."

Lauren laughed. "How long were you married?"

"From 1964 till 2013. Forty-five wonderful years." The laugh lines in the corners of her eyes deepened.

"Isn't that forty-nine years?"

Bonnie grinned. "Yeah, but four of them were just average." She chortled gleefully. "Just kidding. Forty-nine years with the man of my dreams. I'm a fortunate woman. Sit down, sweetie. You've got to be hungry after all that driving."

"I am," Lauren admitted. "But I hate that you went to all this trouble cooking for me when you're on crutches."

"Oh, don't worry about that. I always have a stash of casseroles in the freezer, just in case. You never know when a neighbor might fall sick or something. I thawed a rhubarb pie, too. It's in the oven now."

As they ate the casserole, they talked about Lauren's trip. Bonnie reminisced. "The first time Tim and I drove the Alcan, I wondered what in the world we'd gotten ourselves into. Back then, driving that road was an adventure in itself. Some parts weren't even paved, and the frost heaves could toss your car around like popcorn."

"Much better now, then," Lauren said. "It was a beautiful drive. Just long."

When Lauren had cleared her plate, Bonnie offered seconds. "Once we finish eating, you can pick your bedroom. I'm in the one downstairs, for obvious reasons, but there are three upstairs. Like Goldilocks, try out the mattresses until you find the one that's just right. We want you to be comfortable."

"You're so kind to me." After all her doubts, Bonnie's generous welcome was such a relief that Lauren felt hot tears gathering in her eyes. "Why are you doing all this?"

"All what?" Bonnie looked genuinely mystified. "Thawing a casserole?"

"That, and letting me live here, in your house, and letting me run goats on your farm. I know we agreed you'd share the profits, but we both know it might be a while before the profits amount to anything. I have enough money to build the herd and pay for feed and vet bills, but I couldn't have afforded to lease a farm, too. You're making my dream come true."

"Oh, honey, it's nothing. Other than letting a neighbor cut hay, nobody's used these pastures since Tim died, and the upstairs bedrooms are empty. Besides, I have my reasons for wanting a roommate."

"Well, tomorrow it's my turn to cook. Okay?"

"Sounds good to me. Now, that pie isn't going to eat itself. Why don't you take it out of the oven and get some ice cream from the freezer? You like rhubarb?"

"I've never tasted it."

"Ah. You're in for a treat."

THE NEXT MORNING, Lauren woke to the sound of crutches thumping in the hallway below. She could barely remember her head hitting the pillow before she'd fallen asleep. An embroidered sampler on the wall reminded her not to put off till tomorrow what she could do today. Good advice.

She pushed a faded patchwork quilt back and swung her feet onto the braided rug beside the bed. According to her phone, it was only six thirty, but already sun peeked around the edges of the curtain. She opened them wide. The breeze coming through the window smelled of grass, and earth and sunshine.

By the time Lauren made it downstairs, Bonnie was standing in front of an open refrigerator, leaning on one crutch. "Let me help," Lauren offered.

"I have fresh eggs from my neighbor's chickens. I used to keep hens, but with only myself to feed, it didn't seem worth the trouble."

"Maybe we'll start a flock," Lauren responded. "Just as soon as I get the fences repaired and the goats established. How would you like me to cook these eggs?"

"Scrambled please. If you're cooking, I'll make you coffee."

"None for me, thanks. I'm afraid I'm a tea drinker."

"Really?" Bonnie's eyes lit up, as though Lauren had delivered wonderful news. "Me, too! I knew this relationship was meant to be. I have some wonderful Irish Breakfast a friend brought back from her trip to Europe. I was only making coffee because I thought you would want it."

"I hope you didn't buy coffee just for me."

"Oh, it won't go to waste. My grandson practically lives on the stuff."

"Does he live nearby?"

"In Anchorage. But he visits often—" Bonnie turned on the water to fill a kettle, but the end of her sentence sounded like, "whether I want him to or not."

Lauren thought it best not to explore Bonnie's family dynamics before they'd had their first cups of tea. She found the skillet and scrambled eggs while Bonnie popped bread in the toaster and brewed a steaming pot. They sat down at the scrubbed pine farm table. Bonnie's mug read, in faded letters, *If Mom says no, ask Gran*. Lauren's had a picture of a rooster.

Once they'd finished clearing the dishes, Lauren went to check on the goats and, at Bonnie's direction, survey the farm. What she found was a little discouraging. Except for the hayfields that had been mown every year, the pastures were overgrown. The fence posts weren't in bad condition, but some of them sagged, and three-strand barbed wire might have been fine for cattle, but it wasn't going to hold goats. Especially Spritz. The good news was, goats were browsers, so they were better suited to eating the weedy trees and shrubs that had sprung up than grazing animals like cows and sheep would be. And there seemed to be plenty of room to expand as her herd grew.

Lauren planned to start small. Because she didn't have to buy or lease land, the money she'd saved would be enough to purchase a small herd of goats and pay for their feed and care for a year or two. By that time, if all went as planned, she should be earning enough to live on and pay Bonnie a share of the profits.

Although it looked like at least some of her goat-buying money was going to be directed into new fencing. If she bought the materials and did the labor herself, it shouldn't cost too much. She'd passed a building supply store yesterday on the way out. She checked the time. If she hurried, she could pick up fencing and be back in time to make lunch for Bonnie and herself.

She started back to the farmhouse, but noticed at the corner of one field that the trees seemed particularly dense. These were old white-barked birch trees, not the saplings that had grown up in the last seven years. She stopped to check it out. Threading her way between the trunks, she discovered a one-and-a-half-story log cabin tucked within the forest. Moss covered the roof, and a cow parsnip grew through the front steps, but the cabin seemed largely intact, although obviously abandoned.

Lauren loved old buildings, especially cottages and cabins, but she didn't have time to poke around inside today. She had farm chores to do. As Bonnie would no doubt say, "That fence isn't going to fix itself."

The building supply had the welded wire fencing she needed, and after sharing a peanut butter sandwich with Bonnie, Lauren spent the afternoon installing it. By the end of the day, she'd managed to fence off a small corner of the pasture so that tomorrow she could let the goats forage while she worked on the next section. She checked her watch. It was late, and Lauren had promised to cook. Fortunately, she had pasta, bacon and eggs, and parmesan cheese left over in her camper's ice chest. Tomorrow, she could go grocery shopping.

When Lauren entered the mudroom, she could hear Bonnie talking. "Yes, she's here. Delightful girl." There was a chuckle. "Oh, I know, but that's what he gets for being bossy."

Lauren deliberately turned on the water to wash her hands and to let Bonnie know she was there. When she stepped into the kitchen a moment later, Bonnie was hanging up an old-fashioned wall phone. She smiled at Lauren. "How did the fence building go?"

"Not bad." Lauren held up the sack of groceries she'd collected on the way in. "I hope you like spaghetti carbonara."

"Sounds exotic." Bonnie laughed. "Don't worry. I like everything."

"How's your ankle today?" Lauren reached into a cabinet for a pan to boil water.

"Better every day, I think."

"I'm glad. Say, I came across a cabin over on the north corner. Is that part of the farm?"

"Ah, you found it." Bonnie gave her an approving smile. "Yes, it is part of the farm, and it has a very interesting history."

"Oh?" Lauren set the water on the burner and turned on the flame under it. "Is it very old?"

"It was built by the original homesteaders, who came to the Matanuska Valley in 1935 as part of the New Deal."

"That's fascinating."

"Oh, that's not the interesting part." Bonnie settled into a chair and rested her elbows on the table. "In 1899, gold was discovered in Nome, and it started a gold rush."

Lauren frowned, trying to remember the map of Alaska she'd studied when she was planning the trip. "Nome's not around here, is it?"

"Oh, no. It's on the coast by the Bering Sea, more than five hundred miles from here, and not on the road system. But prospectors flocked to Nome and one of those prospectors was James K. Bradley, who later married the sister of the territorial governor of Alaska."

"I gather he was successful?" Lauren set

a large skillet on another burner to fry the bacon.

"He was indeed. In fact, the first gold he discovered was one of the ten biggest nuggets ever found in Alaska. It weighed seventy-eight troy ounces and was known as Bradley's Heart, because it was more or less heart shaped."

"And he built his fortune on that nugget?"

"Well, no. He considered Bradley's Heart to be his lucky charm and refused to part with it. He found more gold, and from his experience in the Klondike gold rush, he knew the surest path to riches was to sell supplies to the prospectors. He sold his gold, all except Bradley's Heart, and established an outfitter business in Nome, and later in Fairbanks. Then he moved on to real estate. The Bradleys are still major players in Alaska."

"So what does that have to do with the cabin?"

"Ah, I'm coming to that. This house was built in 1955, and the family moved out of their cabin and left it empty. In 1965, James Bradley was living in the best hotel in downtown Anchorage. He was in his nineties by then, still in good health, but he knew he couldn't last forever. A good friend was trying to stir up interest for an Anchorage museum. They talked about it, and Mr. Bradley decided he would give Bradley's Heart to his friend, to be displayed in the new museum when it opened. But that never happened."

By now, Lauren was standing transfixed, waiting for Bonnie to tell more. Bonnie waved her hand at the boiling water. "Don't you need to add the spaghetti?"

"Oh, right." Lauren stirred the pasta into the water, set a timer, and turned off the burner under the skillet. Then she turned back to Bonnie. "What happened to the nugget?"

"Well, despite his wealth, James Bradley didn't like to waste money. It was only half a mile from the hotel to his friend's house on Ninth Street, so he took the gold nugget out of the hotel safe and tucked it into his coat pocket, intending to walk there. But somehow, word got out."

"Someone stole Bradley's Heart?"

"Yes. He'd only gone two blocks when a masked man held him at gunpoint and demanded the nugget. Mr. Bradley resisted. He used his walking stick to try to fight off the bandit, but the man knocked him to the ground and wrestled the nugget from his pocket. By that time, someone had seen them struggling and ran toward them, but the bandit fled."

"Wow. Was the old man okay?"

"No. He broke a hip in the fall. He offered a huge reward for the return of the nugget, but he died three months later from complications related to the break. He swore that his luck had deserted him when he lost Bradley's Heart. In the meantime, state troopers searched for the bandit, and were eventually able to locate him here, holed up in that cabin."

"Here? On your farm?"

"It wasn't our farm then. It still belonged to the original homestead family. But all the children had grown up and moved off and the parents decided to retire to Anchorage. They sold off their cows, but they kept the farm thinking one of the children might change their mind, so there was no one living here at the time. Tim and I bought the farm three years later."

The timer went off. Lauren held up a hand. "Hold that thought. I need to make the carbonara, and then I want to hear the rest of this story."

Ten minutes later, they sat down to plates of pasta. Bonnie took a bite. "Mmm. This is good."

"I'm glad you like it," Lauren replied, "but tell me more about Bradley's Heart. Did the Bradley children honor their father's wishes and donate it to the museum?"

Bonnie shook her head. "They never recovered it. The robber, whose name was William Golson, by the way, refused to talk. The Bradley family doubled the reward. People came from all over, trespassing on the farm, trying to find where he'd hidden the nugget, but nobody ever did. I think that was one of the reasons the owners agreed to sell the farm to us. They were concerned with all the treasure hunters and nobody living here someone might get hurt and they'd be liable."

"Did you have trouble with that?"

"Not too much. Tim posted no trespassing signs, and by then most of the fortune seekers had moved on to greener pastures. Occasionally we'd see signs that someone had been digging somewhere in the middle of the night, but that soon tapered off."

"Were you ever tempted to try to find the nugget yourself?"

Bonnie developed a sudden fascination with her plate. For several seconds, she busied herself twirling spaghetti around her fork. When she finally looked up, she studied Lauren's face for a few beats before she spoke, almost in a whisper. "I was close once. At least I thought I was. Turns out, I was wrong."

"What happened?"

Bonnie shook her head. "Suffice it to say, I learned my lesson. Next time I'll make sure I have the real thing before I go public."

"Next time?"

Bonnie raised her chin and looked at Lauren. "I'm going to find that nugget if it's the last thing I ever do."

CHAPTER THREE

PATRICK PICKED UP his car from long-term parking at the airport, stopped by his house in Anchorage just long enough to pack a suitcase full of not-work clothes, and headed toward Palmer. If Gran had dismissed the aid he'd hired—and Patrick was 90 percent sure she had—he was going to be spending his two weeks off with her. Because until her ankle had healed, she shouldn't be living alone.

Even then, she shouldn't be out on the farm by herself. What if she slipped on the ice trying to shovel her walk and couldn't make it back inside the house? Cell phone service was spotty at the farm, and that was assuming she'd even bothered to charge her cell phone. She might lie there for days.

She needed to move to town, but she wasn't going to like hearing it. To help defuse the tension, Patrick stopped in at the Salmonberry Bakery in Palmer to pick up a half-dozen scones for Gran and a take-out coffee for himself.

The first thing Patrick noticed as he drove up to the farmhouse was an old pickup with a camper shell over near the barn. An even older stock trailer was parked beside it. Gran must be letting someone store their extra vehicles at the farm. No harm in that, he supposed.

The wide lawn looked to be freshly mowed, which was odd. Gran usually mowed it herself with the riding mower, but she couldn't do it with her injured ankle. Maybe she had kept the aid. Patrick grabbed the bakery bag and coffee, trotted up the porch steps, and let himself in. "Gran? It's me. Where are you?"

"In the kitchen, making tea."

He followed the voice. "Good timing. I brought you a teatime treat." He stepped into the kitchen and stopped. Gran was at the table, her foot propped up on a chair and a woman he'd never seen before was at the stove pouring boiling water into Gran's teapot. "Oh, excuse me. I didn't realize you had company. I'm Patrick O'Shea."

"Lauren Shepherd." The woman offered a shy smile. Or maybe just a fake one. Either way, she didn't seem overjoyed that he was there. A new aid, maybe? If so, that was a promising development. She broke eye contact and turned away to return the kettle to the stove. A thick ponytail of glossy brown hair hung halfway down her back.

"Patrick is my grandson, Lauren," Gran said. "He works up on the North Slope, two weeks on, two weeks off."

"How interesting." Lauren sounded more uneasy than interested. So why was she here?

"It's nice of you to visit my grandmother," he probed, hoping she would reveal her connection.

"Oh, Lauren's not visiting." Gran said, with a superior smile. "She lives here."

"Are you the new health aid?"

Gran laughed. "Listen to what I'm saying, Paddy. She lives here. Permanently. Lauren is taking over the farm."

"Taking over the farm?" Relief washed over him. "You're buying the farm so Gran can move into town? That's great."

"Oh, I'm not going anywhere," Gran declared. "Lauren and I have an arrangement. We're roommates."

"Roommates." Patrick still wasn't getting it.

"Yes." Gran smiled sweetly. "Lauren is going to turn the place into a goat farm. She's already got three goats and she has plans to get a lot more."

"But what about the Easy Living Apartments in town?"

"What about them? You said I shouldn't be out here all by myself. Well, I'm no longer by myself, so you don't need to worry anymore."

Checkmate. Patrick had to admire the way Gran had swept the legs right out from under his argument. But now she had a stranger living in her house. With only a moment's thought, Patrick could come up with several scenarios as to why a young woman would want to move in with someone two generations older, and none of them boded well for Gran.

Both women were watching him with guarded expressions. If he went on the attack, he'd never get the information he needed. Instead he tried a smile. "Good thing I brought lots of scones."

"Cranberry almond?" Gran asked as she opened the bag.

"And blueberry." Patrick snagged a pair of mugs and three small plates from the corner cabinet.

"I love scones. Tim and I went to England for our thirtieth anniversary, and we would have scones with clotted cream for tea every day. I wish I could find clotted cream here."

"Maybe once the goats are producing milk, I can make clotted cream," Lauren offered.

"Oh, that would be lovely," Gran said, buttering her scone.

"Lauren, cranberry or blueberry?" Patrick asked.

"Oh, um, either is fine. Thank you." Deep green eyes regarded him. Intelligent eyes. But intelligence didn't mean she was honest.

Patrick set a blueberry scone on a plate and pushed it in front of her. "So, Lauren, did you grow up around here?"

"No. I just arrived in Alaska three days ago." Lauren poured tea into Gran's mug, and then into her own.

"Lauren drove up the Alcan Highway."

"From where?" Patrick tried to sound as if he was just making polite conversation.

"Oregon."

"That's a long drive. Where in Oregon?"

"East."

That was suspiciously vague. "I have a friend who used to live in Bend. Were you near there?"

"No, north and east of there. The La Grande area."

Patrick made a mental note to check out Lauren Shepherd from La Grande, Oregon on the internet later. Assuming that was her real name. "Did you raise goats there?"

"Oh, no. I was an office manager in a doctor's office."

"I'm not following. How did you and Gran find each other?"

"On the Goat People forum," Lauren said. Gran nodded her agreement, her mouth full of scone.

"Goat people?" Was this like a cult or what?

"Yes. I volunteered at a shelter in Oregon and they rescued some abandoned goats. I helped care for them and decided I really liked goats, so I started reading up on them and following this forum, Goat People."

"And I happened to come across the forum while I was looking up dairy statistics," Gran chimed in. "Did you know dairy goat herds are up sixty-one percent in a decade? I followed a link and found the Goat People forum. They're such nice people."

Finding lonely elderly people online sounded like a scam. But a goat forum? What were the odds of someone trolling a goat forum looking for victims? "So, you both were on this forum, talking about goats…"

"Bonnie always gave good general advice about dairy farming. I asked lots of questions because I hoped to start a farm of my own someday. And then one day Bonnie sent a private message and asked if she could call me." She and Gran exchanged smiles. "She said if I came to Alaska, we could be partners. She'd provide the land, and I would manage the goat herd."

"And you came? Just like that?"

Lauren shrugged. "Not immediately. I had to give notice, buy a truck and trailer, and plan the trip. But it's been a lifelong dream of mine."

"To raise goats in Alaska?"

"To live on a farm. It always seemed so… solid. Peaceful." Her expression softened, and there was something wistful in her eyes.

"But you've never actually farmed before," Patrick pointed out.

"No." She met his gaze. "I've researched the heck out of it, but I have a lot of work to do to get started. And speaking of work," she stood and put her mug and plate in the dishwasher, "I'd better get back to it. I have fencing to install. See you later, Bonnie."

"All right, sweetie. See you for supper." A spray of wrinkles fanned from the corners of Gran's eyes. "Paddy will cook."

Patrick waited until he heard the mudroom door close before turning to his grandmother and raising an eyebrow. "Are you sure about this?"

"Absolutely."

"Did you do a background check? Get references?"

"I'm sure any of the members of the Goat People would vouch for Lauren in an instant. She's delightful."

"Lots of con artists are delightful. In fact, that's their stock in trade."

Gran snorted. "Lauren, a con artist? What would she be conning me out of? An occasional cup of tea? The girl even insists on buying half the groceries and she's been doing most of the cooking." Gran glanced at her ankle. "She doesn't want me standing for too long."

"Maybe she wants to start out on the right foot, no pun intended. Then, once you trust her, there will be some money emergency, and she'll ask for a loan."

"Do you think I'm senile? I can take care of myself."

"Can you?"

"You say I shouldn't be alone on the farm. Now you say you don't approve of the company I keep." She scowled at him. "You've checked on me. I'm fine. Maybe you should just skedaddle back to Anchorage now."

"I thought I was cooking supper."

"Not if you're going to lecture me like I'm some helpless old lady. I don't need that kind of negativity in my life."

Patrick raised his hands in surrender. "Fine. I'll keep my doubts to myself. But I hope you don't mind if I stick around the farm for a few days."

"If you can behave, you can stay."

Patrick leaned over to kiss his grandmother's cheek. "I'm just trying to look out for you, the same way you've always looked out for me. Remember when you warned me that I was hanging around with the wrong crowd in junior high?"

That drew a small smile. "Was I wrong?"

"Nope."

"I know trouble when I see it. And I know quality, too. Lauren's quality, Patrick. You'll see once you've spent some time around her."

"I hope so." Patrick picked up the last bite of scone and popped it into his mouth, thinking of those clear green eyes and wondering about the thoughts behind them. "I really do."

PATRICK SPENT THE next couple of hours on the internet, checking out Lauren's story. This Goat People forum seemed to be an enthusiastic bunch, and Gran and Lauren popped up often on the threads, although not lately. That made sense if Lauren was driving and Gran was laid up with her foot. Her computer was in an alcove on the second-floor landing. He should ask Gran if she'd like him to move it downstairs.

Other than the forum, Lauren didn't seem to have a lot of presence online. She existed, or at least a Lauren Shepherd age thirty-one had an address in a smallish town in eastern Oregon. There was only one medical clinic listed in the town. Patrick called, but got a recording that the office was closed. He checked his watch. Better get started on dinner.

Patrick enjoyed puttering around the kitchen. Working on the slope and living alone, he didn't get many opportunities, but he often spent part of his two weeks off working on recipes for new soups or attempting to replicate a restaurant dish he'd enjoyed.

Gran had been the one to teach him how to cook. His mother, efficient as always, had adhered to the preplan theory: taco Tuesday, chicken casserole Wednesday, spaghetti Thursday, all made in advance and frozen in batches. Even when they were living in Greece, a food lover's paradise, they'd adhered to her regularly scheduled menus. But during his school breaks spent with Gran, Patrick had learned to improvise, to devise new recipes based on what they found available at the farmers' market or Gran's freezer. And of course, they'd had an endless supply of milk, cream and butter.

He found Gran settled in front of the television, watching a quiz show. When the tile turned, she blurted out the answer before any of the contestants could buzz in. Clearly not senile, but that didn't mean a con artist couldn't use her generous heart against her. He kept that observation to himself. "I'm starting dinner. Any requests?"

"That thing you made last month with the chicken and pumpkin was good."

"The curry? Do you have basmati rice?"

"I haven't used it, so if you had any left, it's still here."

"Good. Does your guest have any food preferences or allergies I should know about?"

She shot him a stern look. "She's not a guest, Patrick. She's here to stay. And no, Lauren seems to enjoy all kinds of food."

"All right then."

Patrick found chicken breasts in the freezer and the rest of the ingredients he needed in the pantry. The curry jar was getting low. He'd have to bring more from his stash at home. He ordered this particular curry blend in bulk from the UK.

Forty-five minutes later, the popcorn fragrance of the basmati mingling with the curry spices had drawn Gran thumping down the hall on her crutches. "How long until it's ready?"

"It's ready now. Do you want to wait for—"

The sound of the mudroom door slamming answered his question. "Never mind, I'll set the table."

A few minutes later Lauren stepped into the kitchen, closed her eyes and drew in a deep breath. "What is that amazing smell?"

"It's a recipe Paddy developed all by himself," Gran boasted.

Why did his grandmother's praise make Patrick feel like he was six years old? He filled a plate with rice and curry and set it in front of Gran before turning to Lauren. "Have a seat. I hope you like coconut milk curry."

"I'm not sure I've ever had it, but if it smells like that it has to taste good." She accepted the plate Patrick handed her and waited while he filled his own and joined them at the table before she tried a bite. "Oh, yeah. This…" She nodded while she chewed and swallowed. "This is delicious. Are you a chef up in Prudhoe Bay?"

Patrick laughed. "No, I'm an electrician. Cooking is a hobby."

Lauren took another bite. "Well, if you ever decide to open a restaurant, I'm there."

Patrick led the conversation with a story or two about growing up, hoping to nudge Lauren into talking more about her own history, but she didn't seem inclined to share. Once they'd finished eating, she helped clear the table.

"Did you get much fencing done today?" Gran asked her.

"Some. I'm going to try to get another couple of hours in before I call it a day. Thank goodness for the long days here."

"Are the goats settling in?"

"Yes." Lauren smiled. "I've got that one corner of the northwest pasture secure and they're really enjoying browsing there."

"Goats are such rascals," Gran said. "We had two when I was growing up. They got into more trouble."

"You grew up in Alaska?" Lauren asked.

"No, in Nebraska. We lived so far out in the country, the sun set between us and town."

Lauren laughed. Patrick scraped the leftover curry into a storage container and carried the pan to the sink to wash it. Something caught his eye outside the kitchen window. A black-and-white animal. "That fence might not be as secure as you think."

"What?" Lauren crowded next to him to peer out the window. "Spritz! Excuse me." She dumped the dishes she was carrying beside the sink and dashed off through the mudroom. A few seconds later she appeared in front of the window, approaching the goat. The goat waited until she was within a foot before ducking under her arm and tap-dancing behind her. Patrick had to chuckle.

"Laugh if you want, but there's nothing more frustrating than chasing loose livestock," Gran said, watching over his shoulder. "Go help."

"Yes, ma'am." Patrick tossed down the dishtowel he'd been using and started for the door.

"Patrick. Take a treat with you."

"Good idea." He grabbed an apple from the refrigerator crisper. Outside, the goat was still playing keep-away with Lauren. Patrick crouched and held out the apple. "Hey, goat. I've got something for you."

The goat looked back and forth between

him and Lauren for a few seconds before she seemed to make up her mind. Dainty steps carried her to Patrick. The goat grasped one side of the apple. Patrick held on, and in the seconds it took for the goat to bite the apple in two, he was able to grasp the halter.

"Thank you!" Lauren hurried over. "Can you hold on to her for just a sec while I grab a lead rope?"

"Sure." Patrick stood and gave the goat the rest of the apple. He scratched the goat's jaw while he waited. She leaned into him, apparently enjoying the attention. He ran a hand down her back and across her rounded rib cage.

Lauren returned and snapped the lead onto the goat's halter. "Come on, Spritz. Time to go." She tugged, but the goat set her heels and leaned into Patrick. Lauren tugged harder. "Come on."

"I'll come with you." When Patrick moved forward, the goat fell into step, walking between them.

Lauren blew out a long breath of air. "You would not believe the trouble this goat has given me the last two weeks."

Patrick looked down at the goat who was nuzzling his hand. He scratched behind her ears. "I don't know much about goats, but this one seems like a sweetheart."

"She is, but she's sneaky. Spritz escaped three times on the trip up. She can pick anything short of a padlock, and she usually takes the rest of the herd with her."

"The rest of the herd being?"

"Two goats at the moment, but I'll be getting more as soon as I've finished the fencing."

They passed the big spruces at the corner of the field. Lauren gestured in the direction of the old log cabin. "Bonnie told me about the cabin and the missing gold nugget."

"Did she mention her big embarrassment?"

"What embarrassment?"

"Never mind."

Lauren gave him a sidelong look. "She did mention something about a mistake and that next time she'd be sure it was the real thing before she told anyone."

"I'll bet she did."

"So what was the big mistake? You can't tease me like that and then not tell."

Patrick hesitated, but maybe it was better she knew. "Okay, but don't mention it to Gran. She's sensitive about it."

Lauren mimed locking her lips and throwing away the key.

Patrick grinned. "When I was a kid, my

sister and I would take our school breaks here. Gran, Rowan and I used to spend our spare time searching for the nugget. I was twelve or so when we found a rock buried near the front steps of the old cabin. It was all sparkly and vaguely heart shaped. Really more of a triangle, but close. Gran was sure it was Bradley's Heart. She took it to the local newspaper reporter and told him all about the history. He suggested they ask an expert, so they took it to the geology teacher at the high school and he informed Gran it was pyrite."

"Pyrite?"

"Fool's gold. It looks a lot like gold, but it isn't."

"That's disappointing."

"But that wasn't the end of it. The reporter ran with the story, and it was published on the front page as 'Local Woman Taken in by Myth in Quest for Gold.' The whole town was teasing her."

"Oh no."

"Gran was livid. Grandy wasn't too happy either, since it sparked a new round of treasure hunters traipsing through the farm. Fortunately, that didn't last much past the first snow."

"I can understand why she was upset."

"That reporter, Anthony Clark, is now owner and editor of the newspaper, and

Gran still refuses to subscribe. He's apologized more than once, but she's holding on to that grudge like she's hanging ten stories off the ground."

"Now I understand what she meant when she said she was going to find that nugget if it's the last thing she ever did."

"She said that?" Patrick stopped. "That explains everything."

"Explains what?"

"I don't know if Gran told you, but I've been trying to get her to move to a senior apartment complex in town, and she's been resisting me."

"I gathered something along those lines earlier."

"Yeah, well now it makes sense. Several of her friends live there, and I couldn't figure out why she was so dead set against it. But now I understand. She wants that nugget, to show the editor he was wrong."

"You think the nugget is here on the farm?"

"Nah. If it were, someone would have found it by now."

"Have you ever searched? As an adult?"

He shook his head. "When we would go looking, Grandy would laugh and say we were wasting our time. He said someone melted down that nugget a long time ago."

"Your grandmother seems to believe it's here."

"She wants it to be, but that doesn't make it true."

Lauren gave a brief nod. They continued into the back pasture, overgrown with weedy trees and bushes. Rolls of welded wire waited along the old fence line. Several posts sagged to one side. Patrick hadn't realized how much the farm had deteriorated since his grandfather's death. He'd made sure Gran's house was in good repair, but he hadn't thought much about fences or outbuildings.

He could see where Lauren had formed a pen in the corner of the pasture. Two more goats called from inside the gate. Patrick patted Spritz's head. "Not that it's any of my business, but why did you acquire goats before you did the fencing?"

"That was a mistake. Someone on Goat People offered me a deal on two French Alpines, so I decided to take them with me instead of waiting to buy up here. I didn't think about all the health certificates and permitting involved to take them through Canada, but I got it done and brought them here. Since this was a dairy farm, I assumed once we got here, the fencing would be functional. It probably was for cows, but…" She shrugged.

As they got closer, the goats' calls became louder, the sounds almost human. Spritz raised her head to listen but she didn't seem to be in any particular hurry to join the others. Patrick looked from the two goats to Spritz. "You mentioned buying two goats—"

"Yeah, I bought two and they threw in Spritz for free." Lauren shot a look of annoyance at Spritz. "I think I understand why." She opened a gate and led Spritz inside with the others, closing it behind her. After a few minutes of walking the perimeter, she stopped between the two posts. "Aha. Here's the problem."

Patrick circled on the outside of the pen to see what she was looking at. The wire at the bottom was bunched up, as though something roughly goat-sized had crawled underneath.

"The staple is loose," Lauren explained. "Could you please hand me that hammer over there and the box of staples?"

"Sure." Patrick fetched the tools and held the fence in place while Lauren set the staple and secured it with two sharp blows. She'd obviously swung a hammer before. "There. With luck that will hold them. Thanks for your help."

"You're welcome." Patrick watched the

three goats nibbling on leaves. "They look healthy. Fat even."

"They're pregnant. They should be dropping kids in another couple of weeks, and then I can start milking soon after."

Patrick nodded. Three goats weren't a farm, but they were a start. "Are you coming back to the house now?"

"No." She shielded her eyes and looked toward the sun, still well above the horizon. "I'm going to put in some more time on the fencing. I've only got this little pen done, and I want to have the whole section secure before I get any more goats."

"I'll help." Patrick picked up the hammer and waited for her to lead him to her work area.

"Oh, no. This is my job."

"I want to."

"Why?"

Patrick decided to tell her the truth. "It sounds like my grandmother might not have been as upfront with you as she could have about the condition of the farm. It's only right I help you bring it up to specs."

"This isn't Bonnie's fault. I never asked about pasture conditions."

"But still." Patrick grabbed a roll of fencing and carried it to the point where she'd stopped.

"You don't have to do this."

"I know." Patrick picked up her leather work gloves and handed them to her. "Are we going to argue about this, or are we going to build some fence?"

Lauren looked at him, and then at the rolls of fencing waiting to be installed. "Let's build some fence."

CHAPTER FOUR

THE NEXT MORNING Patrick made pancakes
for breakfast. Every time he and Rowan
would come to visit, Gran would make pancakes the first day, cheerfully explaining to
Grandy that they were the grandkids' favorite. They weren't. Patrick liked pancakes well
enough, but Rowan liked waffles better, and
they both preferred the bacon and egg break-
fasts that were standard fare on the farm.
Still, after Gran had made such a fuss, they'd
never had the heart to tell her so. It was only
later that Patrick figured out pancakes were
Gran's favorite breakfast, and she'd assumed
it was theirs, too.

A board in the hallway creaked. Gran
made her way into the kitchen using only
a cane rather than the crutches she'd been
using the day before.

"Hey, look at you." Patrick pulled out a
chair.

Lauren stepped in from the mudroom. She'd

already been out to take the goats to pasture. "Your ankle must be feeling stronger."

"I'm feeling stronger all over," Gran declared. "It must be the good care I'm getting." She smiled at Lauren and then looked pointedly at Patrick.

He didn't rise to the bait, instead he dished up stacks of pancakes and set them in front of each of the women. "Tea?"

"Please." Gran poured a generous amount of syrup over her plate. "I taught Paddy how to make pancakes," she told Lauren.

Lauren took a bite. "They're very good."

"Thanks." Patrick and Gran spoke in unison. Patrick laughed and got tea for them both. "What are your plans today?"

"I'm still fencing," Lauren said, "but I'm running low on staples. I might pop into town this afternoon."

"Today is Tuesday," Gran said and frowned.

"Tuesday?" Patrick tried to think if she had a doctor's appointment or something. Then he remembered. "Tuesday is your yoga day, isn't it?"

"I haven't been the last two weeks, since the doctor said I shouldn't drive." Gran scowled down at her foot. "I hope Crystal doesn't disband the class while I'm out. The

Mat Mates were already at the minimum number."

Patrick had planned to assist Lauren with her fence building, but Gran clearly missed her friends. Suddenly, he saw an opportunity. At least two of Gran's best friends from her yoga class lived in the senior apartments in Palmer. Maybe if they joined his campaign to get Gran to move… "I'll take you."

"You're busy. Besides, I can't do much with this ankle." Her eager expression belied her words.

"I'll bet your instructor can give you some modified exercises. And even if she can't you can still spend time with your friends, right?"

"Well if you really don't mind…"

"It would be my pleasure," Patrick assured her.

"In that case, eat fast," Gran commanded briskly. "The class starts at seven-thirty."

"I thought you met at ten."

"We used to, but Molly teaches a class in calligraphy at eleven every other Tuesday, so we had to reschedule, and this is the only timeslot Crystal could give us. Besides, this way we can all go for tea or coffee at the Salmonberry Bakery afterward."

"Somehow I doubt you stick to tea or coffee." He was familiar with her sweet tooth.

"Well, what's the use of doing yoga if you can't consume a few empty calories? Lauren, would you like to come? The girls would love to meet you."

"I wish I could, but I have fencing to install. Maybe next time."

"I'll bring you a scone. Blueberry or cranberry?"

Lauren smiled. "I don't think I'm going to need any scones after this breakfast."

"Blueberry it is." Gran struggled from her chair, grabbed her cane and limped down the hall toward her bedroom. "I'll just put on my yoga pants."

"I'll pick up those fence staples for you," Patrick offered Lauren, as he set his pancakes aside to eat later. "How many do you need?"

"Three boxes. Thanks." She took another bite. "These really are excellent pancakes."

"I know. Gran really did teach me to make them." Patrick refilled his coffee cup. "I'll help with the fencing when we get back."

"You don't have to—"

"I'm almost ready," Gran called. "Patrick, could you bring the car around?"

"Duty calls." Patrick grabbed the keys and headed out the door, whistling.

As PATRICK HAD expected, the "girls" at the yoga studio greeted Gran as though she were visiting royalty. Despite Gran's urging, they'd arrived a few minutes late and the class had already started, but that didn't stop the ladies from rushing over to dispense hugs and greetings. There were five other ladies in the class, all about Gran's age. The instructor was a relative youngster, looking to be in her late fifties.

"My, my. Look at this handsome man. This can't be little Paddy," the round woman wearing a bright pink leotard that almost but not quite matched her hair exclaimed.

The tall thin woman in black and white frowned. "Bea, you've only lived in Palmer for ten years, and Patrick has been a grown man for that entire time."

"Yes, but I've seen Bonnie's pictures from when he was a little boy." She squeezed Patrick's cheek. "You were adorable."

"Thank you," Patrick said, amused.

"You remember Molly, Alice, Bea, Rosemary, and Linda," Gran said. "And Crystal, our instructor, of course.

"Of course. Good to see you, ladies." Patrick had met them all at one time or another but other than Molly, Gran's best friend since forever, he wouldn't have been able to match names to faces. The woman in black and white was Alice, Rosemary wore her gray hair in a braid down her back, Bea had the pink hair and Linda was the quiet one with silver glasses.

Alice turned to Gran. "Did the goat girl make it?"

"She did. She even brought three goats with her."

"What's she like?"

"What kind of goats?"

"What's her sign? Are you compatible?"

Questions were flying fast and furious, until the instructor clapped her hands. "Ladies, I know you have a lot of catching up to do, but I have another class after yours, so…"

"We'll talk after," Gran promised her friends.

After helping Gran unroll her mat and watching for a few minutes while Crystal helped Gran find an alternate position that didn't stress her ankle, Patrick slipped out the door. The trip to the hardware store to pick up staples didn't take long, so he strolled along the block. Most of the stores weren't open yet, but the bookstore, art gallery and a new arts and crafts co-op offered window displays.

Across the street, an upscale foods store boasted of fancy pastas, gourmet cooking gadgets and specialty cheeses. A possible market for Lauren's goat milk? He'd have to mention it. After glancing at his watch, he returned to the yoga studio in time to meet Gran's group filing out on their way to the bakery next door.

Patrick held the door for them. "Mind if I join you ladies for coffee?"

"We insist," Bea said with a coy smile.

Patrick accompanied the women to the bakery, pushed two tables together on the patio and fetched an extra chair for Gran's foot. Once they were all seated, he borrowed a pen from Gran's purse and grabbed a paper napkin. "What does everyone want? I'm treating today."

The announcement had the desired result of oohs and aahs. Patrick went inside to order. When he returned, the women were talking with animation, something about the farm, but as soon as they spotted him, they went suspiciously quiet.

He set the drinks carrier on the table and passed out pastries, setting aside the blueberry scone Gran had promised Lauren.

Once everyone was served, he settled between Molly and Alice. "Molly, I heard you moved into the Easy Living Apartments a year or so ago. How are you liking it there?"

"Oh, very much. We have activities, you know. I'll be teaching a calligraphy class later today."

"The gardens are lovely," Rosemary said. "There's a perennial garden, a butterfly garden, and this summer they've added raised planters so that residents who want to can plant vegetables. Completely organic of course."

"That's good to hear. How long have you lived there, Rosemary?"

"Three years now. I love it."

"I think I've almost convinced my husband we need to move there," Alice said. "He hates to give up the house, but his arthritis makes it hard to get up and down the stairs, and the apartments are all single-level."

"I've been telling Gran she should move there, too," Patrick said, expecting the ladies to jump in with encouragement.

Instead they all stared at him. "Why?" Molly asked.

"Well, so that she can participate in all the activities—"

"She goes to the ones she's interested in.

You don't have to be a resident," Bea explained.

"And she'd get to spend more time with her friends," Patrick continued. "She's alone out on the farm."

"Not anymore," Molly pointed out. "Now she has the goat farmer."

"Yes, but Lauren can't be at the house all the time."

"That's a good thing," Linda said. "Everyone needs quiet time to read and reflect."

"Lauren is such a pretty name," Bea remarked. "I can just picture her with her goats, like one of those shepherdess statues. Is she pretty, Patrick?"

All heads turned in his direction. Patrick had the feeling this was some sort of trap, but he didn't see a way out. He thought of Lauren's long shiny hair, her bright eyes, the contented smile whenever she worked outside, even digging postholes. He kept his expression neutral. "Sure, I guess. I haven't really noticed."

From their chuckles they saw right through him. He tried to redirect the conversation to his original topic, "But about the senior apartments…"

After a brief pause, Alice turned to Gran and commented, "Did you see in the paper that they're moving the route on the Independence Day parade?"

"What's wrong with the old route?" Gran asked, and all the women jumped in to share opinions.

Meanwhile Molly leaned closer to Patrick and patted his arm. "It's no use," she whispered. "You're not going to push Bonnie into anything she's not ready for."

"But don't you think she'd be safer and happier in the apartments with you?" he whispered.

Molly gave a gentle smile. "I think that Bonnie has earned the right to make her own decisions. She'll move to town when she's good and ready. You might as well accept it."

Patrick nodded in resignation. The verdict was in, and he'd lost.

LAUREN TOOK A long swig from her water bottle and watched Patrick lift the posthole digger high before jamming it into the ground once more. Annoyance and gratitude warred within her as she realized he could dig three or four postholes in the time it took her to do one. Gratitude won. With two of them working over the last six days, the fencing project was moving ahead. She'd never have expected

Bonnie's grandson to give up his days off from work to do manual labor for her.

Especially since he didn't trust her. Oh, he was pleasant enough but now and then, ever-so-casually, he'd ask something like, "Who was that doctor you worked for in Oregon?" The receptionist at her old job had texted to let her know Patrick had contacted them, claiming that he was considering hiring her and asking for references. Lauren told them to answer whatever he asked. She had nothing to hide.

Lauren couldn't really blame him for being suspicious. If Bonnie were her grandmother, she'd be protective, too. Finding Bonnie on the forum was like suddenly discovering a fairy godmother to grant your fondest wish. After saving and scrimping for ten years, Lauren had almost saved up enough for a down payment on a small farm. But that didn't include a budget for livestock, feed and expenses while she got established. It probably would have taken another ten years to save up that much. With a single phone call, Bonnie had waved a magic wand and changed her life.

"Want some water?" she asked, holding up Patrick's bottle.

"When I'm done." Patrick's biceps bunched

again as he lifted the filled digger from the hole. Bonnie had explained that he worked twelve-hour days for fourteen days straight when he was on the slope, but he must somehow fit a few visits to the gym into that schedule. Lauren doubted you developed muscles like that stringing wire, or whatever it was electricians did there.

They'd almost completed the northwest pasture. It had gone more quickly than she'd anticipated. Most of the original posts were intact. The posthole Patrick was digging now was to jog around a boulder so that they could secure the fencing all the way to ground level. Once they'd finished the pasture, Lauren planned to start on the barn. She was already moving the goats into the barn every night to protect them from predators. Once she started milking, she'd need to bring them in twice a day, and the barn needed to be spotless.

Patrick laid the diggers down and set the new post in place. Lauren carried her shovel over to fill in around it. "Looking good. Thanks."

"No problem." He released the post and helped her tamp down the fill with his heavy work boots. She handed him his water bottle, and he gulped down half of it at once. "Shall we break for lunch?"

She'd been hoping to finish the section first, but if he was hungry... "Sure, okay."

He glanced at his watch. "I know it's a little early, but we've been out here for four hours, and I want to check on Gran."

"Oh. Good idea." Lauren felt a twinge of guilt for not thinking of that. Bonnie hadn't said so, but it was clear from her interaction with Patrick that part of her motivation for inviting Lauren to live at the farm was to get her grandson off her back. Which meant Lauren needed to convince Patrick she'd keep a responsible eye on Bonnie and she fully intended to do that. "She's getting better. This morning, she was just using the cane for balance, rather than support."

"Yeah, that's encouraging." Patrick went to claim the denim jacket he'd left hanging on a fence pole near the goats' pen. Spritz raised up on her back legs to greet him. He gave her a pat before turning to join Lauren on the path to the farmhouse.

They passed the old cabin on the way. Lauren smiled. "It must have been a blast, you and Bonnie searching for treasure together when you were a kid."

"It was," Patrick admitted. "Even then I

didn't really believe there was treasure, but it was fun to pretend. Gran and Rowan were all in. And then when we found that pyrite—we thought we were rich. Even though it didn't turn out to be real, it was exciting."

"You were lucky."

"We were." Patrick smiled at some memory. "I still am. Gran and Grandy were the reason I moved to Alaska and went the electrician route rather than college. My parents weren't too happy, but I knew this is where I wanted to be. Besides, they had my sister, Rowan, to follow in their footsteps. I like my job, and I love the life here."

"You live in Anchorage?"

"Yes, I have a house—well, a duplex. My renter keeps an eye on things and mows my lawn, which works out well while I'm on the slope. So how about you? Did you grow up in Oregon?"

"Not exactly. We moved around a lot."

"Oh yeah? Me too. My parents were in the diplomatic corps."

Lauren gave a short laugh that even to her own ears sounded forced. "My mother was… not." Not unless she was some sort of ambassador of short-lived romance. Her mom must have fallen in love with a dozen different men by the time Lauren graduated from high school, and every time it meant a different school in a different place.

Patrick paused as though he expected her to elaborate, but her childhood was the last thing Lauren wanted to talk about. "Where did you live with your parents?"

"Denmark, Greece, Croatia, Indonesia." Patrick ticked the places off on his fingers. "The DC area for training between postings. My other grandparents live in Virginia, so we stayed with them sometimes. What other places did you live besides Oregon?"

"Are you asking for conversational purposes, or because you want to check up on me?"

A flicker of guilt passed over Patrick's face. "I'm not—"

"Much of a liar." Lauren had to laugh. "Listen, I can totally understand why you'd be suspicious. Heck, I was suspicious. If I hadn't been interacting with Bonnie for months before she contacted me with the offer, I'd assume it was some sort of scam. If you want, I'll give you the information to run a credit check and a list of prior employers you can ask for references."

"I already contacted the doctor's office where you used to work," Patrick admitted. "They have only good things to say about you."

"I know. They told me."

"The animal shelter where you volunteered says you're extremely dependable."

"You called them, too?"

"I did. Sorry if it seems like I was going behind your back."

"Seems like?"

"Okay, I was going behind your back. I apologize. I should have been direct and asked for references instead of sneaking around."

"Apology accepted. Like I said, I understand why you'd want to protect your grandmother."

"Yeah?"

"Is that why you've been out here working with me for the past few days? To try to catch me doing something shady?"

"Maybe a little." Patrick winced. "Mostly I wanted to see if you were what my grandfather used to call a 'gentleman farmer' or if you were willing to get your hands dirty."

"And the verdict?"

Patrick reached for her hand and turned it upward, exposing the scrapes and rough spots she'd developed despite her leather work gloves. His touch was gentle as he ran a finger over the callus that was developing on her palm. "I'm certain Grandy would approve of your work ethic."

"What about you?" She suddenly needed to know.

"What about me?"

"Do you approve of my work ethic?"

"Yes, I do. Honestly, I know nothing about goat farming, whether you're doing the right things or whether goats are even a viable option in Alaska, but I'm convinced you're willing to put in the time and effort. And in my experience, that's the biggest part of success."

"Thank you."

"What for? Digging a few postholes?"

"For giving me an honest chance."

"You know I've been worried about Gran being here alone, and she's made it clear she's not ready to move. If you can keep an eye on her and make sure she's safe while you build this goat business, I think we've got a win-win situation."

Lauren nodded. "I think so, too."

EXCEPT FOR MEAL breaks and afternoon tea with Gran, Patrick spent the rest of the day working with Lauren. The sun was low in the northwest when Lauren drove the last staple in the fencing he'd stretched in place beside the gate. She clipped the wires and he followed behind, turning under the ends so there were no sharp edges.

Patrick took off his gloves and brushed his hands together. "Done."

Lauren shot him a grin. "Feels good, doesn't it?"

"It does. Are you going to let the goats into the big pasture now?"

"Not until tomorrow. Right now, they need to go to the barn." She crossed the field to the goats' pen. Patrick followed.

Two goats stood waiting at the gate, but Patrick didn't immediately see Spritz. Lauren frowned. "Has she gotten out again?"

"Let's check the pen first," Patrick suggested. "She could be hiding behind some bushes or something. You go that way. I'll take the other side." He headed clockwise along the fence. After a few feet, he spotted the goat between a rock and a bush, pawing at the ground. "Here she is."

Lauren came to join them. "Hey Spritz, what's up?" She moved closer and stroked the goat's head. "Are you okay?" She ran a hand down the goat's back and squeezed the base of her tail.

"What are you doing?"

"Checking her ligaments. According to what I read, they soften just before labor."

"Are they soft?"

"Maybe. I'm not sure what they feel like normally."

"Didn't you say the goats weren't due for a couple of weeks?"

"That's what I was told, based on when they put the buck in with the does. Although we were talking about Biscotti and Muffin. They threw in Spritz later, and knowing her escape tendencies, she might have decided to visit the buck early. Anyway, I suspect she might be kidding soon."

"What should we do?"

"First of all, let's get them all to the barn." Lauren snapped a lead rope to Spritz's halter, but the goat stomped her foot and refused to move.

Patrick went to join them. He scratched Spritz behind the ears. "Wouldn't you rather do this in a nice clean barn, Spritz?" The goat rubbed against his leg.

"She seems to like having you nearby," Lauren said. "Do you mind leading her?"

Patrick was a little bemused to be the goat's choice, but he supposed it was a compliment. "Okay." He took the rope and Spritz obediently followed him to the gate. Lauren snapped a rope onto one of the other goats and let the third follow behind. Slowly they made their way toward the barn.

They were still forty yards away when Spritz stopped and pressed her head hard against Patrick's leg, panting.

"Yes, she's in labor," Lauren said.

"Maybe I should carry her to the barn," Patrick suggested.

"Are you sure? She weighs as much as I do."

"Not a problem." Patrick waited until the goat stopped panting and lifted her into his arms. She settled against him, laying her head on his shoulder.

Lauren gave her an encouraging pat. "You're doing great, Spritz."

Patrick staggered a bit under the goat's weight, but he managed to get her to the barn without incident. He set the goat gently on her feet and stopped to catch his breath. Lauren quickly cleaned out an unused stall and spread clean straw across the bottom. Spritz willingly followed her into the stall, pawed at the straw until it was arranged to her satisfaction, and lay down against the wall.

Patrick turned to Lauren. "What do you need now? Boiling water? Diapers? Whiskey?"

Lauren laughed. "According to what I've read, we just need to stand back and let nature take its course. Spritz has done this before, after all."

"Good to know someone here has experience."

"Speaking of experience, your grandmother might have some good advice."

"Great idea. I'll go tell her what's happening."

"I'll be here."

Gran had already changed into her pajamas, but she insisted on getting dressed and accompanying Patrick to see the goat. "Get a stack of old towels out of the ragbag in the mudroom," she instructed.

The barn was a fair distance from the house. Patrick wondered if he might have to carry his grandmother there like he had the goat, but Gran was moving well, if slowly, with her cane. When they reached the barn, Lauren stood outside the stall, watching. The other two goats, in a pen across the aisle, were pressed up against the fence watching, too.

"I think it's almost here," Lauren said softly.

"Let's see." Gran came to stand beside her. "Yes, anytime now." Patrick fetched a plastic lawn chair that had been stored in the barn, brushed the cobwebs off, and set it up for Gran. She settled into the chair without ever taking her eyes off the goat.

Spritz dragged her leg back and forth across the straw and gave a sound that was halfway between a bleat and a human groan. A blob appeared. "It's coming," Lauren whispered. Several groans later, the blob slid onto the straw, wiggled, and a miniature hoof tore the sac away, exposing a tiny black-and-white goat. It was like a magic trick.

Spritz curled her neck around to sniff the baby, and then gave it a good lick across the nose, like any mom washing her kid's face. Gran handed Lauren a towel. "If it doesn't upset her to have you nearby, you can help her dry the kid."

Lauren stepped inside the stall. She stroked Spritz's neck and then slipped over and wrapped the towel around the new baby goat, all the while murmuring about what a good mother Spritz was. If Patrick didn't know better, he'd assume Lauren had done this dozens of times before.

Spritz seemed to welcome the assistance. In fact, Patrick could have sworn she was basking in the compliments about her mothering abilities and her new baby's beauty.

"It's a girl," Lauren announced, holding up the white goat with dark speckles. "What shall we name her?"

"Are you sticking with the pastries theme?" Gran asked.

"Why not? Chocolate Chip Cookie?"

"Chip for short," Patrick declared.

One of the goats in the pen bleated, presumably in approval. Spritz lurched to her feet and came to lick the baby in Lauren's lap. A few minutes later, she began groaning again. Before the day's official end, Chip, Pizzelle and Snickerdoodle crowded under their mother, enjoying their first meal.

"Congratulations," Gran told Lauren. "You've just doubled the size of your herd."

Lauren laughed. "I guess so." Covered with dirt and grime, Lauren brushed a strand of hair back from her cheek, leaving behind a smear of something Patrick chose not to identify, but a proud smile lit up her face, and her green eyes sparkled. "They look good, don't they?"

"Beautiful," Patrick agreed. "Absolutely beautiful."

CHAPTER FIVE

SATURDAY MORNING, Lauren checked each goat before taking them to browse in the pasture. From what she could tell, no more newborn kids would be arriving in the next few hours. Her herd was up to an even dozen now. Biscotti had given birth to twins and Lauren had bought four more goats from a local farmer: one pregnant doe and one with two kids. After a few days of togetherness, they seemed to have blended into a cohesive herd.

Since Spritz had milk left over after feeding her triplets, Lauren had milked her for the first time this morning. She'd learned to milk goats by hand when the shelter where she'd volunteered had taken in the herd of rescue goats, but she wasn't particularly fast. It was a good thing the secondhand milking machine she'd ordered would arrive soon, because milking an entire herd of goats would take forever. Spritz didn't seem to mind, though, munching her grain ration while Lauren extracted the milk.

Lauren led the herd to the pasture and closed the gate. Spritz gathered her family together and stood in front of the gate where she looked at Lauren as though she was waiting for something. But what? She'd had her grain. Lauren had even given all the goats carrots as treats. Their water supply was clean and fresh. The three kids took advantage of Spritz standing still to score a little bonus breakfast. And still Spritz stared expectantly at Lauren. She was probably wondering what happened to Patrick.

He'd gone yesterday, back to his job. After all the backbreaking work he'd put in at the farm—digging postholes, unloading feed sacks, and at his grandmother's request, spading a vegetable garden that had clearly been abandoned for years—he was probably happy to get back to his real job so he could get some rest.

It felt odd, just Lauren and Bonnie sharing dinner last night. It shouldn't have; sharing a house with Bonnie was what she'd signed up for. Nobody said anything about a grandson staying in the bedroom down the hall from her. She should be glad he was gone, if for no other reason than that she didn't have to worry that she was taking too long to shower in the only second-floor bathroom. "He's at work, Spritz, all the way across the state for two weeks. I'm not sure if he's coming back to the farm after that or not."

Ironically, if he didn't, that probably meant he'd finished his background check and decided Lauren wasn't a threat to Bonnie. If he did return, it was likely because he was still keeping an eye on her. Lauren wasn't sure which to root for.

Spritz reached over the gate and lipped at the latch. "Don't even think about it." Lauren removed the bandana she'd used to tie back her hair that morning, looped it around the gate and the post beside it, and tied a tight square knot. "Next time I'm in town, I'm buying one of those new latches that takes two hands to operate."

Spritz let out a *blah* noise that probably summed up her feelings about unreliable people who abandoned the herd and goat herders who didn't understand her need to roam free. She turned and trotted away, the three adorable kids trip-trapping after her.

Lauren made her way to the farmhouse, where Bonnie had breakfast ready. She was still walking a little gingerly, but no longer felt the need to use the cane inside the house.

Lauren poured tea, while Bonnie spooned up bowls of oatmeal.

"Any new babies today?" Bonnie asked.

"No, and I'm not seeing signs. I was thinking of making a run into Anchorage today. I milked Spritz this morning, and it occurs to me that I'll need to do something with the milk until the goats are producing large enough quantities to make cheese making worthwhile. So I thought I'd buy some soap making supplies."

"Soap? From milk?"

"Yes. I took classes in cheese making, and as a bonus the instructor spent a day teaching us how to make goat's milk soap. They're very high-quality soaps. I've been working weekends on a goat farm in exchange for milk and using it to experiment, coming up with my own recipes for cheese and soap. I thought soap might be a source of income while I'm waiting for cheese to age."

"That's a great idea."

"Also, I need to check into what forms and permits I'll need to produce and sell cheese."

"I can't help you there. Tim always handled that. He was good at organization and paperwork. Kept detailed records of every cow we owned, when she was bred, how much milk she produced, vet records, all that stuff, as well as all the government permits. Good thing, because all those picky details would have driven me mad. I'm more of a big-picture person."

"He sounds like an excellent farmer. I've started a database for my herd on the computer."

"Tim eventually switched to the computer, but for the first few years, he kept his records by hand. I'll show you his book sometime. It's a thing of beauty. Oh, by the way, there's a Department of Agriculture office in Palmer. In fact, there's a craft supply store on the same street, so you might find what you need there."

"That would save time. I'll check there first. Thanks."

"You're welcome. If it's not out of your way, you might pick up something from the bakery for our teatime."

Lauren smiled. "I'll do that."

Lauren turned on the radio in the truck, catching an upbeat tune that reflected her mood. If Bonnie was right and she could find the supplies she needed, she might even be able to give Spritz a second light milking this evening, which would hopefully yield enough milk for a sample batch of soap.

The ag office was just where Bonnie had

described, and so was the craft store half a block away. Lauren was able to buy all the supplies she needed, including some cute soap molds shaped like forget-me-nots, the state flower of Alaska. Bonnie would love them.

Afterward, she stopped by the agriculture office. A smiling woman at the front desk greeted her. "Our most popular handouts are on the table there. Most are available online, too."

"Thanks." Lauren scanned the table, seeing flyers on everything from encouraging beneficial insects in the garden to tips for growing giant vegetables to enter in the state fair, but not what she was looking for. "I need the form to apply for a milk permit."

"Milk permit?"

"I have a goat herd and plan to sell milk and goat cheese. I assume I'll need to get veterinary and facilities inspections."

The woman suddenly wouldn't meet Lauren's eyes. "Um, I'd better let you talk to the extension agent."

"Okay. Do I need to make an appointment?"

"Wait here a minute. I'll see if he's available."

Lauren waited, shifting from one foot to the other. Eventually, the woman came back. "He said you can go on in." Something about her shaky smile gave Lauren the feeling she wasn't going to like what the agent had to say.

LAUREN DRAGGED HERSELF into the mudroom. She'd hardly gotten started, and now it was all over. How was she going to tell Bonnie?

"Lauren, is that you?"

"Yes, it's me." Lauren stopped to remove her shoes.

"Did you find the soap supplies you were looking for?"

"Yes. They had everything I needed." Lauren padded into the kitchen to find Bonnie at the table with an open book in her hand and a cup of tea beside her. "Oh, sorry, I forgot to go by the bakery."

Bonnie used a paper napkin as a bookmark and closed the book. "That's okay. Probably better for me anyhow." She eyed Lauren for a few seconds. "It's not just the bakery, is it? What's wrong?"

"I...that is—"

"Sit down, honey." Bonnie reached behind her for another mug and poured from the pot in the center of the table. "Drink this first."

"Thank you." Lauren sipped the tea. Afternoon tea with Bonnie had become something she looked forward to every day. She would miss this.

"Now, start at the beginning, and tell me what has you so upset," Bonnie said.

"The beginning, huh?" Lauren drew in a deep breath. "I guess that would be my business plan. I told you how I've been saving up for a farm ever since I got my first job. Once I decided on goats, I've been preparing. I took cheese making classes, worked part-time at goat farms, and I read up on all the rules and regulations for goat dairy farms in Oregon. My plan was to start small and build on my successes."

"I know how much preparation you've done. That's why I made my offer. I felt like you could make something of this farm."

"And I appreciate it. When you offered to let me move up here and use your farm, it was like a miracle." Lauren could feel hot tears crowding her eyes, but she blinked them back.

"So, what's the problem?" Bonnie asked.

"The problem is my lack of research. I just assumed that the rules in Alaska would be similar to those in Oregon. But they're not. In Oregon, if I had regular health and safety inspections, I could make cheese from unpasteurized goat milk as long as it's a type of cheese aged more than sixty days."

"But not in Alaska?"

"No. Alaska has much stricter laws about milk pasteurization."

"I didn't realize," Bonnie said slowly. "Our milk went to the local creamery to be processed, but it went out of business not long after Tim died."

"The agent says it's fine for the owners to use the milk. Apparently, some farmers sell shares in their herds, and distribute the raw milk to the owners. But that doesn't cover cheese, which is the direction I wanted to go."

Bonnie thought for a few seconds. "Do you have a philosophical objection to pasteurization?"

"No, just an economic objection. I can't just boil the milk and call it good. The equipment I'd need to get a Grade A certification would cost a fortune, and I'd need a whole lot more goats to make it worth the investment, even if I could afford it. Which I can't."

"What about the soap? Does it have to be pasteurized?"

"No, there didn't seem to be any regulations about that."

"Could you use the milk to make soap for now, and save up for the equipment you need?"

Lauren shook her head. "I can't see how soap sales would even cover my ongoing expenses, much less allow me to save for equipment. I could get a job, but our deal was that you would get a share of a real business, not just a hobby."

"I don't care much about money," Bonnie said. "Tim was a big believer in life insurance, and I used his policy to buy an annuity. That means I get a comfortable monthly check, but unfortunately, I don't have a lump sum to spend on dairy equipment."

"I didn't mean to suggest—"

"I know you didn't. I'm just thinking out loud. There's got to be a way."

"I'm not seeing it. Maybe I should try to sell the goats I have and see if they've filled my old job back in Oregon." Lauren could return to her original plan, and in another decade—or a little longer because of the money from her savings she'd already spent on fencing, truck and trailer—she'd be ready to start farming there.

"Don't do anything yet. Give me some time to come up with a plan." Bonnie reached over to squeeze Lauren's shoulder. "I want you to stay."

"I want to stay, too." Not just for the farm, but because Bonnie was becoming like the grandmother she'd never known. "It's just—"

"I know. But don't panic. We'll think of

something." There was worry in Bonnie's smile, but also reassurance. "In the meantime, you can teach me how to make soap."

Tuesday morning, Lauren put the goats out to pasture again. Still no signs of labor among the pregnant does. The kids were growing stronger every day, prancing and playing. Lauren smiled at their antics, thinking how much she would miss them.

When she returned to the farmhouse, Bonnie was waiting with a travel mug of tea and a piece of toast. "No time for breakfast. I'm late for yoga. Will you come today? I want you to meet my friends."

"I need to…" Lauren trailed off, realizing that if she wasn't staying, there wasn't anything she particularly needed to do. If she couldn't keep her goats, there was no need to reinforce the pens around the barn or clear out the stalls where she planned to install the milking machine. She might as well go with Bonnie if it made her happy. "Never mind. I'd love to come."

"Good." Bonnie smiled in satisfaction. "Yoga's like tea. It makes everything better. Especially with friends. The women in my class call ourselves the Mat Mates."

"Cute. I've never done yoga. What do I need? I do have yoga pants."

"Put them on. I have a spare mat. I'll meet you in the car."

Once they arrived, Bonnie led Lauren into a studio with muted lavender walls and a polished wood floor. Six other women were already there. "Everyone, this is Lauren. She's my guest today. Crystal, Lauren's never done yoga before."

The instructor gave a graceful wave of welcome. "We're happy to have you, Lauren." Bonnie rattled off the names of her friends so quickly that Lauren had no idea who was who, but it didn't seem to matter, because class was beginning.

Crystal, the instructor, played some soft flute music and instructed them to start in what she called comfortable pose, but Lauren's elementary school music teacher had called crisscross-applesauce. Then they moved to forward fold. Lauren followed along as best she could with the rest of the class. It was a little intimidating when eighty-year-old women could hold the plank position better and longer than she could. Toward the end of class, Lauren was feeling it in her core, but the rest of the women seemed to be breezing through the routine, even Bonnie with her bad ankle and two of the others who had complained of stiffness at the beginning of class. If yoga guaranteed Lauren could move like these women in another fifty years, she was all in.

Once they'd finished class, Bonnie herded Lauren and the other ladies to the bakery next door. They each chose a pastry and drinks and settled at a table outside under a grove of trees. Lauren sipped her tea, expecting to make small talk. Instead, the woman nearest her said, "We understand you're in a bit of a pickle."

"How did—"

"I told Molly." Bonnie nodded toward the kind-faced woman sitting next to her, "about our little dilemma, and she told the others."

"I've contacted my state senator and asked that she look into Oregon's dairy laws," the woman next to Bonnie said. "But change is always a slow process."

"Alice was personal assistant to the governor," Bonnie told Lauren. "She has contacts."

Across the table, one of the women donned the glasses that had been hanging from a chain and pulled a yellow legal pad from her bag. She jotted something on the paper. "That was six governors ago. We'd better not count on help from the current lawmakers.

They've got their hands full already. Bonnie says you'll need new equipment to meet commercial standards. How much money are we talking about?"

Lauren named the figure the extension agent had estimated. Alice whistled. "That's not chicken feed. Plus, you'll no doubt have legal expenses and inspection costs."

"The *MatSu Valley Voice* had a story about someone who won a grant by entering some sort of invention in a contest. Have you invented anything?" the pink-haired lady asked.

"You read it in the *Valley Voice*? I'd trust anything from that rag about as far as I could throw the editor," Bonnie scoffed.

"Now, Bonnie, Anthony Clark shouldn't have written that story about you, but that was a long time ago." The woman with a gray braid down her back spoke in a gentle voice. "You'll never be at peace until you've learned to forgive."

"Well, I'm just glad we have a local paper, even if it's weekly," pink hair said. "And since you refuse to read it, Bonnie, how would you know if it's any good?"

"Ladies, we've wandered off topic. We're here to solve Lauren's problem." Molly smiled at Lauren. "Bonnie has told us all about finding you on the forum, and how she wanted to help you realize your dream. We want to see you succeed. So, we thought we'd do some brainstorming. Linda, what have you got so far?"

The lady with the notepad consulted her notes. "Alice talked to a state senator. Bea suggested a contest for inventors. Rosemary is pro forgiveness."

"Rosemary has a good point, but it doesn't really apply to Lauren's problem," Molly commented.

Bonnie reached into her tote bag. "This is a sample of some goat milk soap Lauren and I made yesterday."

"Oh, very nice," Rosemary reached across the table for the flower-shaped soap. "The texture is lovely. How did you get this blue color?"

"From red cabbage leaves," Lauren explained. "Boiled down and concentrated, they make a sort of intense blue syrup."

"I have a booth at the Saturday Market in Anchorage," Rosemary said. "I sell honey, along with beads and crystals. If you'd like, you can come along and sell your soaps there. Can you have enough by Saturday?"

Lauren had intended to make cheese with Spritz's milk this week, but if she couldn't sell the cheese and she could sell the soap, why not? "This soap won't be cured for another month or so, but if I use a water discount, I could have some ready for the Saturday after next. In the meantime, I have some I made in Oregon and brought with me that I could sell this week. Thank you."

"The soap is a good idea, but where can we get our hands on some serious money?" Bea mused.

"I'm considering looking for a job," Lauren said. "If I get up early enough, I'd have time to milk the goats before I leave and then after I get home, and I'd have weekends for maintenance and projects. Eventually, I might be able to save up enough—"

"But that would leave Bonnie alone all day," Alice pointed out. "If you do that, Patrick will be nagging her to move again."

"I'm not leaving the farm. Not until I find that nugget and stick it in Anthony Clark's face," Bonnie growled. "Once I do that, we can talk about forgiveness."

"The nugget! Of course." Molly beamed. "You and Lauren just need to find that nugget. How big is it?"

"A little over five pounds," Bonnie said.

"With the price of gold at around fourteen hundred a troy ounce, fourteen and a half troy ounces in a pound—" Linda scribbled on her pad "—it would be worth somewhere in the neighborhood of a hundred thousand dollars."

"Last I heard, the family had offered to double that amount as a reward for its safe return," Alice said.

"So, there you are." Molly declared. "Find the nugget, and you're golden."

All six of them were looking at Lauren, waiting for her to agree. She took another sip of tea to buy herself a moment. Were they really suggesting treasure hunting as a viable option? "If we were to find the nugget on Bonnie's farm, the reward would belong to Bonnie."

"I don't care about the reward," Bonnie said. "I just want to make Anthony Clark eat his words. If you'll help me hunt for the nugget, you can keep the reward."

"I can see you're hesitant," Alice said to Lauren. "But why not give it until the end of summer? If you find the nugget, your problems are solved. If you don't, are you worse off than you are today?"

Maybe she was right. If Lauren concentrated on making milk soap from the goats she had now, she could probably meet the goats' feed and vet bills while they hunted.

Bonnie watched her, her eyes wide and encouraging. Lauren smiled. "Okay. Yes. Let's do it!"

"All right!" Bonnie held up her hand. Lauren laughed and slapped her a high five. The ladies cheered.

Linda wrote *Find Nugget* on her notepad and underlined it. "Excellent. And if you're going treasure hunting, I know someone you should talk to. I'll set up a meeting ASAP."

CHAPTER SIX

EARLY SATURDAY MORNING, Lauren checked the new gate latch she'd installed and took inventory of her herd. All her remaining pregnant does had given birth the past week, and six new baby kids had joined the family. Of the twelve kids now wandering about in the pasture, nine were female which boded well for her future milking herd, assuming she still had the herd at the end of the summer.

Between the births, the arrival and setup of the new milking machine, and scrambling to produce enough soap to sell at the market, Lauren and Bonnie had found very little time to devote to treasure hunting. But Linda had arranged a meeting with a historian in Anchorage after the Saturday Market closed. Maybe he would give them something to go on.

Just as Lauren reached the house, she spotted a car coming up the drive. A Subaru so ancient it was hard to distinguish the color pulled up in front of the door, and Rosemary climbed out. "Ready to go?" A slight breeze ruffled her ankle-length cotton skirt and caught at the hem of her cardigan.

"Sure. Let me just grab my boxes and see if Bonnie needs anything before we go."

"I'm just fine." Bonnie stepped onto the porch carrying one of the soap boxes. "You two go ahead. But if that booth that sells the peanut butter fudge is still there, you might pick me up a quarter pound."

"Will do," Lauren promised as she gathered up the other box and set it in Rosemary's car. "Are you sure you don't want to come?"

"No, I'm going with Molly to buy some seedlings and help her with her planter boxes today. You can give me a hand with planting our vegetable garden tomorrow afternoon if you like."

"It's a date. See you later." Lauren shut the tailgate of the Subaru.

"Oh, by the way," Bonnie said, "if you should talk to Patrick before he comes back from the slope, let's not mention the nugget."

"Why would I talk to Patrick?"

"I don't know but if you do, keep the plan to yourself. It's better explained in person."

"I won't say a thing," Lauren promised as she climbed into the passenger seat and shut the door. "Wonder what that was about."

Rosemary chuckled. "I suspect she probably let something slip last time Patrick called, and she's worried he'll call you to check up on her."

Lauren laughed. It was sweet, how Patrick worried about his grandmother. The drive to Anchorage took about an hour. It was Lauren's first trip to the city and the high-rise hotels and office buildings downtown were a big change from Palmer. The market was bigger than she'd expected, filling a large lot not far from the train station on the edge of downtown. Down below she could see ocean, with a snow-capped mountain range on the other side.

She helped Rosemary set up a tent and tables, and then spread their wares for shoppers to see. "I sell honey from my own bees and two other beekeepers as well. There's a little initial on the price tag of each jar of honey," Rosemary explained. "As you sell them, keep track here."

"How about the beads and jewelry?" Lauren asked, looking over the colorful stock.

"They're all mine, but I try to note each sale to help with inventory. You'll probably want to do the same with your soaps. Nice labels."

"Thanks." With Bonnie's help, Lauren

had designed and printed out bands from her computer to wrap the soaps.

"'Now and Forever Farm.' I like it. I don't suppose your phone is set up to take credit cards?"

"No." Darn, Lauren should have thought of that.

"Don't worry, mine is. We'll just keep track and settle up later. Here come our first customers."

A pair of high school–age girls greeted Rosemary by name and stopped to look. "What's new?"

"I just got in these Himalayan beads." Rosemary pointed at some long beads with coral and turquoise inset among an intricate silver design. "And the goat's milk soap is new."

"Milk soap?" One of the girls picked up a bar. "It's pretty. Can I smell it?"

"Sure. I have some unwrapped bars so you can feel and smell it." Lauren reached under the table for her samples.

The girl sniffed it and handed it to her friend. "Nice."

"My grandma would love this," the other girl said. "I'll take a bar." She picked up a wire bracelet with a pink-and-green stone. "What does this one do?"

"Fluorite is good for focus and mental clarity," Rosemary replied.

"Just what I need. I'm taking my driver's exam next week. I'll take it, too."

After the girls left, Lauren took a closer look at Rosemary's jewelry. "I didn't realize the stones in your jewelry have special meaning."

"All stones have meaning," Rosemary replied. She picked up a keychain with an odd, shiny stone with many facets attached. "Even pyrite, fool's gold, offers power and protection. Many crystals offer healing."

"Do you really think so?"

"I do." Rosemary smiled. "The mind and the body can't be separated. If a crystal helps focus the mind on healing, then isn't that all for the good?"

"I never thought of it like that."

Rosemary snapped her fingers. "Blue lace agate." She picked up a pendant with a polished blue stone hanging from a leather cord. "Insight and communication. That's what you'll need for your treasure hunt." She slipped the cord over Lauren's head.

"Insight, hmm? I could definitely use some help with that." Lauren picked up the stone to examine the white and gray bands that ran across the clear blue. "It's very pretty." She reached for her wallet.

"It's a gift," Rosemary said.

"Oh, but I—"

Rosemary laid a hand on her arm. "It gives me joy to be able to give you this gift. Your job is simply to accept it and say thank you."

Lauren could feel her cheeks growing warm. "Thank you."

"You're welcome." Rosemary smiled and patted her hand.

They got busy with customers after that and didn't have a chance to talk much more until the end of the day. Lauren did find a few minutes to locate Bonnie's peanut butter fudge and pick up gyros for Rosemary and herself from one of the food trucks.

By the end of the day, Rosemary's inventory of honey had diminished considerably, and Lauren had sold out of soaps. A quick calculation assured Lauren that the profits from the soap should be enough to keep the goats fed for another week. If she could increase production over the next few weeks, she might even be able to put a little aside. But the market ran only through the summer, and goats ate all year round.

She and Rosemary packed the car, and Rosemary drove her to the address Linda had given them with five minutes to spare. A brown picket fence with the house number faced the street. "Just give me a call when you're done and I'll pick you up," Rosemary told her.

"You're not coming in?"

"No. I have errands, and besides, this quest belongs to you and Bonnie. Good luck."

"Thanks." Lauren fingered the stone Rosemary had given her as she watched her drive away. A quest. She liked that. Not some pie-in-the-sky dream, but a concrete goal that—with enough hard work and good luck—was achievable.

She turned and walked under a curved arbor and into the front yard. The historian lived in an ordinary-looking home with an extraordinary garden. Instead of a lawn, the sidewalk bisected beds of flowers and ferns. Pink tulips underplanted with tiny purple pansies bordered the white railing on the front porch. An enormous basket of pink-and-white fuchsias dangled like a chandelier from the beam overhead.

Lauren stepped onto the porch and rang the bell, disturbing a fluffy white cat who had been sunning himself on a bench cushion. He stretched, and then jumped down and wound around her ankles. By the time the door opened, she was holding the cat, tickling him under his chin and making him purr.

"Ah, I see you've met Bastet. You must be Lauren. Come in."

"Hello, Professor Jankowski. Thanks for meeting with me." Lauren set the cat on the floor, where he dashed between the man's feet and disappeared into the house.

"Albert, please. Let's go to my study." He led her through a sunny parlor and into a cozy room with a scarred wooden desk and two yellow wingchairs in front of a fireplace. Other than the fireplace and window, every vertical surface was covered with overflowing bookshelves. A round table between the chairs held a book titled *Lost Treasures of Alaska*.

He motioned that she should sit and picked up the book. "I was pleased when Rosemary told me you were taking up the search for Bradley's Heart." He opened the book to a marked spot about halfway through and handed it to her. "This was what I found. You can read it later."

Lauren could feel his eyes on her as she skimmed the first page of the chapter. "James Bradley sounds like quite a character."

"Indeed." Albert gave an encouraging smile. "One thing I've learned in my studies—treasures are seldom found by random searches. Most of the time, it's examining the history of the characters involved that solves the mystery."

"Interesting. I've wondered why anyone would carry a valuable gold nugget in his pocket with no protection. My friend Bonnie says James Bradley was notoriously cheap—"

"Ah, yes." Albert chuckled. "He had quite the reputation for thrift. They tell the story that while traveling in the Lower 48, he once drove fifty miles out of his way to avoid going over a toll bridge. However, my theory is that he didn't use a taxi or a bodyguard on the day he transferred the nugget because he felt there was no need, since his appointment with Jack Harrison, the intended recipient, wasn't public knowledge."

"That doesn't look good for Harrison," Lauren said thoughtfully, "although why would he rob the man who was already giving him the nugget?"

"Oh, I can think of several reasons, the most obvious being he could keep it for himself rather than donate it to the museum. However, I'm fairly certain that Harrison had nothing to do with the robbery. Were you aware that William Golson, the convicted robber, worked at the front desk of the hotel where Bradley was living?"

"Really? So, Golson may have gotten wind of the exchange in advance."

"Golson was, in fact, the employee who retrieved the nugget from the hotel safe for Bradley. No one was there to witness the conversation, but it wouldn't have been out of character for Bradley to mention his plans. He was a friendly fellow."

"That makes sense."

"What fascinates me is Golson's history. Prior to this robbery, he had no criminal background. The hotel manager states that he was a hardworking and reliable employee. In his job, Golson would have had opportunities to pilfer, but there's no evidence he ever had, nor that he was prone to violence. In fact, according to the police record, Bradley states that the masked robber was polite, almost apologetic in fact."

"I thought the robber assaulted him and broke his hip."

"One newspaper reported it that way, but the police report contradicts that story. According to Bradley, he handed over the nugget, but then he tried to grab the gun and was injured in the struggle when he fell. Golson could have shot him, but he dropped the gun and ran instead. Overall, he seemed to be a peaceable man. And yet, something drove him to commit robbery."

"Do you have any theories about what it might have been?"

"My only clue is from the arresting officer. You remember, Golson hid out in an abandoned cabin near Palmer for three weeks before the troopers caught up with him."

"Yes, my friend Bonnie owns the farm where the cabin sits."

He nodded. Linda must have explained that. "When the officer arrested him, he reports Golson was crying, muttering something about a woman."

"You think Golson committed the robbery to impress a woman?"

"It wouldn't be the first time."

"Who was the woman?"

"That, we don't know. I've not been able to interview anyone with more than a nodding acquaintance with Golson."

"I've been wondering—why Palmer? He committed the crime in Anchorage. You'd think he'd either hide out there and continue to show up at work to throw off suspicion, or he'd try to get as far away as possible."

"Familiarity, perhaps? He attended high school in Palmer. Golson was orphaned at the age of fifteen and went to live with his grandparents. His grandfather was a farmhand, and they lived in a small house on the dairy farm where he worked. Golson would have ridden the same school bus as the children who lived in the cabin where he hid out, so he knew it was there."

"Would he have known it was abandoned?"

"I have to assume he did. His grandfather had died, and his grandmother moved in with a relative in Soldotna by that time, but perhaps Golson had friends in Palmer he visited. Golson died in prison three years after his trial, and his grandmother died shortly afterward, so I wasn't able to interview her."

Lauren glanced at the chapter again and then set the book on the table. "Do you believe the nugget is hidden somewhere on the farm, or are we kidding ourselves?"

The professor gave a wry smile. "Well, that's the sixty-four-thousand-dollar question, isn't it? Or more like two-hundred-and-fifty-thousand, which is the reward the Bradley family was offering, last I heard. Many journalists at the time assumed Golson had already handed off the nugget to an accomplice before he left Anchorage, but that doesn't ring true to me."

He picked up the book, turned it over in his hands and set it down. "Golson was not a habitual criminal, and he was a loner. If the first he knew about the nugget transfer was when Bradley removed it from the hotel safe the evening before, that would have only given him about twelve hours to find an accomplice. Not likely. I think he probably hid the nugget, and certainly, given the time frame, the area around the cabin is the most obvious place. When his fingerprints matched those on the gun, he pled guilty to robbery but refused to divulge the whereabouts of the nugget. He probably planned to serve out his sentence and go after it."

"But he died first."

"Yes."

Lauren stood. "Thank you so much, Profess—Albert. This has been…illuminating."

He laughed. "I'm always thrilled to hear I've shed light on any subject." He handed her the book. "This is for you."

"Thank you. For everything."

"My pleasure." He shook her hand. "Good luck and keep me apprised. Although if you're successful, I'm sure the whole state will be talking about it."

Lauren smiled, thinking of the newspaper editor. "Bonnie would love that."

CHAPTER SEVEN

MONDAY MORNING, Lauren had four goats to milk. Three of the goats had already learned the routine, but this was the first time Muffin had ever been milked, and she wasn't sure she was too happy about the idea.

Lauren stroked the goat's head and fed her a piece of carrot while she got used to standing on the milking platform. Meanwhile, Lauren glanced around. Yesterday afternoon, she and Bonnie had searched the nooks and crannies throughout the north end of the barn, even opening up the high hayloft door to let in sunlight as well as fresh air. They were working under the theory that Golson might have wanted a secure, all-weather hiding spot for the nugget and since Bonnie and her grandkids had searched the cabin dozens of times, the barn was the next logical choice.

There had been a moment of excitement when they'd found a rounded rock with a clef through the middle tucked into a knothole, but it seemed too small and a quick comparison with an online mineral guide made it clear the rock was granite, probably placed there to block a mouse hole. Today they planned to investigate the south end of the barn. That, along with soap making and goat care, should pretty much fill the day.

Muffin shifted her weight, signaling that she might be considering escape, but the bucket of grain Lauren offered proved to be incentive enough for the doe to stand more or less quietly while Lauren washed her udder, hand stripped a sample of milk to inspect and then attached the milking machine.

Lauren's cell phone rang, startling her. She seldom got a signal anywhere on the farm. Thinking it might be Bonnie, Lauren stripped off her gloves and reached into her pocket, answering on the fifth ring without looking at the caller ID. "Hello?"

"Lauren, it's Patrick."

"Oh, hi." Her heart did a little double beat upon hearing his voice. What was that about? "How are you?"

"Fine. Hope I didn't catch you at a bad time."

"I'm at the barn so you're likely to get dropped at any time."

"I'll talk fast. First, a guy I work with up here is good friends with the people who own the reindeer farm outside Anchorage."

"I've heard of it."

"It's a nice farm. Touristy, but nice. Anyway, Sam happened to know that the owners of the farm there got a good deal on hay bales and if you want, they're willing to split the load with you." Patrick quoted a price that was significantly lower than she'd been paying at the feed store.

"If it's decent quality hay, that would be awesome." Lauren watched Muffin fidget and was ready to intervene if necessary, but then the goat settled down and went back to munching on her grain.

"They're good farmers, so I'm sure they checked the quality before they bought it. I'll text you the contact information. Also, I was wondering if Gran is doing okay."

"She's doing well. The doctor says she can drive now, which makes her happy."

"That's good to hear. It's just that last time I talked with her, I got the idea she was hiding something."

"Like what?" Now Lauren's heart flipped to fast-forward. She was not a good liar.

"I don't know." Some static interrupted. "…afraid she'd gotten bad news from the doctor and didn't want to tell me, but if he gave her permission to drive—"

"Yeah, I was with her at the appointment. He said her ankle looks good as new."

"Okay. She's not doing anything dangerous, is she? You know she was messing around at the old cabin when she fell and sprained her ankle in the first place. What with old logs and tree roots, it's difficult to get through the woods there. Gran shouldn't be taking chances at her age."

"As far as I know, she hasn't been near the cabin." Not yet anyway. They were concentrating on the barn for now.

"Okay, good. Well, I do feel better knowing that you're there with her. I'll see you next Saturday."

"Oh, you're coming to the farm when you get back?"

"Yes, I…" The sound cut out.

"Okay, see you then," Lauren replied just in case he could still hear her before she ended the call. Lauren realized she was smiling. Shouldn't she be seeing Patrick's return as a sign that he still didn't trust her? But he did say he felt better knowing Lauren was there with his grandmother, so maybe he did. Either way, Spritz would be happy to see him.

As annoying as Bonnie found Patrick's protective instincts, Lauren thought it was nice that he would be so concerned about his grandmother. It was nice that he was thinking of Lauren and arranging deals on hay, too.

Lauren stopped the milking machine, leaving plenty of milk behind for Muffin's twins, and led her down the ramp. "See, that wasn't so bad. Next time will be easier." She returned Muffin to the pen, where her two kids greeted their mom with joyful leaping and prancing.

Knowing they were about to make the move to the pasture, the goats surged forward, bleating softly. But there was another noise as well—sort of a whimper. Lauren stopped to listen. It came again, but it didn't seem to be coming from any of the goats in the pen. Leaving them inside, she stepped outside the barn. At the corner of the barn, a bush moved, and two dark eyes looked at her.

Since the eyes were only nine inches above the ground, Lauren felt safe moving closer. Leaves rustled as the bush moved again, and she realized it was a dog, wagging its tail against the twigs. "Hey, pup. What are you doing here?"

At the sound of her voice, the tail wagged harder. Lauren reached in and gently lifted the dog from the bush. Its long body and stubby legs branded it a dachshund, but it was smaller than average, and its skin pulled tight over its ribs. White hairs mixed with the black on the dog's muzzle and ears.

"Are you lost?" The dog gave another little whine. Inside the barn, the goats bleated, demanding to know why they weren't on their way to browse.

"Tell you what, doggo. I'm going to leave you with Bonnie for a little while, and then I'll see what we need to do about finding your people." She carried the dog to the house through the mudroom and opened the kitchen door. "Look what I found."

"Oh, my goodness." Bonnie shook her head, sadly. "Some people."

"What?"

"They think if they don't want a dog anymore, they can just drop it in the country and somehow it will be able to take care of itself. Lucky this little guy didn't get killed by a moose or something, but he certainly hasn't been eating well."

"He could be lost."

"Could be," Bonnie agreed, taking the dog into her arms. "But I doubt it. No collar."

"Can you keep him for a little bit while I run the goats out to pasture?"

"Sure. After that we can take him to the animal shelter."

"A shelter?" Lauren asked in dismay. She suspected older dogs weren't the most likely to be adopted.

"On the farm, you can't afford to feed animals that don't pay their own way. A shepherd dog to herd the goats would make sense, but not a little dog like this. Besides, the shelter can see if he's microchipped."

"I guess." It was Bonnie's house, after all. Lauren watched the dog for a few seconds before tearing her eyes away from his sweet face. "I'll be back soon."

Once Lauren had the goats moved, she returned to the farmhouse and slipped inside. From the mudroom, she could hear Bonnie's voice, "You like that, don't you? Cottage cheese has lots of protein. Yes, that's a happy boy."

Lauren washed her hands and stepped into the kitchen to see the little dog's face buried in a plastic tub and his tail wagging at warp speed. "I thought he was going to the shelter."

"Oh, he is," Bonnie said, "but I needed to clean out the refrigerator anyway, and there was a dab of cottage cheese left in the bottom of the container."

"Um-hmm." There had been well more than a dab, but Lauren wasn't complaining. "I ate while you were milking, but your breakfast is keeping warm in the oven."

"Thanks." While Lauren ate, Bonnie stroked the dog's head. He sat in her lap, his contented expression indicating this was a lifestyle to which he would like to become accustomed. Lauren ate and put her dishes into the dishwasher.

Bonnie set the dog on the floor and got to her feet. "Come on. We need to take you in now before we get attached to each other." The dog licked her ankle, and Lauren suspected it was too late for that.

Bonnie held the dog in her lap while Lauren drove. The dog lay his head across Bonnie's arm and drew in a breath, as though memorizing her scent. At the shelter, Bonnie carried him to the front desk. "We had a stray show up on the farm today. Has anyone reported a lost dachshund?"

"Let me check." The friendly woman at the front desk typed something into her computer. "No, no reports yet." She cast a professional eye. "Looks like he's been on his own for a while. Let me check for a microchip."

She took the dog and disappeared for several minutes. When she returned, she shook her head. "No chip. Looks like you're with us, buddy."

Bonnie pressed her lips together for a moment. "You know, I was thinking. It's possible his owner is out of town and doesn't know he escaped from whoever is supposed to be taking care of him. I could keep the dog for a little while. Like a foster home. And then if someone claims him, you can call me."

"If you want to become a foster for us, we'd need you to fill out some forms and take some training. In the meantime, we'll need to log the dog into the system—"

"Or I can just take the dog home. I mean, I haven't officially surrendered him yet."

The woman smiled. "That's true."

"You can write down my phone number, and if the owner should happen to contact you, you'll know where to find me."

"Works for me." The woman returned the dog to Bonnie. He snuggled against her and wagged his tail.

Lauren scratched behind his ear. "Well, I guess we should be going. I need to stop off at the feed store and pick up a few things."

"I thought you'd stocked up last week."

"I did." Lauren grinned. "But that was before we added our latest staff member."

"Staff member?"

"Sure. Maybe he can't herd goats, but he's good for mental health, and that has to be a plus for the farm, right?"

Bonnie laughed. "Or as Rosemary would say, he puts out good vibes."

"Exactly."

Bonnie snapped her fingers. "Wilson."

"What?"

"We should call him Wilson. After the Wilson brothers in the Beach Boys. They sang 'Good Vibrations.'"

"Perfect." Lauren passed a hand over the dog's head. "Absolutely perfect."

MONDAY AFTERNOON'S SEARCH of the rest of the barn didn't yield any gold nuggets, but Lauren managed to combine the search with clearing a spot to store the hay that was coming. Wilson found the various barn smells fascinating. Once he flushed a mouse, but it escaped into a mouse hole. Wilson spent the rest of the afternoon staring at that hole, but at the end of the day, he was happy to accompany Bonnie into the house for dinner.

Tuesday morning, Lauren tagged along with Bonnie to yoga. She'd decided if yoga could keep her as fit and flexible as this group of octogenarians, the membership fee was money well spent. She did a little better this week, with Crystal praising her posture during mountain pose although Lauren was nowhere near being able to keep her balance for standing pigeon. At the end of class, Crystal asked Lauren to stay for a few minutes.

What did she want? The class was billed as senior yoga; maybe Crystal wanted her to move to a different class. Lauren mentally rehearsed her arguments on why she wanted to stay, while the other ladies rolled up their mats and filed out of the room, calling goodbyes to Crystal. Or maybe Crystal just wanted privacy to inform Lauren she was hopeless and should quit now.

So, Lauren was completely taken aback when Crystal's first comment was, "I hear you have some baby goats."

"Yes, twelve of them, actually."

"I was wondering if you might be interested in a joint venture. Have you ever heard of goat yoga?"

Lauren had not, but when Crystal explained it, she could see the attraction. Doing yoga with baby animals scrambling around and climbing on the participants would guarantee smiles and laughter. "That would be great."

"Do you have an area we could use?"

Hmm, the layout of the barn didn't lend itself to a group activity. She and Patrick had cleared the growth between the house and barn, but the gravel service wasn't suitable for yoga, although they could use it for parking. "It would have to be the front lawn. It has a picket fence around it, which should contain the kids, although I'd need to build a gate under the arbor. I'd have to clear everything with Bonnie first, though. It's her house."

"Of course. Do you think we could be ready by Sunday afternoon? Weekends would encourage people from Anchorage to drive out."

"I don't see why not." Lauren listened while Crystal laid out the details and then made her way to the bakery, where the ladies had already settled in at their table.

"We got you tea and an oatmeal cookie," Bonnie said, patting the empty chair beside her. "What's up? I can almost see the butter churning in your head."

"How would you feel about using your front yard for goat yoga?" Lauren explained Crystal's proposal. "She'll handle the class and the money. I'd just need to build a gate and supervise the goats."

Bea clapped her hands. "Goat yoga looks like so much fun! I've seen pictures."

"It's fine with me," Bonnie told Lauren. "But you're the one who has to do the work. Are you sure you want to take this on?"

"It's another revenue stream," Lauren pointed out. She laughed. "And Bea is right. It'll be fun."

"Then we need to get busy," Alice announced. "I'll talk with Crystal and get specifics about prices and times. Bonnie, you should call your insurance agent and make sure you're covered for liability. Molly, could you design a poster? Bea, you can visit the stores in town and hang the posters in windows. Linda can get the word out on the internet."

"Wait," Lauren said. "Aren't we rushing this?"

"If your first session is this Sunday, there's no time to waste. We want this to be a success, don't we?"

"Um, yes?"

"Then let's get moving." Alice looked pointedly at Lauren. "Don't you have a gate to build?"

"Yes, ma'am." Lauren tucked the oatmeal cookie in her pocket for later. Alice was right; there was no time to waste.

BETWEEN MILKING, soap making, and preparation for the yoga activity, the next few days passed in a blur. Friday morning, Lauren had just set a batch of creamy white milk soap out to cool when she heard a vehicle approaching. As she stepped onto the porch, a red pickup with a picture of a sleigh on the door and an enormous trailer behind pulled to a stop in front of the house.

A woman around Lauren's age jumped down from the truck. "Hi, are you Lauren? I'm Marissa Allen. Chris says about a fourth of this hay belongs to you."

"Yes, thanks." Lauren had almost forgotten about the hay. "Can you drive it over by the barn?"

"Sure." Marissa made a U-turn at the barn and slowly backed the trailer toward the big doors, turning her wheels and then overcorrecting and turning the other way. The trailer ended up crooked, but in the general area. She grinned when she got out. "Sorry. I'm getting better, but trailer backing is not my forte."

"Mine either," Lauren said, remembering the trip through Canada. "This is close enough."

A boy scrambled down from the truck and

looked around with interest. Marissa laid a hand on his shoulder. "This is my son, Ryan."

"Hi, Ryan. Let me grab some gloves and a cart, and I'll get it unloaded."

Lauren fetched the equipment while Marissa uncovered her load and climbed to the top of the stack. When Lauren returned, Marissa started tossing down bales.

Ryan picked up a bale and set in on the cart. "Do the French Alpines we saw in the pasture belong to you?"

Lauren set a bale beside Ryan's. "Yes, they do. You really know your goats."

Ryan shrugged. "We have some goats at the reindeer farm."

"It's sort of a petting zoo," Marissa explained. "We have several different breeds."

"That sounds fun. Do you have other animals?"

She listened to Ryan list their pig, rabbits and chickens, breed by breed, while they loaded the cart. Once it was full, Lauren rolled it into the barn and, with Ryan's help, arranged the bales in a straight line.

When they returned Marissa had tossed down several more bales. "I noticed you have quite a few kids. If you're planning to sell the males, we could use a gentle wether in our herd, right Ryan?"

The boy nodded eagerly. "We have a Swiss Alpine named Heidi, but no French Alpines."

"I do have three males," Lauren said. "I handle them often, so they should grow up to be good with people. And they're about to be exposed to a lot more people." She explained about the goat yoga while they loaded the cart again.

"Goat yoga!" Marissa laughed. "That's hilarious. I have got to try this. When and where?"

Lauren shared all the details. "This Sunday afternoon is our first time to try it."

"Can I come?" Ryan asked.

"Sure, why not?" Marissa said. "You'd probably be great at yoga."

"Other than the instructor, you may be the only ones there," Lauren said. "We have no idea if anyone else would be interested."

"Oh, I'll bet they will be." The back quarter of the truck was now empty. Marissa tucked the tarp around the remaining load and secured it. She jumped down and started picking up bales and loading them onto the cart.

"I can do the rest," Lauren said. "I don't want to keep you. Just let me run in and get my checkbook."

"No problem. We're happy to help." Together they moved the bales into the barn and set them into place. Once they had the bottom layer set, Lauren climbed up and started stacking the next level, while Marissa and Ryan handed up bales until they'd built a tall pyramid of hay.

Lauren climbed down and examined the pile. "Thanks so much. This will really help."

"Happy to do it. A developer bought a farm over by Wasilla and sold off all the livestock, so they had no need for the stored hay and gave us a good deal. Trouble is, we don't really have room for all of it, so I'm glad we found you."

"Me, too! Would you like to come inside for a drink while I write you a check?"

"Can I go see the goats instead?" Ryan asked.

Marissa chuckled. "Actually, I'd like to see the goats, too."

"In that case, you two go ahead along that trail. I'll get the check and meet you there."

"Great."

When Lauren arrived at the pasture, carrying three bottles of cold water, she spotted Ryan sitting on the ground, letting three of the kids climb all over him. Lauren handed him a bottle and a few baby carrots, which brought even more kids running to him. He laughed.

Meanwhile his mom was petting Biscotti

and seemed to be examining her. She turned to smile at Lauren when she handed her the water. "Thanks." Marissa took a drink. "They all look really healthy. I gather you're not bottle feeding the kids."

"No, it seems better to let the mothers do it. I know there are some advantages, and they say bottle-raised kids can be more comfortable around people."

"Yeah, but this way they learn from their moms. I'm a wildlife biologist, as well as a farmer, so I tend to like to do things the natural way as much as possible." Marissa accepted Lauren's check and tucked it into her pocket. "Come on, Ryan. We'd better get home. It's not that long until feeding time."

"Okay." He scrambled to his feet, gave each of the kids an extra pat or cuddle, and walked over to Lauren. "Thanks for letting me see your goats."

"Thank you for all your help with the hay."

"You're welcome."

Lauren latched the gate behind them, and they returned to the truck. Marissa and Ryan climbed in. "We'll see you Sunday. Stop by the reindeer farm sometime if you get the chance."

"I will. Thanks for everything." Lauren watched them drive away. Then she took a minute to gaze in satisfaction at the stack of hay, reaching from the floor all the way to the bottom of the hayloft. She supposed she could have stored it up there, but she wasn't sure how to operate the block and tackle, and she had plenty of room at floor level. She wasn't using too much hay right now, with the goats out browsing all day, but come winter, the goats would go through it.

Of course, that was assuming she was still there this winter. It was entirely possible she'd be the one selling excess hay if they didn't find that nugget. She took a deep breath. Think positive. Next week, she and Bonnie could concentrate on the nugget. Assuming Patrick didn't get in the way, once Bonnie told him what she was up to. But when it came down to it, what could he do? Bonnie had a mind of her own.

Right now, Lauren needed to cut and wrap some soap. And then put a coat of paint on the gate she'd built for the front yard. Then it would be time for the evening milking. But next week—next week they would go treasure hunting.

CHAPTER EIGHT

PATRICK MOVED A load of work clothes from his washer to his dryer and checked his watch. Yesterday during his lunch break, he'd found a voice mail from Gran on his phone, asking him to pick her up at the Saturday Market at three. The message was a little garbled, something about Rosemary and a wedding. When he'd called back, he got her answering machine and left a message that he would be there.

He'd flown in from the slope around noon, grabbed lunch and done a few chores. Now he had less than an hour left to sort his mail, finish his laundry and pack for the farm. It was starting to become routine, spending his weeks off at Gran's instead of doing his own thing. Funny thing was how much he was looking forward to it. The weather was beautiful this weekend, and he'd heard there was a good salmon run on the Kenai, but he'd rather be weeding his grandmother's garden and doing farm chores with Lauren.

"Lauren," he whispered to himself. Just saying her name made him smile. He'd had his doubts, first about her intentions and then about her abilities, but she'd proven to be both honest and competent. With the information she gave him, he'd been able to run a background check and wasn't surprised to find it blemish free, with an excellent credit score to boot. Despite her lack of experience, she'd been right in there when the goat gave birth, doing all the right things. Lauren was an impressive woman.

By the time he'd thrown a few clean clothes into a bag, his dryer was buzzing. He finished folding the laundry with five minutes to spare. He grabbed his bag, carried it to the garage, and started to open the back of his big SUV when his gaze fell on the Jeep parked in the next stall.

With its snap-on canvas cover and go-anywhere suspension, the vintage Jeep Wrangler that had originally belonged to Patrick's grandfather was the ideal summer car, at least in Patrick's view. Gran loved that jeep, and yoga kept her flexible enough to climb in and out. Why not take it?

He threw his bag into the back, drove downtown, and parked near the market. Gran had said to meet at the southwest corner of the parking lot, but he didn't see her there. He did see a familiar figure though. Lauren waited beside a geranium-filled planter, a breeze blowing her hair away from her face and flattening the ruffly skirt she wore against her legs. Patrick realized he'd never seen her legs before. He'd been missing out.

He started toward her. She looked in his direction, and he could tell the moment she recognized him. Her eyes brightened and a smile bloomed on her face as he approached. "Hey."

"Hi." He looked around but all he saw was a tote bag and two cardboard boxes at her feet. "Where's Gran?"

"She was playing bridge with Molly, Alice and Linda last time I talked with her. Why, is she missing?"

"I got a message to pick her up from the Saturday Market. Something about Rosemary and a wedding."

"Oh, no, that's me. I rode in with Rosemary, but she's staying in Anchorage overnight to go to a wedding, and I need to get back to the farm for milking. Sorry, I hope I'm not putting you out."

"Not at all. Is this your stuff? Looks like you had a successful shopping day." He reached down for the boxes, which were surprisingly light.

"Oh, I wasn't shopping. I was selling soap. Did Bonnie not tell you about that?"

"No." He gave a wry smile. "I get the idea there are lots of things she hasn't told me about. Come get in the car. I want to hear all about this soap."

She grabbed her tote and followed him. When he stopped at the Jeep, she grinned. "Wow. I've never ridden in one of these."

"The ride's a little rough, but it's fun."

She touched the canvas cover. "Does this come off?"

"Yep. The outdoorsman's convertible. We'd better leave it on for the highway, though, but we'll open these side panels since it has no air-conditioning."

"Sounds like fun." She stored her tote in the back and hoisted herself onto the passenger seat.

Patrick pulled out of the lot and made his way through downtown traffic until they stopped at a light on Sixth Street. "So, tell me what you're selling at the market."

"I'm using the goats' milk to manufacture fancy soaps. You probably know Rosemary sells honey and crystals, and I'm sharing her booth."

"I knew Rosemary was a beekeeper, but I didn't know she was selling at the market now. Her honey's great. Is your booth doing well?"

"It is. I've only been doing it for two weeks, but I've sold out both times. The tourists seem to like the soaps as little souvenirs. I'll have more milk this week, so that means more soap to sell in a couple weeks once it cures."

"Glad to hear your milk production is rising." The light changed and Patrick pulled forward. The wind whipping through the open panels drowned out any reply she might have made. At the next stoplight, Patrick tried again. "So, Spritz and the kids are good?"

"All the goats are. We're up to a dozen kids now."

"Wow. Sounds like I missed a lot. But why soap? Wasn't your plan to make cheese?"

Her expression changed to one of frustration. "I've run into a bit of a snag there."

"Oh? What happened?"

The light changed and they pulled forward. Over the roar of the wind, Lauren called, "I'll tell you later."

They'd reached the highway now, so Patrick was going to have to wait until they made it to the farm. Maybe driving the Jeep hadn't been the best idea. His regular SUV would have insured a nice quiet ride where they could talk, and he could learn more about this woman who had moved into his grandmother's life, and by extension into his.

On the other hand, Lauren did seem to enjoy riding in the Jeep, tucking her hair behind her ears and watching the scenery go by. She had an interesting profile, gracefully curving and yet strong, like a drawn bow. She laughed and waved when they passed two people sitting out on an old couch overlooking the highway. They waved back.

Almost an hour from the time they'd left the market, he pulled up in front of the farmhouse. Under the arbor leading into the yard, a new gate blocked his path. Before he could ask Lauren about it, a small dog dashed down the front steps and ran up to the fence, barking frantically. Which explained the gate.

"Who's this?" He leaned over and let the dog sniff his hand.

"I see you've met Wilson." Gran approached at a more reasonable speed, but with no sign of a limp, he was happy to see.

"Wilson, huh?" Patrick stepped inside the gate and hugged his grandmother. "Where did he come from?"

"He just showed up out of nowhere." Gran scooped up the dog. "Lauren didn't have the heart to turn him in at the shelter."

Hearing a strangled snort, he looked over to see Lauren covering her mouth and silently shaking with laughter. He could guess why. Gran liked to think of herself as tough, but he knew all about her generous heart, and that dog looked pretty darn comfortable in her arms. "I see. Hello, Wilson. Nice to meet you." He scratched under the dog's chin. "The Easy Living Apartments in Palmer allows pets, you know."

When that piece of information was greeted with nothing but stony silence, Patrick decided to change the subject. He looked around at the freshly mown lawn, and if he wasn't mistaken, new pillows on the porch swing. "The place looks good."

"We've been sprucing up. Did Lauren tell you about tomorrow?"

"Tomorrow? No."

"Come sit on the porch, then. I'll make us some tea, and we'll catch up."

"I brought your favorite from the market," Lauren told Bonnie. "I'll just get the package out of the car."

"Oh look, you brought the Jeep." Bonnie turned to Lauren. "He loves that car. Tim bought it new the year Patrick was born and turned it over to him on his twenty-first birthday."

"Wow, he didn't tell me that. That's cool."

"I'll get the tea. Meanwhile, Patrick, why don't you bring in your suitcase and leave the Jeep behind the barn? We'll be needing this parking space tomorrow."

"Okay." Patrick parked and walked back to the house, wondering what they would need parking for. With Gran, one never knew. A few minutes later, they were all sitting in rocking chairs on the front porch, sipping Earl Grey and sampling peanut butter fudge. Patrick waited until Gran had finished the last of the fudge before asking, "So what's this big event tomorrow?"

"Goat yoga," Gran said.

At least that's what he thought she said, but those two words didn't go together in his mind. "Come again?"

"Goat yoga," Lauren said. "It's like regular yoga, but with baby goats. It's a thing."

"I don't get it. The goats do stretches…?"

"No, the people do the poses and the goats interact by climbing on them, like they do each other. You'll see."

"Okay. How many people are coming? Just Gran's regular yoga class?"

"Oh no. This is a business venture," Gran explained. "Crystal and Lauren will split the proceeds. We've been advertising all over town."

"Very entrepreneurial." Patrick smiled. He hoped Gran and Lauren weren't disappointed. After all, how many people could possibly be willing to pay money for the privilege of having a goat walk on them? But far be it from him to burst their bubble. "I'll look forward to it. So, goat yoga and goat soap. It sounds like you're making things happen, but you never told me the problem with the cheese making."

"Well…" Lauren drew in a deep breath and explained how laws in Alaska differed from those in Oregon and made the prospect of goat cheese manufacturing much more complicated and expensive. "So, if I want to make cheese, it's going to take a huge investment in time and money."

"I'm sorry to hear that. Are you eligible for any sort of small business loan or grant?"

"The extension agent wasn't aware of anything like that," Lauren said.

"But we have a plan." The way Gran raised her chin made Patrick suspect he wasn't about to like this plan. "We're going to find the nugget."

"What?"

"The nugget. Bradley's Heart. We're going to find it and Lauren can use the reward money to get the equipment she needs."

"No!" Patrick spoke louder than he'd intended. He lowered the volume but kept his tone firm. "No. I don't want you risking your health chasing rainbows."

Gran raised her eyebrows. "You say that as if you have a vote. You don't."

Patrick turned to Lauren, who seemed to be shrinking away from him. "Look, I understand you're desperate for money, but that doesn't mean you can put Gran—"

"I assure you," Gran broke in, "that Lauren didn't put me up to anything. This is my idea, and Lauren generously agreed to help."

"But—"

"Paddy, you know those senior apartments you've been trying to get me to move to?"

"Ye-es," he answered slowly, sensing a trick.

"Well, I think it's a good idea." Gran's smile was sweet only on the surface, with steel underneath. "But only after I've found Bradley's Heart. I've heard Anthony Clark is making noises about selling the paper and retiring, and I want to shove that nugget in his face before he does."

Patrick stopped to consider. Maybe this could work out. "So, you're saying that once you find that nugget, you'll move to the apartments." He wanted it on the record.

"That's what I'm saying."

"And in the meantime, Lauren will be here to…" Patrick almost said babysit but decided that wouldn't go over well. "To assist."

"Exactly."

"Maybe we—" Whatever Lauren had been about to say was drowned out by loud bleating. A goat stuck her head over the new gate. "Spritz! How did you get out? The new latch I installed is supposed to be goat proof!"

The goat used her nose to flip open the horseshoe-shaped fork latch on the gate and skipped up the sidewalk to the porch, three kids right behind her. She tripped up the steps and pressed her head against Patrick's chest. Bemused, he stroked her neck and looked questioningly at Lauren.

She shrugged. "What can I say? She likes you." Then she jumped up. "Oh, no. Spritz probably let the rest of the goats out. I hope they didn't get far." Lauren dashed to the gate and stopped. "I see them. They're at the barn." She checked her watch. "It is almost milking time. Come on, Spritz. Let's go."

The goat made no move to leave. One of

the kids jumped into Patrick's lap. He ran a hand over the soft fuzz covering the kid's adorable face. Okay, maybe he could see why people would pay to play with goats. Gently, Patrick pushed Spritz away, returned the kid to the floor, and stood. "I'll come, too."

Spritz and the kids were perfectly happy to accompany Patrick and Lauren to the barn. Lauren had left one of the big sliding doors open, and from a distance, they could see the other goats milling around inside and out. A distinctive brown goat ran around from behind the barn to the door and disappeared inside. A minute later, she did it again. Odd. Patrick didn't remember a back door on the barn, other than the hayloft.

They reached the barn, only to discover goats scrambling up a huge stack of hay that wasn't there when Patrick left. One kid reached the summit and leaped from the haystack to the empty hayloft above. Wow, they had good balance.

A sudden sound, somewhere between a bleat and a scream sounded from behind the barn. Patrick and Lauren both ran outside and around the barn. The sound came from Patrick's Jeep, where one of the kids seemed to have climbed onto the roof and gotten caught. Before they could get there, another kid leaped from the hayloft and landed on the roof, like a net under a high wire, before scrambling down.

"Oh, no." Lauren had reached the screaming goat, who had somehow punctured the canvas cover and had his legs stuck. Patrick got inside the car and worked the legs loose while Lauren held on to the kid and kept her from jerking away until they could get her untangled. The moment she was free, she hopped down and ran around the barn, presumably for another turn.

When Patrick got out of the car, Lauren faced him, wide-eyed. "Patrick, I am so sorry. I had no idea—"

A sudden bleat drew their attention upward. One of the grown goats seemed to be shouting a warning before she jumped and landed on the roof with a thud. The canvas made a ripping sound as she pulled her foot back through a hole in the canvas and jumped down.

Patrick pulled the keys from his pocket, jumped into the Jeep, and drove several yards away. He got out and looked at the shredded cover and then up at the hayloft opening where three goats loudly expressed their displeasure at having their game interrupted.

Lauren stood below, holding one kid in her arms and staring helplessly at him.

And Patrick just had to laugh.

DESPITE THEIR VANDALISM, none of the goats seemed worse for the wear. In fact, the kids chased each other around the pen while their dams took turns at the milking stand as though nothing unusual had happened. Lauren felt terrible about Patrick's car, especially knowing it had been his grandfather's. But he didn't seem all that upset. In fact, he'd laughed until tears ran from his eyes.

Now he was sitting in the pen with the goats, letting the kids climb into his lap. Lauren could have kicked herself for not thinking about the haystack being a ladder to the loft above. She'd deliberately left the sliding doors on the hayloft open a few feet to allow the warm air to escape, never dreaming her goats would see it as a diving platform.

She finished milking Biscotti and returned her to the pen. The next doe stepped forward. Lauren always milked them in the same order, and each goat knew when it was her turn to set up. Lauren did a cleaning wash, hand stripped and examined the milk and then attached the milking machine.

Patrick had let himself out of the goats'

pen and was watching her. "You're really good at this."

"I've been practicing," she said. "Twice a day."

"No, I mean at the whole thing. Taking care of the goats, managing the farm, finding ways to make it pay."

She shrugged. "Except for when they escape and ruin your car cover."

He waved that comment away. "It could have happened to anyone. Are you as good at cheese making?"

"I do make good cheese," Lauren could say with confidence. "I've been working on my formulas for three years now, and my Gouda took first in a competition."

"Three years? That's a long time."

"Not especially." She laughed. "Some Goudas are aged three years, but mine is ready in about six months. I brought some samples with me. Now that I'm getting more milk, I'll probably start a batch this week."

"You're serious about looking for the nugget, aren't you?"

"Yes. I talked to a historian last week—"

"What historian?"

"His name is Albert Jankowski. He taught history at Alaska Pacific, and he wrote a book called *Lost Treasures of Alaska*, including a chapter about Bradley's Heart. Linda arranged the meeting."

"I see. And what did this historian have to say?"

"He said the key is to understand the personalities involved, in this case the robber, William Golson. Dr. Jankowski thinks the most likely scenario is that he hid the nugget while he was hiding out on the farm."

Patrick grinned. "No wonder Gran is so gung-ho. Especially since you need the reward money."

"I don't want you to think I coerced Bonnie into—"

"No, I know. She's had that bee in her bonnet since long before you arrived. That's how she hurt her ankle, you know, hunting for treasure. Not that she admitted it." Patrick blew out a breath of frustration. "She's right though about me having no say in the matter. Gran is going to hunt for the nugget, whether I agree or not. At least she has you to help. Maybe you can keep her out of trouble."

"I'll do my best."

"I know you will." Together they put hay in the rack and checked to make sure the water was clean before Patrick gave Spritz a last pat and locked the pen.

When they got back to the house, Bonnie

was in the kitchen, turning something in a cast iron skillet.

Patrick's eyes widened. "Is that fried chicken?"

"And mashed potatoes. Or at least they will be once you mash them." Bonnie handed him a pot and a tool. "Were all the goats present and accounted for?"

"They were fine. Patrick's car—not so much." Lauren filled Bonnie in on the hayloft debacle.

"Goats." Bonnie shook her head, but she was laughing. "Cows never would have pulled something like this."

Patrick laughed, too. "Good thing. I'd have been replacing a lot more than a canvas top if a Holstein dropped onto my car."

"I'll pay—" Lauren started to apologize again, but Patrick stopped her.

"Don't worry about it. The top was old and worn. I'd probably have replaced it next year anyway. Put the money into your equipment fund instead." Patrick added milk and butter to the pot and began mashing. "Lauren and I had a little talk about the nugget," Patrick said to his grandmother oh-so-casually.

He glanced at Lauren. She gave a little head shake, trying to telegraph *leave me out of this*. The last thing she needed was to be involved in an argument between him and Bonnie. He flashed a smile before returning his attention to his grandmother. "You're serious about moving to town once you find it, aren't you?"

"I am." Bonnie plunked a platter of fried chicken in the middle of the kitchen table. "But only after I've made Anthony Clark eat his words."

"Okay, then." Patrick set out plates and silverware. "If it's that important to you, I'm on board."

Bonnie, who had been reaching into the refrigerator, stopped and poked up her head. "You won't keep trying to talk me out of it?"

"On the contrary." Patrick took the three-bean salad from his grandmother's hands and set it on the table before turning to face her. "Starting today, if you'll let me, I'm joining the treasure hunt."

CHAPTER NINE

PATRICK TUCKED A bookmark into the book Lauren had lent him last night and set it on the wicker table. Despite all the time he and Gran had spent searching for the nugget when he was a kid, he'd never really heard the whole story of Bradley's Heart. He read over Lauren's notes from her interview with the author, as well. While the odds were still long, Patrick had to admit their chances were better than he'd originally thought. The nugget could well be somewhere on this farm.

Gran propped the screen door open and backed through it, carrying a plastic-wrapped tray holding small bits of carrots. "Pat, could you move that table from the porch to over by the gate? Lauren and I thought the yoga people might want to feed the goats treats for photo ops after class."

Patrick set up the table and took the tray from her. "When is all this happening?"

"In a little over an hour. I hope Lauren and Crystal get a good turnout. The Mat Mates have been trying to spread the word." She ran a critical eye over the yard, stopping to pick off a few spent pansies. "Could you rig up something to cover the flowerbed, so the goats won't eat the plants? Maybe laundry baskets or something? The rugosa roses will be okay if they nibble a little, but I don't want them ruining my peonies. They're almost antiques. I transplanted them from the cabin."

"I'll see what I can do." There was probably some of that woven wire fencing left. "Where's Lauren?"

"In the barn, I think."

When Patrick arrived at the barn, he found Lauren tying ribbons onto the baby goats. A brown-and-white-spotted kid with a blue polka-dotted bow around his neck like a bowtie jumped onto a big goat's back. The kid tilted his head to examine the newcomer and gave a little bleat. Patrick chuckled. "How many layers of cute can you add before we're in danger of cuteness overload?"

"I don't know, but we're pushing the limits today." Lauren tilted a red bow over a white kid's ear and smiled at the result. "We're just going to have to take the risk."

Lauren was looking pretty cute herself, with her hair braided and tied with a ribbon. Patrick reached to brush a stray bit of hay off her cheek and found his finger lingering on her soft skin. Her eyes seemed even brighter than usual. Almost luminous.

They locked gazes for a long moment before Lauren spoke, in a slightly higher voice. "Did you, um, need something?"

"Hmm?" Patrick blinked, realizing he'd been standing there, grinning at her. "Oh. Yes. I'm looking for something to put over Gran's flower garden to protect the plants. Did you have any fencing left?"

"Oh, I didn't think of that." Lauren's smile dimmed a little. "Makes me wonder what else I might have forgotten. Anyway, yes. There's a roll of wire over there in the corner. Thanks."

"No problem. I'm sure everything will go fine." He lifted the wire to his shoulder and carried it to the doorway, but he couldn't resist one more look back to see Lauren still watching him. She smiled, and he waved before carting the fencing to the house, where he erected a temporary cage over the bed in front of the porch. Just as he finished, a minivan drove up and parked in front of the yard, and the instructor from Gran's yoga class got out.

"Hi. I don't suppose I could convince you to unload a couple of tables for me?"

"I can do that." Patrick followed her to the liftgate and pulled out the first of three long folding tables. "Where do you want them?"

"Lined up outside the yard, I think. We need a place for people to leave their shoes and bags. I put up a sandwich board beside the driveway so people will know where to turn in."

Two more cars pulled up and all of Gran's friends from yoga class piled out. "Hi, Patrick. Are you doing yoga with us today?"

He shook his head. "I'm just the help."

Gran came out the door and called a greeting. Wilson ran from behind her, tail wagging. All the ladies bent down to shower him with attention.

Another car pulled up and parked, this one with three young women Patrick didn't recognize. "Are we in the right place?" one of them asked. "We're looking for the goat thing."

"You are, but it doesn't start for another forty minutes," Crystal told her.

"Oh, that's okay. We came from Anchorage and wanted to get here early to make sure we got in. Where are the goats?"

"I'll go check on that," Patrick told them. In the barn, he found Lauren snapping leads onto the mamas. "Your first customers are here, looking for goats."

"Already?" Lauren checked her watch. "I wanted to get them in the fenced area ahead of time. Here, since there's traffic would you mind carrying the kids while I lead Spritz?"

A couple who looked to be in their forties and a mom with three children had joined the three women before Patrick and Lauren arrived. A chorus of aahs rang out when they spotted the baby goats. As soon as Patrick set them down on the grass, they began bouncing their way over to inspect the new people, who all dropped to their knees to pet the goats.

It took four more trips to bring all the goats and kids to the yard. All the parking in front of the house and barn was taken, and people were beginning to pull off beside the driveway, even though the start time was still twenty minutes away. The people in the yard had already passed out all the carrots, and Crystal was silently counting to estimate the number of mats she could fit on the lawn. Lauren, standing with Gran, Crystal and Gran's friends, was beginning to look a little panicked.

"The Olsons have that empty field where they cut their winter wheat," Patrick said to

Lauren and Gran. "Maybe they'd let us use it for overflow parking, and I could shuttle people here."

"Gina Olson is right over there," Gran said. "I'll ask her now."

A woman about Patrick's age and a preteen boy walked over to Lauren. "Hi."

"Marissa!" Lauren beamed. "Thanks for coming. Hi, Ryan. Ladies, this is Marissa Allen and her son Ryan. They're from the reindeer farm."

"Quite a crowd," Marissa commented.

Lauren's gaze swept over the pandemonium. "Yeah, a little more than we bargained for."

"What can I do to help?"

"Really? Thank you. Maybe help wrangle goats? Make sure they don't escape and encourage them to mingle."

"And pick up poop?" Ryan suggested.

Gran had returned from her errand in time to hear him. "That would be most helpful," she told the boy. "I'll get you gloves and bags in just a sec." She turned to Patrick. "Gina authorized use of their field, so you'd better start directing traffic over there and arrange a shuttle."

"Take my van. The keys are in it," Crystal said. "We already have all the people we can fit into the yard. Tell anyone who isn't already in the yard that we'll be doing another session in an hour. Half price."

"I'm on it," Patrick said.

"I'll make a sign," Molly volunteered.

"I'll stand at the road and direct traffic," Bea offered. In her neon-orange yoga pants and today's glowing green hair, she was equipped for the job.

Crystal climbed the porch steps. "Excuse me. May I have your attention? Please find a spot and roll out your mat. We'll be doing mostly grounded work today, so you won't need a lot of space." Her voice was remarkably serene. "Let's all get comfortable and have some fun."

Patrick spent the next half hour shuttling people from the Olson's field. A few were unhappy to hear the class was full, but most were willing to wait around for the second session. Alice and Rosemary had formed an impromptu petting zoo outside the yard with two of the big goats, one kid and Gran's sausage dog which seemed to keep them entertained. Linda was taking names and accepting payment for session two.

While dropping people off, Patrick caught glimpses of people stretching and goats frolicking. At forty minutes after the official start time, Patrick decided it was safe to assume nobody else would be coming. He gave Bea a ride up the driveway and dropped her off near the gate before double-parking Gina's van behind Alice's car.

He walked to the fence to watch the class. Crystal told the group to move to downward facing dog. Almost fifty rumps rose in the air, which seemed to be an invitation for the baby goats to spring off the ground onto their backs and climb. The sounds of laughter almost drowned out Crystal's voice, but she didn't seem to mind. One lady sat quietly on her mat, stroking an adult goat that snuggled against her leg. Spritz came to greet Patrick, and he scratched her neck absently while taking in the scene.

Lauren, Marissa and Ryan scurried around the edges of the yard, redirecting goats that tried to rear up on the fence or nibble at someone's clothing. Gran brought out another tray of carrots. Crystal had the class move to their hands and knees. The kid with the polka-dotted bow climbed onto someone's back, and then used it as a launching pad to leap from back to back all the way across the yard, leaving a wake of giggles behind him.

At forty-five minutes after the start time,

Crystal ended the class to give everyone time to pet the goats and talk before the next class. Patrick circulated, volunteering to snap pictures. He captured dozens of joyful smiles and the goats seemed just as happy. Two kids decided that since class was over, they'd sneak a little snack from mama, which delighted the crowd.

He saw Lauren over in a corner, stroking a goat's head and talking to one of the participants. She must have been answering questions about goats, because her smile sparkled with enthusiasm. Patrick felt a not-unpleasant ache in his chest, watching her. Lauren belonged here, on a farm. If the only way to make her dream happen was to find the nugget, then that's what they'd do.

The class clearly wanted to linger, but Crystal was a pro, herding the people out of the yard as efficiently as any sheepdog while still making them feel welcomed. Marissa positioned herself near the gate and grabbed one kid who tried to sneak off with her new friends. Lauren shook some alfalfa pellets in a bucket, attracting all the goats away from the gate. The next class poured in, eager to join in the fun.

Crystal led them to sit cross-legged on their mats while they stretched their necks and shoulders. A fawn-colored kid with black markings climbed into one woman's lap and snuggled against her for a nap. The others were wide awake, though, bouncing around the yard, climbing and leaping from person to person, and just looking adorable. Patrick snapped quite a few photos on his phone, thinking Lauren might want them for future advertising.

Patrick had joined Gran on the porch to take some pictures from higher up when Crystal dismissed the class. One of the participants, someone Gran knew from church, came to say hello. He caught sight of the book Patrick had left lying on the porch and chuckled. "You're not still looking for treasure, are you Bonnie? I remember what happened last time."

Gran stiffened, but before she could give the blistering answer she was no doubt composing, Patrick picked up the book. "Actually, this is mine." He opened the book to an earlier chapter. "Have you heard about the lost gold mine around Fairbanks? It's fascinating."

"I do remember hearing about that." The man started talking and Patrick just had to edge him away from Gran and listen until the man's wife came to claim him and Patrick could begin shuttling everyone back to their cars.

At the end of the day, Patrick, Lauren, Crystal, Gran and Gran's friends gathered around the big oak table in Gran's seldom-used dining room and ate takeout pizza Bea had fetched from town. Patrick had no idea how much cash they'd raked in that day, but he'd seen an impressive stack earlier when Crystal had handed over Lauren's share.

"So, takeaways," Crystal said. "We obviously need to sell a limited number of tickets in advance. The demand is higher than our capacity."

"Porta potties," Molly suggested. "Once class broke up, we had twenty people wanting to use Bonnie's downstairs bathroom. She can't have strangers wandering the house unsupervised."

"The advertising obviously worked," Alice commented. "Linda, whatever you were doing on the internet, keep doing it. At least half the people here today were from Anchorage."

"More like two-thirds," Linda said. "I asked when they signed in. I also collected email addresses of people interested in hearing more, in case you want to put out a newsletter. I think it was that gorgeous poster Molly designed that caught their eye."

"It is beautiful. I'm going to frame a copy and hang it in my bedroom," Lauren said.

"There's a thought." Alice tapped her index fingers together. "Molly could sell numbered editions of the posters as souvenirs."

"So, same time next week?" Bea asked.

Lauren looked at Crystal, who nodded. "Same time next week." Crystal smiled. "Ladies, I think we have a hit on our hands."

LAUREN RETURNED AFTER the morning milking the next day to find Patrick and Bonnie at the kitchen table, heads together over the treasure book. Patrick looked up and smiled. "Hungry? I have an asparagus and cheddar frittata in the oven."

"Sounds delicious. What are you looking at?"

"Patrick was reading some of the other stories in this book and that gave him an idea on where to search," Bonnie told her.

Using oven mitts, Patrick removed a cast iron skillet from the oven and set it on the trivet in the center of the table. "Gran and I searched all the nooks and crannies of the cabin years ago, and we checked for trap doors and loose floorboards."

"Did you ever find anything?"

"A few things," Bonnie said. "Mostly trash. A half-full bottle of some snake oil tonic. Oh, and we found a wooden box, but it was locked. It's in the attic."

"And you didn't force it open to see if the nugget was inside?"

"It wasn't nearly heavy enough to be holding gold," Patrick explained.

"And it was too pretty to break," Bonnie said. "Someone had painted fireweed on the top. I meant to see if a locksmith could unlock it without breaking it, but I never got around to it."

"Anyway—" Patrick cut the frittata into wedges and set one on her plate. "We searched all the obvious places, but until I read about it in this book, it had never occurred to us that with so much time on his hands, Golson might have fashioned a hiding place in the chinking between the logs. I thought if you have time today, we could take a look."

"Sounds good to me." Lauren had been curious about the old cabin, but since Bonnie had assured her it had been thoroughly searched many times, she hadn't visited. "I need to make soap this afternoon, but I'm free all morning." She looked over at Bonnie. "You're not going?"

Bonnie frowned. "Patrick doesn't think it's safe for someone as fragile as he seems to believe I am."

"Hey, I never said you were fragile. I just said the sixty-four earthquake left the floors buckled and uneven, and that you didn't much enjoy your time on crutches. If we find anything, I promise we'll take pictures so you can see exactly where it was and how we found it."

Bonnie sighed. "I suppose you're right. The important thing is finding that gold."

CLOUDS GATHERED IN the sky and spruce trees surrounding the cabin cast a thick shade, giving a twilight feeling to the area around the cabin. Lauren instinctively moved closer to Patrick. Her eyes hadn't fully adjusted when she caught her toe on a hidden root and stumbled forward, grabbing Patrick's arm to catch herself.

He steadied her. Once she was back on her feet, he took her hand and led her forward, probably just to make sure she didn't trip again. But it still felt nice, holding his hand. "Watch the steps. Some of the wood is rotten."

Stepping carefully, she followed him through an empty door frame and into the cabin. He was right about the floor buckling, and the whole cabin seemed to be tilting slightly to the south, but the wood of the floors seemed sound inside. The main level of the cabin was all one room, with the remains of a kitchen at one end.

Stairs ran up the back of the room. Only a few shelves and a crude table remained, but Bonnie had told her the family abandoned the cabin when they built the farmhouse, so they would have moved their good furniture with them.

Patrick dropped her hand so that he could shrug out of his backpack. Immediately, Lauren missed the feel of his touch. She gave a mental head shake. They were here on a mission that would allow her to finance her dream. She couldn't allow herself to be distracted.

Patrick pulled out two heavy-duty flashlights and handed her one. "If he really did hide the nugget between the logs, it's going to take some time to find it. I figure the first step is to inspect all the walls, inside and out."

"What are we looking for?"

"Anything that looks different from the rest." Patrick shined his light at the strip between two of the logs. "Different color, different texture, something that might indicate Golson removed the original chinking and replaced it."

"Chinking?"

"The stuff that fills the gaps between logs to keep the wind out. They used Portland cement for chinking in this cabin."

Lauren ran her finger over the rough line. "Wouldn't it have cracked and fallen out over time, and been repaired?"

"Probably. But checking each repair has to be faster than trying to remove every bit of chinking in this house."

"Good point. How many rooms upstairs?"

"Three as I remember." He probed the wood on the stairs. "Careful. The stairs seem sound, but the railing is loose."

The upstairs was divided into three modest rooms, presumably bedrooms. One had a crumbling foam pad pushed into the corner. Lauren pointed her flashlight upward. "How do we know he didn't hide it up there?"

"Good question." Patrick peered up at the low ceiling. "I guess we don't. But, as far as I know, nothing's been taken out of this cabin since then except for a few tin cans and that box Gran found under a floorboard. No stools or ladders. He'd probably have been working from floor level. I wonder how tall he was."

"Tall. The professor showed me a picture. About your height, or maybe a little taller."

"Maybe we should concentrate our search at what would be a comfortable level for me to work then."

Lauren shined her light along the wall at shoulder height. "According to Golson's employer, he was careful and detail oriented. He had plenty of time. I think he would have found an out-of-the-way spot less likely to attract attention."

Patrick paused to consider and then nodded. "I think you're right. Let's concentrate on dark corners and awkward spots first. Upstairs, you think?"

"That makes more sense to me." She reached for the pendant Rosemary had given her and gave it a rub.

"That's an unusual necklace," Patrick commented. "What kind of stone is that?"

"Blue lace agate. Rosemary gave it to me. She said it brings insight."

"Sounds like Rosemary." Patrick chuckled. "I suppose we can use all the insight we can get. Let me know if it starts glowing or anything."

They set to work, with Patrick inspecting the corners and spots around where the roof beams met the walls. Lauren started in on the low spots. Several times, she studied a random divot or smudge in the chinking, only to decide the color and stroke matched too well. The earthquake had knocked large chunks of chinking to the floor, but nothing seemed to be hiding in or behind them. An hour later, she'd inspected only a small section of the bedroom where they were working.

A little light trickled through the small dusty window at the end of the room. Patrick had tried to open it earlier, but it was stuck closed. The stagnant air grew warmer, even on a cloudy day.

"I'll be right back." Lauren went downstairs to fetch two water bottles from Patrick's backpack and returned to hand him one.

"Thanks." Patrick unscrewed the top and took a swig. "That hits the spot."

Lauren took a long drink from her own bottle. "If it takes this long just to inspect the seams, imagine how long it must have taken to build the cabin."

"A lot of work went into this one." Patrick patted one of the logs. "And if not for the earthquake, it could still be inhabitable. The original settlers learned to be good craftsmen."

"Do you know who lived here?"

"A family named Aberg. They were part of the original Matanuska Colony who homesteaded this place."

"Like a religious colony or something?"

"No, it was a government project, part of the New Deal. They chose about two hundred families from the upper Midwest to move to Alaska and build a farming colony. It was a big thing at the time, and quite an honor to be chosen. I imagine the colonists sometimes wondered if it was a blessing or a curse, but a few of the original families are still here. The Abergs hung on until the late 1960s, when they sold to my grandparents."

She and Patrick continued working. An hour passed, and then two. Finally, about a foot from the door, Lauren noticed a patch of chinking was slightly lighter in color and had a different texture. "Maybe this is something."

Patrick came to look. "Yeah, definitely a patch job. Could you hold the light, please?" He pulled a folding knife from his pocket and used the blade to probe along the edges. Then, removing just a layer at a time, he continued until he uncovered what looked like a wad of paper.

Lauren's heart kicked up a notch. Could this be it? Could the nugget be hidden behind the paper? Or maybe it was a map, showing where to find it. "Can we get it out in one piece?"

"I'll try." Patrick continued to scrape along the edges until the paper came loose and fell to the floor. Nothing seemed to be behind it except more chinking.

Lauren turned her light on the paper. Dust and grime coated the outside. Patrick grasped a protruding corner and gingerly smoothed the paper open, revealing black-and-white pictures of various frilly aprons, nipped in at the tiny waist of the smiling model. Prices listed below each picture ranged between one and two dollars.

Patrick pointed to print in the bottom corner. "Sears, Roebuck, and Company. Probably from their Christmas catalog."

Lauren suppressed a sigh. She'd known it couldn't be this easy. "So sometimes a patch is just a patch."

"Looks like." Patrick checked his watch. "Guess we'd better head back to check on Gran and have lunch."

"Good idea. She's got something in town this afternoon, so we don't want to hold her up."

"What's Gran got going on in town?" Patrick asked as they walked to the house.

"She didn't say. Something with Linda, I think."

Before they went into the house, Patrick stopped to dust the cobwebs and dirt from his clothes. Lauren did the same. "Turn around," he directed. When she did, Patrick picked something from her hair.

"What was it?"

Patrick flicked something into the rose bush. "You're not afraid of spiders, are you?"

"It was a spider?" Lauren's hand flew to her hair to check for more nasty bugs. She knew spiders were mostly harmless, even beneficial, but knowing wasn't the same as believing.

"It wasn't a spider. Nope. No spiders in that cabin." Patrick managed to say it with a straight face.

Lauren laughed, thinking of all the cobwebs they'd brushed away. "Seriously, what did you pick out of my hair?"

"A, uh, ladybug. Yeah, pretty sure it was a black ladybug." Patrick opened the mudroom door and held it for her.

"Ladybugs aren't black."

He grinned. "This one was." He washed his hands.

"How many legs did it have?" Lauren asked when she took her turn at the sink.

"I didn't have time to count."

A spate of barking ended the ridiculous conversation and continued until Patrick opened the door to the kitchen and assured Wilson it was just them and not burglars there to steal the cookie jar. Bonnie was at the counter, spreading mayonnaise on bread. "Oh, good. I have a class at one, but I didn't want to leave without asking how the search is going."

"Well, so far we found that ladies in the forties apparently needed special aprons for entertaining, as well as for practical use," Patrick said.

Bonnie chuckled. "How did you come up with that information?"

"A page from a Christmas catalog, stuffed in the wall," Lauren explained. "Other than that, we came up empty. But there's a lot more house to cover. We'll find it."

"That's the spirit," Bonnie said. "It's got to be somewhere."

"What's this class you're taking?" Patrick asked while setting plates on the table.

"Linda is teaching a genealogy workshop, and I said I'd be there." Bonnie pulled a pitcher of iced tea from the refrigerator.

"I didn't know you were interested in genealogy." Lauren took three glasses from the cabinet.

"I'm not particularly, but Linda's an expert. It's her first time teaching, though, so all the girls are going to support her. If you weren't so busy, I'd have you join us."

"I wish I could, but I need to get that soap made this afternoon."

"And I said I'd help," Patrick added quickly. Lauren didn't remember him saying so, but he clearly wasn't in the mood for a genealogy lecture. "Take an umbrella. It's supposed to rain."

"Are you leaving Wilson with me?" Lauren asked.

Bonnie smiled down at the little dog who, as usual, stood right beside her foot, his now-glossy coat catching the light. "No, I think I'll take him. The girls always make a fuss over him."

"And this is the dog you almost dropped at the shelter?" Patrick asked his grandmother.

"Shh." Bonnie laughed. "We don't talk about that anymore. Do we, Wilson?"

CHAPTER TEN

ONCE BONNIE WAS out the door, and she and Patrick had cleaned up the kitchen, Lauren collected her soap-making equipment from the cabinet in the mudroom and laid it out on the countertop.

"What should I do?" Patrick asked.

"You really want to help?" Lauren tied her rubber apron over her clothes. "I thought that was just an excuse to avoid tracing your ancestors."

"No, I want to see how it's done. I've always been curious about how soap is made."

Lauren raised her eyebrows. "Always?"

"Well, always since I found out you were making it."

She laughed. "All right, if you want, you can get the goat milk out of the freezer in the barn. Bring six ice cube trays for the first batch."

"It's frozen?"

"Yes, because the lye will scorch milk if

it's not cold enough. Trust me, I know what I'm doing."

Patrick touched her shoulder while he passed behind her. "I do. Trust you, that is." And with that enigmatic remark, he headed for the barn.

Lauren looked up from measuring coconut oil to watch him out the kitchen window. Did he mean he trusted her to know what she was doing with the soap, or in general? And why did the idea of his trust cause a warm, happy feeling to bubble up in her chest?

She returned to her ingredients, measuring carefully, but a few minutes later she checked the window again. Patrick was returning, carrying the stack of trays. The summer sun had added a few lighter streaks to his brown hair, turning it almost an old gold color.

He carried the trays to the countertop and watched while she dumped the milk cubes into a large bowl and set it inside a larger bowl of ice. "What should I do now?" he asked.

Lauren pulled on her rubber gloves. "You should turn on the kitchen exhaust fan." She adjusted her goggles over her eyes. "And put on some goggles."

He picked up the extra goggles and backed

up several feet. "Are you going to blow something up?"

"No, but when you're dealing with lye, there are certain safety procedures you need to follow." Slowly, she poured the lye flakes into the milk cubes, using a potato masher to combine the ingredients. Once all the lye had been added, she mixed and stirred until she was sure it had been dissolved. "Okay, you can come closer now."

"I didn't realize soap was so dangerous." Patrick approached slowly. "Should I have been wearing goggles in the shower all these years?"

Lauren laughed. "No, the saponification process means the lye reacts with the acid in the fat and they combine to form soap. As long as all the lye is completely dissolved, and it is, it won't irritate skin. In fact, the milk fat will make this soap extra gentle and creamy."

"Nice."

Patrick was an excellent assistant. Lauren didn't know why that should surprise her after his help on the fence, but it did. Reading through the recipe she'd clipped onto the upper cabinet, he anticipated which utensil or ingredient she would need next and had it at the ready. She finished mixing in record time.

"Okay, if you'll bring me one of the molds from the shelf over the freezer, this is ready to set."

"Aye, aye, Captain." Patrick brought one of the flat molds and watched while she poured in the soap and used a spoon to create a whipped cream texture on top. He handed her the dividers which she pushed into the soap, forming eighteen bars. By the time she'd finished, he had another mold ready to go.

"Okay, that's it," Lauren said, taking off her goggles. "We just need to put these in the refrigerator in the barn for a few hours, and then let them set for several days. In the meantime, I have the ones I made week before last to wrap and label."

"You refrigerate soap?"

"Cooling it down quickly helps keep the surface from developing an ash layer. Then it needs to sit for a couple of weeks to let some of the water evaporate and form bars."

"You really know your stuff. Where did you learn all this?"

"I took a class." Lauren picked up one of the filled molds. Patrick grabbed the other and walked with her to the barn.

"How long have you been planning this?" Patrick asked.

"Planning what?"

"The goats, the cheese making, farm life."

"The goats, about six years. I took my first class in cheese making three years ago. The farm…" Lauren thought about it. She'd started a special savings account nine years ago, but when had she first decided she would someday own a farm? She shrugged. "All my life."

They reached the barn before Patrick could comment. Lauren set her soap down to rearrange the milk bottles from that morning so that she could fit all three molds of soap inside. Then she removed an old sheet she'd used to cover curing soap and, with Patrick's help, loaded those molds onto the lawn cart.

He insisted on pushing it back to the kitchen. "There's a lot of back and forth in this process."

"I know. If we—" She stopped herself, remembering her pledge to think positively. "When we find the nugget and get the reward, I'll want to set up a commercial kitchen in its own building near the barn."

She could see the "but" on Patrick's lips, but instead he nodded and carried the soap into the kitchen. She retrieved the labels and wrap from the storage closet in the hallway. Patrick picked up a label and smiled. "Now and Forever Farm. I like it. It has kind of a fairy-tale feeling."

"Thank you."

"Where did you come up with the name?"

Lauren looked up. Patrick was watching her with genuine interest in his eyes. Denim blue eyes, like his grandmother's, although Bonnie's had faded to stonewash while Patrick's were a true indigo. When people at the market had asked about the name, Lauren had waved the question away with a nonanswer, but something in Patrick's gentle tone made her decide to share the truth. "I was ten years old, and I was starting a new school. Again."

Patrick nodded as if he understood. Maybe he did. He'd moved a lot, too, as a child. But not for the same reasons. The empathy on his face encouraged her to continue.

"My mom was addicted to romance."

"What do you mean? Like, she read lots of romance novels?"

If only. "No, I mean she loved to fall in love. She would meet someone and somehow, she just knew that this man would be the love of her life. To show her true love, she was willing to give up her friends and quit her job and move across the country to be with him. Whatever it took to be happy. And quite often, they were happy together. Just not for very long. When it was over, her first response was to start over someplace new."

"And she dragged you along with her?"

"Yes." Lauren studied the label—the stylized mountain in the background, with a fence and a tree forming a peaceful scene. "It could have been a lot worse. They were good guys. Most of them went out of their way to be nice to me. I wasn't neglected. It's just that it was always…temporary."

"You could never settle in and get comfortable because you knew it wouldn't last," Patrick said with the certainty of a shared experience. He moved closer, resting his hand on her back.

"Yes." She continued to stare down at the label, but it was starting to blur as the tears welled up. "That year, when I was ten, we were living in a house on the very edge of a small town. Our backyard butted up against a pasture with a couple of horses and a few cows grazing. Reggie, the guy my mom was with then, mentioned that same family had been farming there for four generations. To me, that sounded like heaven. To settle down in one place and stay there, forever.

So, I made up stories about Now and Forever Farm, where I lived happily ever after."

Patrick stroked two fingers down her face and caught her chin, encouraging her to turn her head and look at him. She did, into deep blue eyes that seemed to see right into her, to understand her longing for a place to belong. He leaned closer, pausing a hair's breadth away from her lips. She didn't pull away. And then he kissed her, tentatively at first, and then, finding welcome, more deeply.

He drew back and looked at her, his breath coming faster. Her own heart raced. She reached up to touch his face, to run her hand over the bit of stubble on his cheek. It was softer than she expected. She cupped his face between her hands and pulled him closer for another kiss.

He didn't seem to mind at all.

THAT NIGHT, LAUREN'S comfortable bed was suddenly not. It was too hot, and then too cold. The sheets, the same ones that had been smooth the night before, were too scratchy to bear. And the light! Who could sleep with sunlight still sneaking around the edges of the curtains at—she checked her phone—eleven thirty-nine at night? Her inability to sleep had nothing to do with that incredible kiss.

Yeah, right. She couldn't sell that non-sense even to herself. It was all about the kiss. Well, kisses, but especially the last one, the one she'd initiated. It felt—she had no words for the way it felt. She just knew it made her happy, that she wanted more of those kisses. And that was a problem.

Once a couple had crossed the line into romance, the relationship acquired an expiration date. She'd seen it play out over and over with her mother. Attraction, bonding, a period of happiness and then, inevitably, the breakup, usually involving tearful accusations, charred bridges and finally a broken heart which could be healed only by starting the cycle over again.

Only Lauren had more than a broken heart at risk. The farm belonged to Bonnie. If Lauren got involved with Patrick and it didn't last—and her mother's experience had taught her these things never did—then Bonnie might decide she didn't want Lauren around anymore. Sure, she and Bonnie were friends, but if Bonnie ever had to choose between Lauren and her own grandson, Lauren would be the one to go.

In the O'Sheas' world, family came first. Look at the way Patrick was spending his time off at his grandmother's house when he could be hanging out with friends or fishing or whatever it was he did when he wasn't working or here. And now he'd joined in the hunt for the nugget, for his grandmother's sake. What would it be like to be part of a family like that?

Lauren would never know. She'd never even met her grandparents, and her mother was currently in a relationship with a long-haul trucker, seeing the country from the cab of a big rig. Lauren had received a postcard from her with a picture of a cartoon alien from Roswell, New Mexico last week. The message on the card read Having Fun! They'd been together for almost two years now, probably a new record for her mom.

The charging light from her phone reflected off the pendent Rosemary had given her, lying on the nightstand. Lauren picked it up, rubbing the smooth stone between her fingers. Blue lace agate for insight. She could use some of that right now.

She set the necklace down and moved to the window, intending to adjust the heavy curtains to block out the sun, but instead she opened them wide. Orange, peach and pink painted the clouds in the sky over the barn, where her goats were all tucked in for the night. The mountains in the distance, capped by the familiar profile of Pioneer Peak, seemed to form a wall, protecting this valley and keeping it safe. A nearby owl gave a soft hoot, and then she spotted him, gliding silently to land on the barn roof. Hopefully on the lookout for rodents who might want to get into the goats' grain.

Lauren loved this farm. Even after only a month here, she knew she never wanted to leave this place. That's why she'd agreed to help Bonnie search for the nugget, and that's why she had to put a stop to this attraction she felt for Patrick. There was too much at stake.

That decided, she pulled the curtains firmly shut, climbed into bed and closed her eyes. Morning would come early, and she needed to be sharp if she was going to find that nugget.

PATRICK WHISTLED AS he stirred the batter and sprinkled a few drops of water on the waffle iron to test the heat. He could hear the water shut off upstairs, which meant in a few minutes Lauren would appear, her skin still dewy from the shower, her cheeks pink, her lips soft looking. Kissable.

Gran walked into the kitchen, already dressed for the day, scuttling any chance

Patrick might have had to kiss Lauren before breakfast. Maybe later.

"Did you get those boxes down from the attic?"

"Yes, they're in the mudroom." Patrick poured batter and closed the waffle iron. "Come see if they're the right ones."

Gran carried one of the boxes in and set it on the kitchen table. She lifted out a red bowl with a blue rim and white stars, handing it to Patrick to wash. Next came a tablecloth with the Declaration of Independence as part of the design, and a roll of streamers.

"Good morning." Wilson gave a bark. Lauren had come down the stairs so quietly, she'd startled the dog. She peered over Gran's shoulder at a roll of red, white and blue fabric. "What's all this?"

Gran ran a soothing hand over Wilson's head. "It's bunting, for the fence. Tomorrow is the Fourth of July."

"Are we having a party?"

"I always have the Mat Mates to the farm for a picnic lunch."

"Gran loves to decorate for holidays." Patrick removed the first waffle and started another. "You should see this place on St. Patrick's Day."

"Well, we are Irish."

Patrick laughed. "Your maiden name was Romano."

"My mother was a Dolan, and I've been an O'Shea for more than half a century now." Bonnie removed a cake cutter with a handle shaped like a firecracker. "We still have some of those berries left, don't we?"

"Yes, strawberries and blueberries," Patrick assured her.

"I'll decorate while you and Lauren are at the cabin this morning," Gran said, pulling out a folding banner that read Happy Independence Day.

"Okay, but remember you promised to stay off ladders."

"Of course."

She'd agreed a little too readily. Patrick raised his eyebrows. "Step stools count as ladders."

"No, they don't. Step stools are a completely separate category," Gran protested.

He looked toward Lauren for support, but she was feigning fascination with salt and pepper shakers shaped like minutemen. No help there. "I'm not leaving you alone unless you promise to keep one foot on the ground at all times," Patrick told his grandmother. "I'll hang whatever you need hung later today."

"Fine," Gran huffed. "I'll just put the bunting on the fence this morning."

After breakfast, Patrick and Lauren started for the cabin. Gran wished them good luck and began arranging the striped fabric bunches along the picket fence, muttering something under her breath that sounded like, "...too big for his britches." Lauren gave a sudden laugh-snort so she must have heard it, too. Patrick decided his wisest action was to pretend he hadn't.

As they got closer to the cabin, he could hear the water gurgling. Yesterday's rain must have swollen the streambed. "Before we go inside, let's check the creek. There's a culvert under the road, and sometimes when the water's high, it gets clogged."

"Good to know. I'll remember to check on it when it rains."

Patrick led her past the cabin along an overgrown trail to the creek, which had doubled in width overnight to about four feet. The narrow trail followed the creek to the road, where some leafy branches had jammed against the culvert opening, causing the water to back up into a swampy pool. Patrick pulled the broken branches away and tossed them into the woods, allowing the water to drain freely.

"There. All done."

"Look at this." Lauren was standing beside an ancient cottonwood a little upstream from the culvert. She'd pulled off a broken branch, revealing the spot where someone had taken the time to carve a heart about a foot across in the rough bark. Inside the heart were the initials *B* and *E*.

"Anyone you know?" Lauren asked.

"I don't think so." Patrick came to look. "The *B* could be for *Bonnie*, but she and my granddad, Tim, were married long before they bought this farm, and I don't think she was sneaking around on him."

"Definitely not. Your grandmother talks about Tim all the time. She adored him."

"He adored her, too. They were really good together."

"How about your dad? Did he have any girlfriends he might have wanted to immortalize on a tree?"

"Nope, Dad's name is Kevin. Besides, something about the shape of the letters looks old-fashioned to me. Probably one of the Aberg kids." He took a step closer to Lauren. "Fun to think about them here, probably kissing under this tree."

"Guess we'd better get to work if we're going to inspect all the chinking in the cabin." Lauren turned and started briskly up the trail.

Huh. Either Patrick's flirting ability needed work, which was a definite possibility, or Lauren was avoiding the chance of another kiss. Which seemed odd. She'd been willing, even enthusiastic when they'd kissed yesterday. Maybe she was just focused on finding the nugget.

At the cabin, she went right to work shining her light on the wall where they'd removed the catalog page and slowly moving it along the chinking. Patrick took the hint and found the spot where he'd left off the day before. He found a place or two where the chinking was uneven, but a little probing revealed it was only surface damage.

They'd been at it for almost two hours when Lauren mentioned, "There's a crack in this log."

"There are cracks in most of the logs," Patrick pointed out.

"Yes, but this one is against the grain."

He crossed the room to see. Sure enough, a narrow opening ran across the log. "What's this?" He pointed to a tiny lump.

She shined her light on it and looked closely. "It looks like a knotted piece of string. Should I pull it out?"

"Give it a try."

She tugged, and the string came away in her hand. The loop was broken at the far end, like she'd pulled it away from whatever it was attached to. She ran her fingers over the log. "Maybe this whole piece of log comes out. Do you see another crack?"

"I don't." Patrick opened his pocket-knife. "Let me feel along the opening." His knife blade bottomed out at about an inch in, and he could detect no hollow parts. As he dragged his knife downward, probing the walls, something fell to the floor with a metallic tinkle.

"It's a key." Lauren picked it up and opened her hand to display the tiny barrel key with a toothed protrusion on the end. "Could this open a lockbox somewhere that contains the nugget?" Her voice shook with excitement.

"Maybe," Patrick said. It didn't look more like a regular key that unlocked a room, for instance. "It's awfully small, though. If I were securing a five-pound gold nugget, I'd use a bigger lock."

The hopeful look on Lauren's face slipped a notch. He hated watching that beautiful smile fade. "Hey, at least we found something. Let's go show Gran. Maybe she'll have some ideas."

When they returned to the farmhouse, the entire front fence had been draped with red, white and blue scallops. Gran was on the porch, tying more in place on the railing. It looked like she'd kept her promise and left the overhead parts for him.

"This looks amazing!" Lauren's eyes were wide. "Can we leave it up until next Sunday for the yoga class?"

"Of course, if you think they'd enjoy it." Gran stood up a little straighter. "I wasn't expecting you until lunch."

"We found something. Not the gold, obviously, but this." Lauren held out her hand with the key on her palm. Do you think there's any connection?"

"Hmm, a key." Gran picked it up to examine it. "Oh. Patrick you don't suppose the box we found—"

"The one with the fireweed?"

"Yes. It's in the attic. I'll get it." His grandmother began to move.

Patrick laid a hand on her shoulder. "I'll get it. Ladders, remember?"

"Fine. Go. I think it's over by the old milk cans near the dress dummy."

"I'll be right back."

The box wasn't anywhere near the milk cans. In fact, Patrick finally ran it to ground on the opposite side of the attic, under a carton of sewing patterns. Of course, this was likely the reason Gran had wanted to fetch it herself. He climbed down the folding ladder and followed the voices to the living room, where Lauren was draping streamers from the corners of the room to the central light fixture. "Found it."

"Let's see if the key fits." Gran pushed it in, but she couldn't get it to turn. "I guess it's not the right key."

"Or maybe the lock is just stuck." Patrick fetched the lock lubricant he used on the doors and puffed it into the keyhole. "Now try."

Gran inserted the key once more and this time, after a bit of wiggling, it turned. She lifted the lid. "Looks like letters." She removed the top one, gently unfolded it, and took a minute to skim it. "Love letters. At least this one is."

"What does it say?"

"Let's see. 'My darling Elsa,' yadda yadda. 'Your sweet lips are like roses, your blue eyes like the sky, from your head to your toes-es, your beauty makes me sigh.' Oh, my. That's just terrible."

Lauren laughed. "I can't believe he rhymed *roses* with *toes-es*."

"Hey, give the guy a break." Patrick chuckled. "He was probably desperate for another kiss." He looked toward Lauren. She met his eyes briefly and then looked away. Her cheeks grew noticeably pinker. Kind of like those roses from the poem.

Gran was still examining the letter. "Elsa. Why does that name sound familiar?"

"I wonder if Elsa is the initial from the carving," Lauren said. "Who signed the letter?"

"Just B."

"It is them!"

"Who?" Gran asked.

"Patrick and I found a tree down by the creek with initials inside a heart carved on the trunk. *B* and *E*."

"Was Elsa one of the Abergs?" Patrick asked Gran.

"I can't remember for sure. But I know how to find out. Let me call Linda. She has a subscription to one of those genealogy things on the internet." Gran picked up the phone and dialed.

Patrick tried to catch Lauren's eye, but she had settled on the couch and was busy examining the box and then the letter. Gingerly, she unfolded all the letters and spread them out on the coffee table, sorting them by date. Patrick went to peer over her shoulder.

The rest of the letters seemed to be more of the same bad poetry, but as time went on, it became clear that Elsa had moved on to someone else, and B desperately wanted her back. He reminded her of their history, of his love. Mentioned that money didn't buy happiness, which Patrick took to mean B didn't have much and the new suitor did. The final letter asked her to meet him and elope before she married tomorrow.

"I wonder if she did elope," Patrick said.

"I doubt it. Judging by his letters, she's been consistently clear that she's not coming back to him," Lauren commented. "It's sad."

"Yeah. Poor guy."

"I meant Elsa. She kept the letters. She must have cared for B. It had to have been difficult to tell him she was going to marry someone else."

Gran hung up the phone. "I have the information. Elsa was indeed an Aberg, who married into the Helvig family."

"Helvig. They're the ones who always win the giant vegetable competitions at the state fair, right?" Patrick asked.

"Yes. They're probably the most prosperous farmers in the Matanuska Valley."

Lauren glanced at the letters. "I don't suppose his name started with a B."

"No." Gran glanced at her notes. "Nils Helvig married Elsa Aberg in 1956. They had four children, including one who died in infancy. In March of 1965, Nils and the three remaining children perished in a fire."

"How awful! What about Elsa?"

"Elsa was severely burned. She was able to get her youngest out of the fire, but the baby died two days later."

"It must be tough to recover from something like that." Patrick tried to imagine what it would be like to lose his entire family in one terrible accident.

"Yes," Gran said. "But eventually she did. After she was widowed, Elsa started a career as a painter. Several of her paintings are in the museum in Anchorage, and Elsa Helvig Elementary is named for her. That's why the name sounded familiar to me." She closed the box and looked at the lid. "I'll bet she painted the fireweed on this box."

"It's beautiful," Lauren commented. "I wonder if Elsa was ever in contact with B again after the fire."

"Hard to say. She never remarried."

"1965 was a rough year," Patrick mused. "Elsa lost her husband and children in March, and then James Bradley's nugget was stolen in June and he died in September."

"I can't imagine there's any connection," Gran said.

"No." Patrick glanced up at the streamers overhead. "So, what should I hang up next?"

CHAPTER ELEVEN

INDEPENDENCE DAY DAWNED clear and warm. When Lauren returned from the morning milking, Bonnie served her a plate of French toast with strawberries and blueberries arranged on top in the shape of the American flag.

"Wow, I'm impressed," Lauren told her.

"Wait until you see my firecracker Bundt cake."

"Where's Patrick?" Lauren asked in what she thought was a casual voice, but Bonnie still shot her an amused look before answering.

"He's getting the lawn chairs down from the attic. The parade starts at eleven, but we should leave here by nine thirty to get a good spot. Now eat up. I'm going to go change into my parade clothes."

"Okay." Lauren wasn't sure what constituted parade clothes, but from what she'd seen, her jeans would fit in at almost any Alaskan event. Patrick confirmed this when he carried three folding chairs through the kitchen a few minutes later, wearing jeans and a gray T-shirt with a flag on the front.

"Good morning." He stopped to smile at her. It really wasn't fair. Nobody should have such an irresistible smile.

Which was the main reason she'd spent yesterday avoiding being alone with him as much as possible. Because if he tried to kiss her again, she was going to have to say no. And it was going to be hard to say no to that face. But no one said that they couldn't be friends. She just needed to make sure it stopped there. She smiled back. "Morning. I gather we're leaving for the parade in Wasilla soon."

"That's what Gran tells me. Are you all done with the milking?"

"Yes, and I've turned the goats out to pasture. I'll need to be back for evening milking by around six, but until then I'm free."

Bonnie came into the room, dressed in red-and-white-striped cropped pants, a white top and a blue vest covered with white stars. Tiny red firecrackers dangled from her ears. "Ta-da!"

"You look fabulous!" Lauren said.

"You do," Patrick agreed. "Are you ready to go?" he asked Lauren.

"Two minutes to change clothes. Not everyone appreciates the scent of goat as much as I do." Lauren ran upstairs to throw on some clean jeans and a white shirt with red polka dots.

When she returned, Bonnie had just finished tying a patriotic bow around Wilson's neck. "I almost forgot to get him ready for the parade."

"I managed to talk her out of the top hat," Patrick whispered to Lauren as they carried the lawn chairs to load into the trunk of Bonnie's car.

"I'm sure Wilson was grateful," Lauren whispered back.

Lauren loved the homespun quality of the parade. Floats were created by various organizations and usually crammed on as many costumed people as possible. Sometimes it was hard to decipher the theme, as Lady Liberty mingled with a dancing moose and a giant pumpkin, but their enthusiastic waves and the candy they threw brought cheers from the crowds.

There was a marching band, local dignitaries riding in classic cars, Scout troops, several groups on horseback, and a group from a gymnastics school doing flips and cartwheels down the street. Someone with foresight had put the gymnasts before the horses.

"The Mat Mates should march next year," Lauren suggested.

"Nah, I'd rather watch," Bonnie answered. "Besides, Molly, Rosemary and Bea are already in the parade on the Easy Living Apartments float. Here they come now!"

Two of the ladies were perched on the front seat of a horse-drawn wagon, pulled by a pair of gorgeous Clydesdales. To Lauren's surprise, Bea held the reins. Today her hair was white with blue and red streaks. Beside her, Rosemary tossed plastic balls to the children. Three more people from the apartments occupied the back of the wagon. One sat in a rocker and knitted, the second was typing on a laptop computer and Molly stood in front of an easel, painting a picture. The sign on the side read Pursuit of Happiness, Easy Living Apartments.

Wilson bared his teeth and let out a low rumble to make it clear he was willing to protect Bonnie from the enormous horses if necessary. Bonnie shushed him. "Those horses aren't bothering anybody. Leave them be."

"I didn't know Bea drove horses," Lauren said.

"Did you not? She and her husband were

both teachers in Michigan and worked summers as drivers on Mackinac Island, where motor vehicles are forbidden. When he died about ten years ago, she moved to Palmer to be closer to the grandkids. The horses belong to her son."

Two girls standing near them opened the capsules Rosemary had thrown and pulled out strips of red, white and blue stickers. They immediately stuck stars on each other's faces.

"Your friends have so many talents," Lauren said to Bonnie.

"You don't know the half of it," Bonnie said. "You should see Alice and her husband dance the Watusi."

As the last car of the parade came into sight, Bonnie jumped up and folded her chair. "Let's go." They hurried to the parking lot and managed to beat the traffic out of Wasilla. Back at the farm, Patrick set up a grill and started the coals while Lauren and Bonnie put a picnic table in the front yard under a shade tent Patrick had erected the day before. Wilson stretched out on his belly under the lilac bush.

Bonnie used a navy blue tablecloth set with white plates and red napkins. A second table nearby held a salad made from their garden produce, buns, condiments and a Bundt cake elaborately festooned with red and blue drizzles of icing and star-shaped sprinkles. Lauren added a cheese tray.

"What's this?" Bonnie asked.

"These are all goat cheeses. The Gouda and cheddar I made in Oregon. They've been aging for about six months. The herbed soft cheese is fresh, from our goats. I can't legally sell it, but the rules say I can serve it to my family and you're the closest thing to family I've got."

"Oh, honey." Bonnie pulled her into a hug. "I'm so glad you feel that way."

"What's going on?" Patrick had come out of the house carrying a tray of stuff for the grill.

"Lauren made us this beautiful cheese tray," Bonnie told him, "because we're like her family."

Yeah, that didn't make her sound like a con artist or anything. Lauren was almost afraid to look at Patrick for fear he'd be sitting in judgment, but he was admiring the tray she'd prepared. "Wow, this looks great." He reached for a cheese cube, but Bonnie slapped his hand. "Wait for our guests."

Bonnie's friends arrived all together, all bearing food for the picnic. Rosemary's contribution was a dill and lentil salad. Linda carried deviled eggs, Alice and her husband Ralph brought a tray of chips and dip, and Bea set a platter of puffy cookies on the table. "I made snickerdoodles," she announced.

Molly carried a tall wooden bucket with some sort of crank across the top. "Patrick, could you get the ice and salt from the trunk, please?"

"Sure." He parked his tray beside the grill and went to unload Molly's car. "What kind of ice cream this year?"

"Strawberry." Molly set the tub on the porch. "I've already added the ingredients and the paddle."

At Molly's direction, Patrick layered ice and rock salt between the walls of the wooden bucket and a smaller cylinder inside. When it was full, he began turning the crank, but Molly shooed him away. "Go get Ralph and you men do your grilling. We've got this."

Lauren came to look. "I've never made homemade ice cream. May I have a turn cranking?"

Molly laughed. "I feel like Tom Sawyer. Sure, go for it."

"How long does it need to be cranked?" Lauren turned the handle.

"Twenty or thirty minutes. We'll start to feel resistance when it's frozen hard enough."

A firecracker went off in the distance. The dog ran to the gate and barked. "Wilson, hush." Bonnie shook her head. "Every time there's a loud noise, he runs to the front door or the gate like he thinks someone's trying to break in."

"He's trying to protect you," Bea said. "He wants to warn off the noise before it gets into the house."

"The coals are ready," Ralph called from the grill.

"We have salmon, beef or veggie burgers," Patrick announced. "Rosemary, a black bean patty?"

"Yes, please."

"How about a portabella mushroom topper for that?"

"Sounds good."

Patrick, obviously as comfortable with a grill as he was in the kitchen, took everyone's orders and, with Ralph's assistance, cooked them to perfection while Lauren and the ladies took turns cranking the ice cream. Bonnie brought Lauren's cheese tray to the porch for everyone to munch on.

Alice took some Gouda and a cracker. "Oh, this is excellent. Where did you get this cheese, Bonnie?"

"Lauren made it," Bonnie said proudly, "from goat's milk."

The ladies exclaimed over the cheese as they tasted it. "Hey, don't forget the poor cooks over here," Patrick called. "We want cheese, too."

"Here, Lauren. Take them some." Bonnie pressed the tray into Lauren's hands. "It's my turn to crank."

Ralph collected several cubes of cheese and some crackers. "I'm going to need a plate," he murmured, walking toward the picnic table. Patrick stopped flipping burgers to taste some Gouda. "Hey…" He paused to chew and swallow. "This is good. Really good. I don't know a lot about cheese, but even I can tell this is better than your average stuff."

"Thank you." Lauren had won prizes with her cheeses. She knew it was good. But somehow Patrick's opinion meant more to her. "Try the cheddar."

His hands were busy flipping the rest of the burgers, but he opened his mouth like a baby bird. Lauren laughed and popped in a cheddar cube.

"Mmm." He paused to move some of the burgers farther from the coals. "Would you be insulted if I use some of the cheddar on my burger?"

"Go right ahead," Lauren said.

"Mine, too," Bea called.

"Gouda on my veggie burger," Rosemary ordered.

Lauren had momentarily forgotten that they weren't alone. She didn't want the others to think she and Patrick were...well, Lauren and Patrick. Like together in the same sentence. Feeding him cheese might have created a false impression. She moved a half step back.

"Can I try the white stuff?" he asked.

"Here." Lauren spread the herbed goat cheese on a wafer. This time she set it on a napkin and handed it to him.

"Rosemary?"

"And thyme."

He tried a bite. "Yeah, you have absolutely got to get your cheeses on the market. This is great."

Lauren felt her cheeks grow warm at his praise. Alaskans loved good food. She was sure there was a market for artisanal cheeses here. If only...

"How's the treasure hunt going?" Ralph

asked, as though he'd read Lauren's mind. "Alice was telling me about it."

Bonnie filled them in on the key and the love letters. "I'm not sure what to do with them. Should I contact Elsa's family to return them?"

"Elsa lived to be ninety-eight years old. She had plenty of time to retrieve the letters if she'd wanted her family to have them," Linda pointed out.

"It could be awkward, since she married someone else," Alice agreed. "I'd hang on to them if I were you."

"I wonder what *B* stands for." Bea stopped cranking and Linda took her place. *"Bernard? Bruce?"*

"Bjorn," Rosemary suggested.

"Or it could be his last name. Or a nickname. We really have no clue," Alice pointed out.

"I could check the census on neighboring farms," Linda said. "If you think it would help."

"What we really should be focusing on isn't Elsa, it's William Golson," Molly said. "If we knew more about him, maybe we could figure out where he'd hide the nugget."

"I'll see what I can find," Linda promised. "Molly do you think this ice cream is ready?"

Molly tried the crank. "It's done." She opened the lid to remove the paddle from the tub of ice cream before corking the lid and replacing it. The paddle dripped onto the porch, cueing Wilson to rush over for cleanup. Molly added more ice to the top of the bucket and covered it with a towel. "We should let it ripen for an hour or so."

"Good, because the food is ready." Patrick set a plate of burgers on the buffet table. "Let's eat."

The picnic was delightful, with good food and good conversation. Wilson almost ran his little legs off dashing back and forth under the table whenever he thought he spotted a crumb. After feasting on everyone's offerings, they decided to postpone dessert temporarily. Bonnie sent Patrick on another trip to the attic while they moved the leftovers to the kitchen and took down the tables.

Patrick returned with an ancient croquet set. "Oh good," Alice exclaimed. "I'm much better at this than cornhole."

"I think Alice should have a handicap because she plays golf," Bea said.

"Golf is played with clubs, not mallets," Alice protested. "Entirely different game."

"No handicaps," Molly pronounced. She grabbed a handful of grass stems from the tall grass outside the gate. "We'll draw straws for teams. We need six players."

"I'd like to see Elsa's letters if I could," Linda told Bonnie.

"May I tag along?" Ralph asked. "I'm always interested in local history."

"Sure. Come inside. I need to feed Wilson anyway. We'll play the next round. Have fun." The three of them disappeared into the house, Wilson tagging along behind them.

"That dog never gets more than a foot away from Bonnie," Molly commented.

Lauren smiled. The people from the shelter had called a week after they found the dog to confirm that no one had asked after him. They'd mentioned they had an opening with a foster family, but Bonnie had assured them Wilson had found a forever home with her.

Lauren just wished she could say the same. She loved the farm, loved Bonnie, and would like nothing better than to make this her forever home as well. That was the plan, that she would share the profits with Bonnie and over time, she would buy the farm. Of course, that was before she discovered the cost of certification. If they didn't find that nugget…

"Lauren, you're up." Patrick called.

She gave him a smile. "All right then. What's the object of this game again?"

Croquet turned out to be a more cutthroat game than Lauren would have guessed, but in the end, the team with Alice, Lauren and Rosemary were the winners. Patrick took losing with good grace, which didn't surprise Lauren considering how he'd reacted to the goat's destruction of his car's roof. He touched her back. "I'm getting a bottle of water. Want one?"

"Yes, please." Thoughtful, too. Couldn't he have been rude, or selfish or have some terrible trait that would make it easier for her to resist him? Why did the one man whom she absolutely shouldn't get involved with have to be so appealing?

"Lauren, would you cut the cake while I scoop the ice cream?" Molly asked.

"Sure." Lauren focused on the task at hand. Tomorrow would be enough time to worry about how to put the brakes on her attraction to Patrick, and how to finance the equipment she'd need to make the farm work. Today was a celebration, and she should live in the moment.

That decision made, she cut the cake and handed a slice to Patrick, who had returned to set a cold bottle of water on the table beside her. "Enjoy."

"Thanks." Patrick gave her that adorable smile. "I will."

THAT EVENING, PATRICK set a folded blanket and a bottle of mosquito repellant in Gran's trunk next to the lawn chairs. Somewhere between the farm and town, a whistling rocket zoomed into the air and burst into a red-and-green cluster. Gran's pint-sized mutt let it be known from inside the house that he did not approve.

Lauren returned from the barn, where she'd gone to check on the goats. "The fireworks don't seem to be bothering them, particularly," she reported. "I closed the barn doors so it's really not that loud, and they're settling in their pen for the night."

"Good. Wish I could say the same for Wilson. He's loaded for bear." As Patrick spoke, a pop led to another round of barking. "Are you ready to go watch the fireworks?"

"Can't wait. I love fireworks, even if the sky in Alaska doesn't get completely dark this time of year. I'll see if Bonnie's ready."

Before she could go inside, Gran came out onto the porch, carrying her little dog in her arms.

"I got the blanket like you asked," Patrick told her. "Do you want to take a sweater?"

"I think I'll skip the fireworks this year." Gran shushed Wilson after a bottle rocket set him off again. "I don't want to take him any closer to the noises, and I don't want to leave him home alone."

"Are you sure?" Patrick asked. "We could put him in his crate."

"No, he needs reassurance. You two go on."

Lauren shuffled her feet. "Oh, well, maybe I should stay and help—"

"Nonsense. I'm fine. I've seen my share of firework shows. You and Patrick go and enjoy them."

Lauren climbed into the car, but she didn't close the door. "I feel like I should stay."

"We won't be gone long," Patrick assured her. "We're not going all the way into Wasilla. I know a place where we can watch the fireworks from a distance."

"Okay." She shut the door and he started up the driveway. "That was some picnic."

"Yeah. Your cheese was a hit."

"So was Molly's ice cream. She gave me the recipe. The milk production this evening was the highest yet. I should work on some goat's milk ice cream recipes."

"Gran has an electric ice cream maker. I saw it in the attic when I was getting the croquet set. And if you need a taste tester…" He grinned.

"I couldn't help but notice you went back for second helpings."

"Oh, you didn't see me sneaking thirds when I was cleaning up? I confess, when it comes to ice cream, especially homemade ice cream, I can't resist."

"So ice cream is your one weakness, huh?"

"Oh, I wouldn't say that." He also had a weakness for hard-working brunettes with big goals. Or at least the one who was sitting beside him in the car right now. He wanted to be the hero who helped her find that gold nugget that would make her dreams come true. Trouble was, if it wasn't hidden anywhere in the cabin, he was out of ideas on where to look next.

He turned into the side road and parked in a spot overlooking a cow pasture. "We're here."

"All by ourselves?"

"Looks like. Sometimes there will be another car or two. Most people go to Wonderland Park or Lucille Lake to watch the fireworks up close, but I've always liked to see them from a distance so we can see the whole shape. Do you mind?"

"Not at all."

He opened the trunk. He'd brought chairs for the three of them and a blanket in case Gran got cold. Instead, he left the chairs where they were and grabbed the blanket to spread over the hood and windshield of Gran's car to protect the paint. He gestured. "Your viewing platform awaits."

Lauren laughed and climbed onto the car, lying back against the windshield. Patrick settled in beside her. It was a perfect evening, warm, with a slight breeze to knock down the mosquitos. The air carried the fragrance of cut grass. The first rocket sizzled into the air and exploded into three pink chrysanthemum shapes. Lauren watched, her eyes wide with wonder.

That was one of the things Patrick liked most about her: the wonder. She noticed little things, things that seemed ordinary, and teased out the extraordinary. She didn't just compliment Molly on the ice cream, she'd commented on the balance of flavors, on the texture. Lauren didn't just run goats. She knew each one by name, and their habits and idiosyncrasies. He had a feeling that no matter how large the herd grew, she would always know her goats.

Lauren rubbed her hand over her bare forearm. "Cold?" Patrick asked.

"A little. I should have brought a sweater."

"Come here." He opened his arm.

She hesitated, the tip of her tongue sweeping over her lower lip. He watched, fascinated with the shape of her mouth. After a second, she slid closer and laid her head against his shoulder. She fit just right, tucked in against him.

Another shell fired, this one with whistling rockets spiraling into curlicues in the sky. Lauren moved her head, releasing a floral scent as her hair rubbed against his cheek. If time froze at that moment, if Patrick could stay there forever breathing in her scent, with his arm around her, watching the fireworks light up the sky, he wouldn't complain.

When the last of the sparkles fell from that rocket, she raised her head to look at him. Slowly, he brushed his lips against hers. He felt, rather than heard her contented sigh. She tilted her head, and he kissed her again, more deeply. Somewhere in the distance, a deep boom signaled that another rocket had been set off, but he kept his eyes closed and concentrated on the internal fireworks from that kiss. When he lifted his head, their eyes held for a long moment. And then, with another sweet sigh, she settled against his shoulder to watch.

He wanted more of these moments with her. But if they couldn't find Bradley's Heart, the only way she would be able to chase her dream would be to return to Oregon. And Patrick didn't want that to happen.

Somehow, somewhere, before summer was done, they were going to find that nugget. Patrick would make sure of that.

CHAPTER TWELVE

LAUREN TRIED TO lead Muffin to the milking rack, but the goat planted her feet and refused to move. In the pen, Biscotti gave a disgusted bleat, and Lauren realized why they were upset. She'd inadvertently changed their milking order.

"Sorry, girls." She returned Muffin to the pen and Biscotti took her rightful place on the milking stand. Lauren needed to concentrate on what she was doing. She could worry about Patrick later.

But once she'd started the milking machine, her mind wandered back to him. When she'd decided to delay the difficult talk with Patrick so as not to ruin the holiday, she'd never expected she would be alone with him under the fireworks. She should have stayed home with Bonnie and Wilson. And yet she couldn't be too sorry because if she'd stayed home, she would have missed out on the best kiss of her life. Her cheeks flamed at the memory.

She finished the morning milking and took the goats to pasture. On her walk back to the house, she passed the patriotic decorations they'd left up for the goat yoga classes on Sunday afternoon. Her face flushed again. Would the Fourth of July be forever tied in her mind to those kisses beneath the fireworks? She slipped into the mudroom door in time to hear Bonnie asking for an update on the nugget search.

"We'll continue to check the chinking," Patrick told her. "I've tried to put myself in Golson's head, and I can't think of a more likely place to hide the nugget. It's tedious, but unless you or Lauren can think of something more likely, I think it's our best bet."

"No, over the years, I've already exhausted all the fun ideas. You're probably right, that inch by inch is the best way to search. It's good of you to spend all this time looking. I know you believe your grandfather was right, that the nugget is long gone."

"That was before I read Lauren's notes from the historian. Now that I have, there's a good chance Golson hid the nugget here, somewhere. I'm glad to help."

"Are you helping because of me, or because of Lauren?"

Lauren stopped with her hand on the water

spigot, waiting on his answer. But he just laughed. "Does it matter?"

Lauren washed her hands and continued into the kitchen. Patrick spooned oatmeal into a bowl and set it in front of her. "Hi. How was my good friend, Spritz, this morning?"

"Producing well. She sends her love."

Patrick chuckled and passed her the maple syrup jug. He preferred brown sugar and cinnamon in his. It felt intimate, knowing these little preferences about each other. Like they were family. Lauren wondered if her own mother would remember how she liked her oatmeal. The kettle sang, and he poured boiling water into the teapot before helping himself to a cup of coffee from the coffee maker.

"What's the schedule today?" Patrick asked Bonnie.

"I have a planning meeting about the holiday bazaar this morning, and I thought since Lauren has provided us with all this nice cream, I'd bake up some rhubarb scones for this afternoon's tea."

"Let me know if you need a hand," Patrick offered.

"I can handle it. I've been baking on my own for seventy years now."

"I was thinking more along the lines of tasting," Patrick admitted. "But whatever."

"Oh, that reminds me," Lauren said. "Marissa, from the reindeer farm, is coming by this afternoon. Hope that's okay."

"Of course. You live here, too," Bonnie said. "I'm glad you're making friends. I'll make plenty of scones."

"It's more for business than pleasure. We were talking after yoga last week, and she said she'd show me how to vaccinate the kids, which will save a load in vet bills. She's going to leave a stack of brochures about the reindeer farm for the yoga check-in table."

"Sounds like a deal," Patrick said. "Do you have time to work with me in the cabin this morning?"

"Absolutely. I want to get in as much search time as possible." Assuming he still wanted to work with her once she'd made it clear they couldn't have a romantic relationship. She rinsed her bowl and set it in the sink.

"You two go ahead," Bonnie said. "I'll do kitchen cleanup. Maybe today will be our lucky day."

"Here's hoping." Lauren held up crossed fingers and followed Patrick outside. As they walked along the trail to the cabin, Lauren debated how to approach the subject of their relationship. Maybe she should wait until it came up naturally? Better not. Judging from last night, she couldn't trust herself to make the right call under pressure.

They turned in at the cabin, picking their way through the trees across the rough ground. Patrick stepped over a log and stopped to offer a hand. She hesitated a moment, but he would have done the same for his grandmother or anyone. It didn't have to mean anything. So why did it feel so good?

She dropped his hand as soon as she was over the obstacle. They stepped into the cabin and he headed toward the stairs, but she stopped. "Could we talk for a second?"

"Sure. What's up?"

"I, uh, that is we…"

"Uh-huh?" He leaned forward, encouraging her to continue.

"Last night was…nice."

"It was nice." Even in the shadows, she could see that killer smile aimed at her.

"But—"

"Not liking the but," he murmured.

She drew in a breath and spit out the words. "But it's probably better if it doesn't happen again."

He gave her a puzzled look. "You don't want to watch fireworks with me anymore?"

"You know what I mean."

"Do I?"

"The kissing. The kissing has to stop."

"I thought you said it was nice."

"It was."

He raised his eyebrows. "You don't like nice?"

"Look. You're a nice guy and your kisses are—"

"Nice. Yeah, I got that."

"But I'm not in a place right now to form any attachments."

"So 'it's not you, it's me.' Is that what you're saying?"

"I—yes. I mean, I hope we can still be friends."

"That's what you want?" he asked slowly. "To be friends?"

"Yes."

"But not kissing friends."

"No kisses."

"Why—" He studied her face for a long moment. "Never mind. If that's what you want."

"It is," she lied.

"Fine." He sucked in a breath and let it

out all at once. "I guess we'd better get to work, then."

"You're still willing to help me?"

"We're friends, right? Besides, it's clear Gran won't move to town unless she finds that nugget, and I want her safe."

"You don't think she's safe with me?"

"She's safer in town." He turned and climbed the stairs.

Lauren followed slowly. Did he mean that Bonnie was safer in town because there were more people around if something went wrong, or was this his way of saying he still didn't completely trust her?

Who could blame him? Kissing him one night, backing off the next day, Lauren must come across as a flake. But she'd never wavered in her support of Bonnie, and she'd like to think he understood that.

When she reached the second floor, he was already at work in the third bedroom, shining his light along the top row. She stopped in the middle of the room and crossed her arms. "Bonnie means a lot to me, you know."

He looked over his shoulder at her. "Yeah, she means a lot to me, too, and this nugget means a lot to her, so let's get to searching, shall we?"

Lauren went to the opposite wall and

began inspecting the chinking there but had to stop when tears blurred her vision. She blinked them away, annoyed with herself. Patrick had agreed to everything she'd asked and was still willing to help with the search. She'd gotten everything she'd asked for. So why did she feel like she'd lost?

VACCINATIONS TURNED OUT to be easier than Lauren had feared. Ryan, Marissa's son, was a genius at distracting and comforting the kids while they got their shots. After Marissa had demonstrated the technique on three of the kids, it was Lauren's turn. She chose Chip, one of Spritz's kids, to hold across her lap.

Ryan stepped in with a bottle of Spritz's milk. Chip hadn't ever seen a bottle before, but it didn't take long for him to figure out how it worked. Ryan held the bottle in one hand, while using the other to help hold the kid still so that Marissa could find a loose flap of skin near her back leg.

When the needle went in, the kid dropped the nipple to give a plaintive bleat, but it was over quickly. Ryan let Chip finish the bottle while Lauren rubbed the area to distribute the vaccine and soothe the sting. "I'm going to be a vet when I grow up," he told Lauren. "A big animal vet, not just pets."

"You'll be a good one," Lauren said, sincerely.

"We think so, too." Marissa gave the boy's shoulder a squeeze. "My husband, Chris, is already researching the best veterinary programs." She grinned. "Think of all the money we can save at the reindeer farm if Ryan gives us a family discount."

It took most of the afternoon to get the rest of the kids vaccinated. Afterward, Ryan and Marissa enjoyed some play and cuddle time with the kids in the barn. Lauren laughed when one of the goats climbed onto Ryan's shoulder and rested his front hooves on his head.

It was a nice break, after the tense morning Lauren had experienced. It had been miserable, working in the same room with Patrick all morning in near silence. Lauren had desperately tried to think of a topic of conversation to break the awkwardness between them, but nothing seemed big enough to budge that iceberg. She wasn't sure if Patrick wasn't talking because he was hurt or if, like her, he could find nothing to say. Inch by inch, they'd inspected the entire wall of the third bedroom and been rewarded with nothing but cobwebs, dust and disappointment.

Lauren checked her watch. "We just have time to put the goats in the pasture before we're due to have tea. You'll join us, won't you? Bonnie said she's making scones today."

"That sounds like an offer we can't refuse," Marissa answered.

"What's a scone? Like an ice cream scoop in a cone?" Ryan asked, hopefully.

"Good guess, but no." His mom laughed. "It's somewhere between a cookie and a sweet biscuit. You'll love it."

"And if you don't, we have some homemade strawberry ice cream left over," Lauren told him.

"I like strawberries."

They took the goats to their pasture. As they walked toward the house, Patrick emerged from the trees around the cabin. "Hi, everybody." He must have been climbing around the roofline because cobwebs clung to his hair.

Lauren reached up to brush them off but stopped halfway. Would it send mixed signals to touch his hair? Like she'd trespassed out of the friend zone? She dropped her hand. "You have something in your hair."

The corners of Patrick's mouth twitched. "Is it a spider?"

"A black ladybug," Lauren countered.

"Ladybugs are red with black dots," Ryan insisted.

"You don't say." Patrick shook his head and swept the cobwebs away with his hands. "How did the vaccinations go?"

"It was fairly painless," Marissa said. "Although the goats probably wouldn't agree."

"Let me run inside and get something from the refrigerator," Lauren said as they reached the barn. When she returned with a jar and a bottle of fresh milk, Marissa and Patrick were talking.

"Patrick was just telling me about your problems with the dairy regulations. I'm sorry to hear that."

Lauren tried to make light of it as they resumed walking. "Yeah, it's a setback, but I'm optimistic I'll be able to get the equipment I need to pass the state's rules for a cheese-making operation." No need to mention the whole thing rested on a treasure hunt. Ordinarily, Lauren was the kind of person who planned carefully. She didn't want Marissa to think she'd taken up farming on a whim, and next week would be taking up a new hobby. Why did Patrick have to bring it up, anyway?

But Marissa didn't seem to doubt her planning skills. "You know, if you're putting in a building for a cheese-making operation, you should include a tasting room, like the wineries do. I could see cheese tastings as a tourist draw on weekends."

"What a great idea!" Would the reward from the nugget cover a tasting room as well as all the equipment? If not, maybe she could design the building to be expandable, so as to build it in the future.

Ryan and Marissa exclaimed over the decorations on the fence. They all washed up in the mudroom. The teakettle whistled. When they came into the kitchen, Bonnie was pouring boiling water into a teapot. A platter of scones and a stack of plates and cups were already arranged on a tray, ready to go.

"Hello," Bonnie greeted them. "I thought we'd have our tea outside."

"I brought you a surprise." Lauren handed the jar to Bonnie. "Clotted cream. It's my first attempt, though, so I don't know if it's any good."

"How wonderful!" Bonnie beamed. "Thank you."

Bonnie reached for the tray. "Let's adjourn to the porch, shall we?"

"I'll get that," Lauren said. Patrick went

ahead to hold the door open for everyone, with Lauren coming through last, carrying the tray. Her forearm brushed against Patrick's hand as she passed, and a sudden awareness tingled on her skin. A quick glance at his face revealed that he'd felt it, too.

Surely if she ignored those little flashes of attraction, they'd eventually go away. Lauren set the tray on the table.

Bonnie poured tea and distributed plates, inviting everyone to help themselves. She split her scone and filled it with a smear of raspberry jam and a generous dollop of clotted cream. When she bit into it, her expression went dreamy. "Yes! That's it. That's the taste I remember." She tried another bite. "In fact, I think I like yours even better. Of course, the cream we had in England was cow's milk instead of goat's milk. Oh, Lauren, thank you!"

"You're welcome." A flush warmed Lauren's cheeks at Bonnie's pleasure. "I'm glad you like it. Oh, Ryan, I forgot about the ice cream. Do you want some?"

"That's okay." A drop of clotted cream clung to his chin. "But can I have another one of those scone things?"

PATRICK SET HIS suitcase beside the front door. He could hear Gran in the kitchen, talking to someone on the phone. Once he'd said his goodbyes, he'd head back to Anchorage so he could catch the early plane to the North Slope tomorrow. Usually, he was ready to get back to work at the end of his two weeks off, but this time he felt like he was leaving too much unfinished.

Gran still refused to consider moving to town, and Lauren was no closer to affording the upgrades she needed to start her business. Together, he and Lauren had gone over every inch of the inside of the cabin, up to and including prying up more floorboards, but there was no sign of a nugget.

Gran came out of the kitchen. "All packed up?"

"Yep."

"That was Linda on the phone. She did her genealogy thing and found Golson has a first cousin once removed in Valdez."

"Huh. Not an especially close relative. Any indication this cousin might know anything?"

"No way to know unless we ask. Linda's emailing me the particulars. I'll forward them to you." She handed him a paper bag. He knew without looking there would be a cookie or some other treat inside. Gran was convinced he'd die of starvation between Palmer and Anchorage if it wasn't for her.

"Thanks."

"You're welcome. What's going on with you and Lauren?" The question came out of the blue, but then Gran had never been one to dance around awkward questions.

"Absolutely nothing," Patrick answered honestly, but hearing the edge of bitterness in his voice he tried to inject some optimism. "But we haven't searched the outside of the cabin yet."

"I don't mean the search. I mean between the two of you. You've hardly spoken the last few days."

Patrick had been wondering about that as well. "Maybe you should ask her."

Gran tightened her lips and shook her head. "What did you do?"

"Nothing. I... I kissed her," Patrick admitted.

Gran couldn't have looked less surprised. "And?"

Patrick shrugged. "She kissed me back. Everything was good. But then the next day, she said we should just be friends."

"Why?"

"I don't know. I assume 'let's be friends'

is code for 'I'm not rude enough to say so, but I don't like you.' Am I wrong?"

Gran gave a long-suffering sigh as if it was taking all her patience to deal with such a knucklehead. "She likes you."

"Oh, yeah? Then why is she brushing me off?"

"Why are you asking me? Go talk to her."

"I don't want to make things uncomfortable."

Gran laughed. "The last few days the two of you have been circling each other like a couple of strange dogs with your hackles up. How much more uncomfortable could it get?"

"Good point." Besides, if he didn't ask, he'd spend the next two weeks wondering. "Maybe I will. I assume she's milking?"

"If you hurry, you can catch her." He gripped the doorknob, but before he opened the door, Gran added, "Oh, Patrick?"

He turned. "Yes?"

She straightened the collar on his shirt. "Good luck."

LAUREN WAS MOVING the evening's milk from the cold-water bath to the refrigerator when she heard Spritz's distinctive greeting bleat. She turned to find Patrick leaning over the goat pen, tickling the goat under her chin. "Hi."

"Hello." Lauren added the last bottle and shut the door. "What can I do for you?"

"If you have a minute, I wanted to ask a question."

"All right." She came to stand beside the goat pen. "Is this about your grandmother?"

"No. It's about us."

"Us?" Lauren shifted her weight. It had been hard enough to get through this once. Surely he didn't want to rehash it.

"You said you wanted to be friends."

"Yes."

"But we're not acting like friends. Whenever we're in the same room, it seems like the temperature drops a couple of degrees. Even Gran has noticed."

What could Lauren say to that? She didn't want to damage her relationship with Bonnie, or to make things worse with Patrick. "I'm sorry. I didn't mean—"

"What did you mean? That's my question."

"What did I mean about what?"

Patrick gave Spritz one more pat and took a step closer to Lauren. "Lauren, I like you. I'm attracted to you. Maybe I completely misread the situation but I got the feeling you might like me, too. When I kissed you, you kissed me back. I thought it was mutual. Was I wrong?"

"No," Lauren admitted.

"So, something changed your mind. What?"

"I just think it would be better if we don't become involved."

"Because…?" he prompted.

Fine. If he wanted to know, she would tell him. "Let's look ahead. Suppose we started dating. Maybe things go well for a while. But it doesn't work out. You decide you don't want to be with me. If you think this week was awkward, imagine how that would be."

"There are no guarantees, but I don't see why we couldn't handle it—"

"You say that now, but if you were really mad at me you wouldn't want to see me anymore. Your grandmother would support you. I'd have to leave the farm."

Patrick blinked. "That's what you're afraid of? That I'd force Gran to choose between us?" Patrick gave a wry laugh. "That's not going to happen. Besides, Gran has agreed that if we can find the nugget, she'll move to town, so there's no conflict."

"But if you hated me—"

"I could never hate you." He took a step closer and touched her arm. "Trust me—I'm not a vindictive person. I've dated before, and none of the women I've gone out with ended up being my mortal enemy."

"No?"

"Uh-uh. I can give you references if you need them."

"Or I could ask your grandmother."

"That might work, too. Lauren, you're a special person. I want to know you better, to spend time with you. I want to kiss you. I don't know if it will lead anywhere or not, but I'd like to see where it takes us. Is that a possibility?"

Was it? It would be easy to fall for Patrick O'Shea, but as her mother had demonstrated time and time again, falling wasn't a permanent condition. If they broke up—or rather when they broke up—it could be messy. But would it really be any worse than this last week of tiptoeing awkwardly around each other?

Maybe it was all a moot point. If they didn't find that nugget she wouldn't be staying anyway. Lauren didn't have enough savings to support herself indefinitely, and the Saturday Market and goat yoga were only for the summer. Realistically, this fall, she would most likely be selling her goats and moving back to Oregon. So why not take a chance?

"It's a possibility," she said.

"Yeah?"

"Yeah."

"So just to be clear, when I get back from this next work hitch, you'll go out with me. Agreed?"

She hesitated, weighing her doubts against those amazing sparks she felt with Patrick. Finally, she let out a breath. "Agreed."

He touched her forearm. "Shall we seal it with a kiss?"

Oh, those indigo eyes. "That seems appropriate." She tilted her head, but he didn't immediately kiss her. Instead, he stroked her cheek while he studied her face, as though he was trying to memorize every feature. He let his hands drop to her waist and pulled her closer. She wrapped her arms around his neck. And then, only then, did his lips meet hers in a sweet, sweet kiss.

Somewhere, a thousand miles away, goats were bleating and going about their goat business, but she and Patrick were alone in a world that was suddenly sparkly and bright. He lifted his head, smiled at her, and kissed her once again before releasing her.

"I really wish I didn't have to go to work tomorrow."

"Me too."

"I want to see you as soon as possible when I get back."

"I'd like that."

"You'll be at the Saturday Market, right? How about if I pick you up and take you for a night on the town? Dinner, dancing, movie, bowling, whatever you want."

"Bowling?" She laughed and started to agree, only to remember, "I have to be back for milking."

"Oh, yeah. Okay, we'll grab some takeout from one of the downtown restaurants and bring it with us. Maybe we can go out for dessert in Palmer."

"I'm sorry. I know the life of a dairy farmer isn't terribly exciting—"

"I want to spend time with you. It doesn't matter where."

"In that case," she stood on her tiptoes to brush her lips across his once more, "it's a date."

CHAPTER THIRTEEN

"ROSEMARY GAVE ME a bracelet that's supposed to use acupressure to prevent seasickness, but I think I'll get some pills, too." Bonnie jotted that on her list. "I'll pick them up when I drop Wilson off with Molly."

"Do you get seasick?" Lauren asked her.

"I don't know. I've never been on an oceangoing boat before." Bonnie laughed. "Look at me. I'm as excited as a kid on the first day of summer vacation. Dairy farmers don't tend to travel much, as you know. I wonder if I'll need my passport for the ferry."

"Probably not, since we're not crossing any borders, but I'm bringing mine, just in case," Lauren advised.

"You have a current passport, Gran?" Patrick carried in two dusty suitcases he'd brought from the attic.

"I do. I got it eight years ago. Tim was finally going to retire, and we were supposed to go to Europe. We had a lot of fun planning that trip, right down to which cafés we planned to try in Paris."

"What happened?" Lauren asked.

"He died," Bonnie said in her usual matter-of-fact way. "Anaphylactic shock from wasp stings. He must have stepped on a nest somewhere out in the far pasture. We didn't even know he was allergic."

"I'm so sorry."

"Thank you. I am, too. I guess it goes to show you not to put things off. Tim was really looking forward to seeing the Eiffel Tower." Bonnie gave a little smile, more to herself than directed outward. "I used to tease him, tell him I married a man three years younger than me so I wouldn't be left a widow. You see how that worked out."

"I miss him, too." Patrick put an arm around her shoulders and gave a gentle squeeze.

"I know." Bonnie patted his arm. "But I couldn't have asked for a better husband, or a better father for Kevin and grandfather for you and Rowan."

"What would you say is the secret for a happy marriage?" Patrick asked.

"The big secret, hmm?" She chuckled. "It takes a lot more than one secret, but I'd say it boils down to trust. Everyone has tender places. When you love someone, you're trusting them to be kind and careful with those sore spots. Of course, being human, sometimes we get careless and can't resist poking each other. Love means trusting that even when we hurt each other, we'll stick it out long enough to forgive and heal."

"You've put a lot of thought into this."

"Well I had a long time to think. Tim and I had a lot of good years together."

"Forty-nine, right?" Lauren said.

"Forty-nine. The trip was supposed to be for our big five-O." The wistful look on Bonnie's face lasted only a moment before she turned to beam at Patrick. "But right now, we need to get ready for this trip. I can hardly wait."

"I'm still not sure I should go," Lauren said. "Maybe the two of you should talk to the cousin in Valdez while I hold down the fort here."

Patrick flashed her an indulgent smile. "Marissa assures me the Holmen brothers have filled in at the reindeer farm many times, and she highly recommends them."

"But the reindeer don't have to be milked. And the Holmens are teenagers."

"Just give them a chance. They grew up farming, and their parents are there for backup if a situation should arise. They'll be here in time for the evening milking today. If you're not comfortable once you've seen them in action, we'll make other arrangements. But I really think we should all be there to talk with this relative of Golson's. She says her grandmother held on to every letter she ever received and that sounds promising."

"You're right." Lauren gave a decisive nod. Patrick had been so good to her. Saturday, he'd met her at the close of the farmers' market to help her and Rosemary pack up. Then he'd taken her out for ice cream to eat while they strolled through the gardens of Town Square in downtown Anchorage. Together, they'd chosen food for a picnic under the tree in Bonnie's front yard.

On Sunday afternoon, he'd pitched in with goat yoga. Now that they were selling a limited number of tickets in advance and the goats had learned that time in the yard meant lots of petting and attention, it all ran much more smoothly, but it was still helpful to have an extra goat wrangler.

And now Patrick had not only followed up the lead Linda had given them, he'd made all the arrangements to turn this into a mini vacation, including goat sitting. Lauren shouldn't obsess about her goats. "You really think there's a chance we'll find a clue?"

"I hope so. With that many letters, we may get lucky."

While Patrick had been on the slope, Lauren had been spending all her spare time, except for a few hours one day when she accepted Marissa's invitation for lunch at the reindeer farm, inspecting the outside of the cabin, inch by inch. She'd discovered a few abandoned bird's nests and lots of bugs, but no sign of any hidden compartments. Meanwhile, Patrick had chased down Golson's relative in Valdez and it turned out she had an entire basement filled with family memorabilia and was happy to let them look.

Patrick reached for a rag to dust off the suitcases he'd fetched. "Which one do you want, Gran?"

Bonnie considered. "I'd better take both of them."

Patrick laughed. "We're only going for two nights. You won't need a formal gown for dinner on the ferry crossing."

"I suppose you're right. I'll take that one." She grabbed the handle of the smaller roller bag and dragged it down the hall to her room.

Lauren stepped closer to Patrick and raised on her toes to brush a kiss across his lips.

He grinned. "Not that I'm complaining, but what was that for?"

"For planning this trip and making your grandmother happy."

"She's excited, isn't she?" Patrick smiled in satisfaction. "Honestly, it would save time to drive directly to Valdez, but I thought a triangle with a ferry crossing would be more fun. Like Gran said, she's never done it, and I know you've hardly been away from the farm since you arrived in Alaska."

"You're right. Other than looking over the inlet when we go to the Saturday Market in Anchorage, I've never even seen the ocean in Alaska."

"Well, tomorrow, you will. Let's hope for clear weather."

THEY GOT LUCKY. Only a few picturesque clouds floated in the blue sky over the snow-capped mountains of Cook Inlet as they drove along the Seward Highway. Sunlight sparkled on the water. They passed a blue-and-yellow passenger train on the tracks that ran beside the road.

It was almost a guilty pleasure Lauren felt as she looked out the window at the beautiful scenery. The teenagers Patrick had hired had arrived right on time both yesterday evening and this morning to handle the milking and she had to admit, they seemed quite competent. The goats liked them immediately, which Lauren considered a good sign. Still, as she'd waved goodbye, she'd felt like a new mother leaving her babies for the first time.

"Look." Bonnie pointed. "Belugas."

Lauren followed her finger and spotted the white whales bobbing along halfway across the inlet. She counted five, no six of them before the road curved and she lost her view. They continued to follow the ocean until they reached the turnoff for Portage Glacier.

"Can you see the glacier from the road?" Lauren asked.

"No, you have to take a boat. It's at the end of Portage Lake," Patrick said. "If we didn't have to be in Whittier by noon, I'd stop. Don't worry, though. We'll see glaciers from the ferry today."

"I brought my camera." Bonnie patted the tote bag in her lap. "And the guidebook Linda loaned to me."

They came to a stop behind a line of cars. An A-frame building spanned the road up ahead. "What's going on?" Lauren asked.

"We're at the tunnel, and the train is coming through. We have to wait our turn."

"The cars and the train share the tunnel?"

"Yes, it's only one lane wide. We go this direction on the half hour, the cars from the other direction go on the hour."

Bonnie pulled the book from her bag and thumbed through the pages. "The Anton Anderson tunnel is the longest highway tunnel in North America at 2.5 miles. It was originally only a train tunnel. It opened to public traffic in 2002."

"And there's a town on the other side?" Lauren asked.

"Whittier, a small port town," Patrick said.

"Population 215, most of whom live in a single building," Bonnie read aloud. "Established as Camp Sullivan during World War II, the city of Whittier was incorporated in 1969. The single school serves approximately 38 students."

Patrick gave a little cough that sounded suspiciously like a laugh and shot a fond glance toward his grandmother. Fortunately, she was too busy digging for her camera to notice. "I'm going to get out and take some pictures to document the trip."

"Good idea. We still have twenty minutes before we move."

"Let me get a shot of the two of you in front of the tunnel. Stand right there," Bonnie commanded. They exited the car. Patrick slung an arm around Lauren's shoulders and smiled. Bonnie snapped the photo. "Now turn and point at the sign."

"She must have been a tour guide in a former life," Lauren whispered to Patrick.

"Or possibly a dictator."

Lauren laughed, just in time for the picture.

"Nice. Now I'm going to try to capture the train in the background."

"Let me take some of you and Lauren," Patrick offered, once Bonnie had snapped several more photos.

Bonnie happily handed over her camera and posed for a few shots before they returned to the car. A few minutes later, the line moved forward into the tunnel. The bleak stone walls lit only by rows of small lights made the ten-minute drive through rather spooky, at least in Lauren's opinion. "This wouldn't be a good spot for claustrophobes," she commented.

"It does sort of feel like something from a Poe story," Patrick agreed.

"But just think of all the work they did to dig this tunnel right through the mountain," Bonnie said. "It's remarkable."

Shortly after exiting the tunnel, they arrived in Whittier. The single apartment building rose up three stories in front of the mountain. Other than that, only a few buildings made up the town, nestled in a narrow valley. As they turned toward the docks, the calm water spread out before them between mountains that seemed to rise straight out of the sea. Farther down the coast, an enormous cruise ship waited at a large dock.

The ferry, with its black hull and crisp white upper area, approached the dock where they waited. In a remarkably short amount of time, the arriving cars and passengers had all disembarked, and they'd loaded Patrick's SUV with the other vehicles in the hold. Lauren, Patrick and Bonnie milled about with the passengers, looking out the windows of the observation lounge. A warning blast from a horn sounded, and they were on their way.

"Shall we go on the outside deck?" Patrick suggested.

"Let's. I can get better pictures that way." Bonnie led the way onto the deck and found a clear spot near the railing. A sea otter floated on its back nearby, his round face peering up at them for several minutes, and then with a sudden flip, he disappeared under the water.

Lauren breathed in the ocean scents of salt and fish. Overhead, seagulls called to one another. The ferry ran parallel to the shoreline, where dark spruce trees reflected against the deep blue mirror of the ocean. "This is amazing."

"Beautiful," Patrick agreed. "We couldn't have picked a better day, weather-wise."

"Look at that." Bonnie pointed her camera toward the shore.

A waterfall rushed down from the cliff above, tumbling several stories past boulders and knobs until it splashed into the ocean. Birds circled around it, occasionally diving toward the water.

They passed a seabird rookery—rocky cliffs where hundreds of birds raised their young. The voice over the speaker pointed out seals sunning themselves on some rocks as they went by. They were never far from land, but the water seemed to twist and bend around and between mountains and islands. Lauren wondered how anyone could keep their route straight in this maze, but since this was a routine run for the ferry, obviously they could.

The ship seemed to be making a gradual turn to the left. Soon, Lauren noticed a few chunks of ice floating in the water. They got more numerous as they traveled, until in the distance Lauren spotted what looked like a huge cliff made of ice.

"Columbia Glacier," Bonnie informed them. "The guidebook says it's one of the fastest-moving glaciers in the world."

"Fastest-moving glacier? Isn't that a little like jumbo shrimp?" Patrick mused.

Lauren smiled. "Or frozen hot wings?"

Bonnie chuckled. "I suppose it's all relative." She brought her camera to her eye. "Squish together. I want a picture."

"Do you want me to take one of the three of you?" a friendly woman with a New England accent asked.

"That would be great. Thanks. Here, just push this button halfway down to focus, and all the way to take the picture." Bonnie stepped over to stand beside Patrick. He put one arm around his grandmother and the other around Lauren.

"Say cheese!" As she handed the camera back to Bonnie, she commented to Patrick, "Your wife is lovely."

"Isn't she?" Patrick answered and winked at Lauren.

Lauren felt a strange ache in her chest as the feelings inside her warred. The warm and cozy feeling of being close enough to Patrick that a stranger would think they were married. And then the knowledge that it was only temporary. Sure, some couples, like Bonnie and Tim, somehow stayed together for forty-nine years, but miracles like that didn't happen to people like her. Her mom was proof of that.

And speaking of miracles, it was going to take a big one to make it possible to keep her goats. The end of summer was coming all too soon, and with it the end of goat yoga and Saturday Market. If she didn't have the money for improvements by then…

"Lauren? You okay?" Patrick touched her cheek.

She managed a smile. "Sure. Just thinking about something."

"I'm sure the goats are fine. Once we get to Valdez, you can call and check on them."

"No, I'm sure they're all right. The Holmens know what they're doing."

"Then what is it?"

She hesitated, not wanting to spoil the day. But Patrick was giving her that concerned look—the one that said he wouldn't stop asking until she'd given an honest answer. "It's just that I'm having such a great time, and I'm wondering if it's the last time."

"Hey—" he took her hand "—don't give up yet. We may find the solution to the whole puzzle waiting for us right there in Valdez."

"And if we don't?"

"Then we'll keep looking until we do."

"Orcas!" someone called, and everyone surged forward to look leaving Patrick and Lauren momentarily alone.

He put a finger under her chin and lifted it until she was looking directly at him. "We're going to find that nugget. For you and for Gran. Believe it."

And somehow, looking into his eyes, she did. She brushed a kiss across his lips before tugging him after the crowd. "Come on. Let's go see the whales."

OTHER THAN THE Alaska Pipeline terminal, some brightly colored houses and a few totem poles, everything in Valdez seemed to be a shade of green. Thick grass covered the ground. The spruce trees were taller and denser than the ones in the area around Palmer. Emerald green moss clung to every surface possible.

They had already watched a heavy rain shower that morning while the three of them ate breakfast at the hotel coffee shop, but now the sun was peaking from between the clouds. As Lauren, Bonnie and Patrick made their way to the front door of the address he'd been given, the raindrops clinging to a spiderweb on the porch railing sparkled in the sunlight.

Patrick stopped to appreciate the intricacy of the weaving. Lauren slipped a hand around his arm. "Beautiful, isn't it."

"Yes," he chuckled. "But I'm surprised you think so."

She laughed. "Hey, I have nothing against spiders as long as they keep at least three feet away from me."

Bonnie, meanwhile, had stepped onto the porch and rung the bell. The door opened, and a woman who looked to be around fifty zeroed in on Patrick. "Hello. I assume you're Patrick O'Shea? I'm Debbie Watson."

"Yes, hello. This is my grandmother, Bonnie O'Shea, and this is Lauren Shepherd. We really appreciate you letting us look through your family letters."

"Come on in." She led them through a living room furnished with an eclectic assortment of antiques and into the kitchen. "Everything is in the basement. Can I get you coffee or anything first?"

"We just finished breakfast, thanks." Bonnie told her. "We're eager to get started."

"Then follow me." She opened a door at the end of the kitchen and flicked a switch that illuminated a single bulb over the wooden stairs. At the bottom of the stairs, Debbie pulled a string to turn on another bare lightbulb.

A few scattered chairs, a wicker shelving unit, a rolltop desk and other assorted furniture cast eerie shadows on the wall behind them as the light swayed by its cord. Several folding tables leaned against the wall. Under the staircase, rows of trunks and boxes filled the space.

"Sorry I didn't have time to sort anything out in advance. My grandmother's letters should all be in either this trunk—" Debbie pointed at a brown one with leather straps that had several boxes stacked on top of it "—or possibly in the desk." She frowned up at the swinging bulb. "I've got a portable work light in the garage. I'll bring it down."

"Thank you," Patrick said. He pulled out one of the sturdier-looking chairs and brushed the dust off the seat. "Gran, why don't you sit here while I clear the boxes off the trunk?"

"Or I could check out the rolltop desk instead of twiddling my thumbs. I may be old, but I'm not frail."

Lauren snorted. "Have you not seen her in yoga class?" she asked Patrick.

"Okay, good point."

"It looks like there's a window behind that stack of boxes over there," Lauren said. "Why don't we move them and see if we can let in some natural light?"

Patrick helped her move the boxes from the dingy well window, making it a little easier to read the labels. He and Lauren moved various boxes from the top of the trunk marked Christmas, Dishes, Hats, Costumes and an alarming number labeled Miscellaneous. They stacked them along the far wall as they went.

By the time Debbie opened the door up above to say she'd found the work light, Gran had collected a stack of papers from the desk and Patrick was moving the last box off the trunk. He left Lauren to open the trunk while he carried the work light on a stand down the stairs. Debbie followed, holding a desk lamp.

Lauren gasped. "Look at this." She carefully lifted some sort of cloth from the trunk.

"My grandmother's wedding veil," Debbie said.

Patrick plugged in the shop lamp and the basement was suddenly flooded with light. Lauren held up the sheer fabric to examine it. "The embroidery is exquisite."

"That was great-grandmother's work. My grandmother, my mother and I all wore that veil in our weddings." She gave a rueful smile. "My boys' brides weren't interested. One married in Las Vegas and the other got married on a mountaintop wearing rock-climbing gear."

"Well, it's lovely," Gran said. "It sounds like you're big on family history. What did you know about William Golson?"

"Not that much, I'm afraid. My mother was a first cousin." She sank into the chair Patrick had set out for Gran. He dusted off and set up another one beside it.

"Mom remembered him as a quiet boy, kind of dreamy," Debbie continued. "She didn't know him growing up because his parents had moved to the Lower 48. He was a young teenager when his parents died and he came to Alaska to live with his grandparents. I don't think they were particularly close. Mom said they were pretty old by then and couldn't generate a lot of enthusiasm for raising another child."

Gran perched on the chair beside Debbie and leaned forward. "Is it possible he may have written those letters?"

"That I don't know. Their letters could be in one of these boxes, but I doubt it. No, the letters I told Patrick about would be to my grandmother Elinor, his aunt. He spent a lot of time at my grandparents' farm near Palmer. My mom was already married and living here in Valdez by then, so she didn't know him that well, but her parents liked him. A farmer can always use an extra hand. Mom says my grandmother corresponded with him while he was in prison."

"Were they surprised when they heard William Golson had been charged with robbing James Bradley of his gold nugget?" Patrick asked.

"Shocked. That's what my mother says. He'd never shown any inclination to take anything that wasn't his. They thought at first it was some sort of mistaken identity, but he pled guilty. But he never would tell the authorities what he'd done with the nugget."

"Why do you think that was?" Lauren asked.

"Well, the most likely answer is that he planned to go back for it after he got out of jail. He was sentenced to seven years, but he only made it three before he died of some kind of infection he'd contracted."

"And he never told your grandmother where he'd hidden the nugget?" Patrick asked.

Debbie laughed. "Well if he had, I would assume she would have told someone. The robbery left a big stain on the family. I'm sure she would have wanted to return it. Not to mention there's a huge reward." She pointed to the trunk. "I've been meaning to go through my grandmother's letters, but I haven't gotten around to it. You're welcome to read them. I'll warn you though, she was a prolific letter writer, and she saved every letter she received in return. I'm afraid it's a needle in a haystack."

"Wow." Lauren had lifted a few more pieces of cloth out of the trunk, revealing a solid layer of folded papers. "There must be hundreds of letters here."

"Maybe thousands." Debbie gave a wry smile. "Good luck. I have some things to do upstairs but call me if you need anything. Please be as careful as you can with the letters. They're very old."

"We will," Gran assured her. "Thank you for trusting us with your family's historical documents. We'll let you know if we find anything."

Patrick stared down at the piles of paper in the trunk. Needle in a haystack didn't begin to describe the situation. It was more like looking for a particular spruce needle somewhere on a forest floor.

CHAPTER FOURTEEN

"Do WE HAVE a *Betty* yet?" Lauren searched one of the folding plastic tables they'd erected in the basement.

"There's a *Betsy* in the right corner," Patrick answered. "Better check and make sure I didn't misread the signature."

"No, different handwriting." Lauren stuck a strip of masking tape to the last bare spot on the table and used a marker to write *Betty* on it.

After reading a couple dozen random letters mostly sharing recipes and giving health, weather and crop reports, they'd decided to first sort all the letters by signature before they read any more. With Debbie's permission, they'd set up the tables and created piles for each correspondent.

So far, the biggest piles were from Bear, Snook and Trixie. All those letters were addressed to Pinky. Most of the rest read Dear Ellie or Elinor.

"Ester, B.G. and Willie," Patrick murmured as he put three more onto existing stacks.

"Three more from Betty, and several from Mama. The signature is smudged on this one." Lauren went to hold it under the light Bonnie was using to sort the contents of the rolltop desk.

"I believe that says *Edward*, or maybe *Edwin*," Bonnie guessed.

"We have an *Edger*," Patrick said. "Does the handwriting match?"

Lauren went to compare. "It does. Good. I was afraid we were going to have to start another table."

Lauren went to fetch the next batch. This group contained two postcards from California, one showing "Interesting Hollywood" and the other with redwood trees. Both cards were signed by Trixie and carried a one-cent stamp.

Debbie came down the stairs. "Any luck?"

"Not so far, but we've still got a long way to go," Patrick told her.

"Can you tell us who Bear, Snook and Trixie are?" Lauren asked.

Debbie giggled. "Yes, my family was big on nicknames. Grandma Elinor was Pinky. Her brothers were Bear and Snook. Trixie was her sister. Trixie would have been William's mother."

"From California?" Lauren held up the postcards.

"Yes, Trixie married a soldier and moved to California. They were killed in an accident of some kind." She squared off one pile of letters. "You're getting a lot done. I wanted to see if you'd like to come upstairs for lunch. I have chicken salad for sandwiches."

"You shouldn't have gone to the trouble," Gran protested. "You're already letting us go through your family history."

"Nonsense. If anything, I should be paying you for sorting it for me."

"Well, we're taking you out for dinner tonight," Patrick insisted. "It's the least we can do."

Debbie smiled at him, her cheeks dimpling. "That would be nice."

After lunch they continued sorting. About midafternoon, Bonnie held up an envelope. "It's from the prison."

"What does it say?" Lauren asked.

Bonnie took out the letter and read it. "It's the official letter announcing William Golson's death. The warden sends condolences. He says Golson was a model prisoner. So sad."

Lauren waved her hand at the table. Some

of the piles were almost ready to topple. "All those people, and we haven't yet found anything from William. Do you suppose she destroyed his letters?"

"I doubt it," Bonnie said. "It's obvious she prized the letters people sent her. Maybe we'll find them all together at the bottom."

But by evening, they still hadn't uncovered any letters signed by William. They were probably nine-tenths of the way through the trunk. "I'm starting to think this is a wild goose chase," Lauren said.

"We need a break. Let's take Debbie out for dinner and talk about something else. In the morning we can finish." Patrick set the letter in his hand on a pile. "If we don't find William's letters in the trunk, we can start looking elsewhere."

"You're probably right. Before we go, let me call the Holmen brothers and make sure they knew we'll be gone another night and they need to milk in the morning," Lauren said. "I'll meet you upstairs."

After talking to the oldest Holmen brother, she found everyone gathered in the kitchen. "He says they can do the morning milking, but they have something planned later. So, I'll need to be back in Palmer by six for evening milking."

"It will take about four and a half hours to drive," Patrick said. "That still gives us the morning to work."

After consulting with Debbie, they chose a local diner. While they ate their burgers, shepherd's pie and halibut, Debbie asked about their plans. "On the drive back to Palmer, you're planning to stop at Worthington Glacier, aren't you?" she asked.

"If we have time," Patrick said.

"Leave a little earlier if you have to. The glacier is beautiful, and so is the landscape. We got over seven hundred inches of snow in Thompson Pass last winter."

"Wow, that's, what, almost sixty feet?" Lauren said.

"That's right. We only got three hundred inches in town, though."

"So 'only' twenty-five feet of snow in town." Patrick shook his head. "We get about thirty-eight inches of snow per winter on the North Slope. Big difference."

"Well that explains why Valdez is so pretty and green," Bonnie said.

They'd finished dinner and were waiting for the check when Bonnie told Debbie about the letter from the prison. "It's a shame William's life ended like that. From what the warden said, he was a good man. It's hard to imagine the impulse that landed him there."

Debbie sighed. "My mother said he always felt cursed. First his parents died. The girl he fell in love with spurned him. He lost a job once because his coworker had some mishap and laid the blame on him. And then to die in prison. Poor Billy Goat."

"Did you just call him Billy Goat?" Lauren asked.

"Oh, that was the family nickname. I think his parents called him Billy, you know, short for William. Billy Goat was a nickname my grandparents gave him. I don't know why. Just silliness I suspect."

"Billy Goat," Bonnie repeated thoughtfully.

"B.G.," Patrick said. "Billy Goat, or Billy Golson."

"Did you read any of the letters from B.G.?" Lauren asked Patrick.

He shook his head. "I only sorted them. But there were lots."

"In theory at least three years' worth," Debbie said, "There might be a hundred or more."

The waiter came to their table. "How about some dessert tonight?"

"Just the check, please," Bonnie told him. "We have work to do."

It WAS NO wonder they'd missed that B.G. was William. He seemed to have gone out of his way not to mention prison in his letters. They'd hurried to Debbie's house from the restaurant and read enough to determine B.G. and William were the same person but Lauren, noticing Debbie yawning and Bonnie beginning to droop, had suggested that they get a good night's sleep and start fresh in the morning.

Now that they'd read all B.G.'s letters to his aunt, his personality was beginning to emerge. He seldom complained about his life in prison, only occasionally writing about someone being disagreeable or that the food sure wasn't as good as Ellie's. He often referred to a book he was reading, or a bird he'd seen. Sometimes he even touched on philosophy. One letter had several paragraphs discussing predetermination versus free will.

But he never mentioned the nugget. Lauren's mood sank lower with every letter she read. It wasn't that she'd expected anything direct, like "The nugget is buried beside the seventeenth fencepost from the southwest corner," but she'd hoped for some clue. A mention of his routine while he was hiding out, or of a specific place in his memory. Even a clue as to what he was thinking during that time.

The closest he came was in one particularly melancholy letter, when he mused about why one man would have so much money that he carried around useless but valuable things in his pockets, while others could barely scrape together enough to live on. Perhaps it really was his lucky charm. Later in the letter, he said that it was a shame most women wouldn't look past a man's wallet to see into his heart.

"It doesn't sound as if he had much luck with women," Debbie commented as she read. "I know his high school sweetheart married someone else. It sounds like some other woman must have rejected him later. I wonder if he stole the nugget hoping for enough money to impress her."

Bonnie read over her shoulder. "That might explain why a formerly law-abiding man would suddenly become a robber. I've heard there are only three motives—love, money and power."

"Sad. He doesn't mention a woman's name

in any of the other letters, does he?" Debbie asked.

"Not that I've found," Patrick said, skimming the letters he'd already read. "Wait. In one of the early letters when he was still working at the hotel in Anchorage, he says, 'We've gone out a few times but it's nothing serious.' No name. It's worded like he's answering a question from a letter Elinor had sent."

"Is it dated?" Lauren asked.

Patrick checked. "Yes, not quite a year before the incident."

"Maybe he met someone and she was out of his league," Debbie said slowly. "Working at a nice hotel, he probably met wealthy people quite a lot. I suppose we'll never know the whole story."

"The historian I talked to said something like that." Lauren thought back. "I think the arresting officer says William mentioned a woman. Maybe there are more letters from him here. We still haven't made it to the bottom of the trunk."

They did find three more letters from B.G. but none of them offered much new information. One letter, dated about four years before the robbery, mentioned the incident Debbie had remembered, when William had lost his job on the railroad because a coworker had left equipment out overnight. When it was stolen, the coworker blamed William. William said bad luck seemed to follow him wherever he went.

Once they'd emptied the trunk, Patrick took all the B.G. letters to make copies for their files while Lauren and Bonnie helped Debbie sort the other letters into labeled folders so she would be able to find them in the future.

Lauren noticed a paragraph in one of the letters from Snook. *I tried to help him, but Billy won't listen. He says he done it, so what good would a fancy lawyer do him? Maybe he's right. It might go easier on him if he turns over the gold, but Billy ain't talking. Don't know what else I can do.*

Lauren was starting to feel the same way. They could search the cabin and look for clues in the letters and talk to all the historians around, but if Billy didn't talk to someone, what were the chances they'd ever find the nugget?

THE ICE INSIDE a glacier was like a piece of sky, compressed and compacted into intense blue. Patrick had been to Worthington Glacier before, and he'd really been looking forward to showing it to Lauren and Gran, but now that they were here, it seemed like both women were only going through the motions.

Gran was taking photos, but she hadn't quoted from her guidebook once, and Lauren was staring into the ice as though all the secrets she was looking for might be hidden inside. He came up behind Lauren and slipped his arms around her waist. "Hey. It's not over yet."

She ran her hand over his forearm. "No. I know. It's just—"

"Disappointing. I know. When I talked to Debbie and she said she had letters, I was hoping for more, too. But we've only read over them once. We can study the copies more carefully at home. There might still be information to be gleaned. And if not there, we'll keep looking until we find it somewhere else."

"And if we don't?"

"We will." Patrick wished he could be as sure as he sounded. If they didn't, Lauren would have to go back to Oregon. She'd worked too hard and had too much talent to give up on her dream just because she happened to land in Alaska. He wished he could bankroll her himself, but the equity in his house and his retirement savings wouldn't begin to cover her startup costs.

"The glacier is beautiful," Lauren said. "There's a lot to love about this state. I don't want to leave."

"You won't have to."

"What's this talk about leaving?" Gran had finished taking her pictures and joined them at the mouth of a shallow ice cave.

Lauren fingered the polished agate pendent Rosemary had given her. "If we haven't found the nugget by the end of summer—"

"It's there, somewhere on the farm. I can feel it." When Patrick opened his mouth to answer, Gran held up a hand. "I know, I know. But the more I find out about William, the more certain I am that he must have put that nugget somewhere on the farm. And he was planning to come back for it, so he hid it somewhere he'd be able to locate it again."

"I bet you're right," Lauren said. "It's somewhere on the farm. We just have to be smart enough to find it."

Gran raised her camera. "Now, I want you and Patrick to stand right here in front of the ice cave. A little to the right, so I can see the blue shining through. Now closer together." Lauren leaned against Patrick. He put an arm around her to pull her close, noticing the way they seemed to fit together so well. Gran snapped the picture. "Good. Stay right there. I want a different angle."

While Gran moved farther up the pathway, Patrick whispered, "Feeling better?"

Lauren nodded. "I do. I don't know why. Nothing's changed. But when you and Bonnie say it's going to happen, it gives me hope."

"Hang onto that. Hope and hard work can take us a long way."

CHAPTER FIFTEEN

"WILLIAM SAYS HERE that there's no gold at the end of a rainbow." Lauren looked up from the letter she was reading to gage Bonnie's and Patrick's expressions. "Could that be some sort of clue as to where he buried the nugget?"

"Rainbow…something shaped like an arch…something colorful… I've got nothing," Patrick confessed.

"I suspect he was writing metaphorically." Bonnie pointed to the one she was reading. "Here he says love is an illusion, a reflection of one's own self in a rippled pond. It sounds poetic, but I'm not sure what that means."

"Maybe he means he wasn't really in love with the woman he stole the nugget for, just with his own image of her," Lauren suggested.

"You're probably right. Too bad. Love, real love, is the greatest gift of all. Tim and I—" Bonnie paused to smile at something in the distance only she could see. "He brought so much joy into my life. He knew me, more than anyone else ever did. I'm not perfect—"

"You're not?" Patrick teased.

Bonnie swatted his shoulder. "No one is perfect, but Tim loved me, even the parts of me I wasn't so fond of. And I loved him. That's how it's supposed to work."

"Well it certainly worked for you." Patrick leaned over to give his grandmother a peck on the cheek. "And you must have been a good example because it seems to work for my parents, too."

Bonnie grinned. "Ah, when Kevin met Renee, he never knew what hit him."

"My mom is like a force of nature," Patrick explained to Lauren. "Dad is part of the diplomatic service and has an important title, but Mom is the one who makes things happen. He adores her."

Lauren could see where Bonnie's son would have learned to appreciate strong women. What would it have been like to have grown up in a family where people stayed married and love lasted a lifetime? She still found it hard to grasp. "Where are your parents now?" she asked Patrick.

"Tokyo. My sister is there, too." He looked toward Bonnie. "You know, you could visit them in Japan if you want. I'm sure Lauren could take care of the dog while you were gone."

Lauren started to agree that she'd be happy to dog sit Wilson, before she remembered that trips took time to plan, and she didn't know how much longer she could afford to remain at the farm.

"Maybe I will," Bonnie said. "With the dairy farm, we never traveled, and once Tim died, I didn't want to travel alone. But if they were there to meet me—"

Patrick smiled. "We should plan that."

"First things first. We're concentrating on the nugget right now. Once Bradley's Heart is back where it belongs, and Lauren has the money to set up the farm the way she needs to for her cheese-making operation, and that darn editor at the newspaper has eaten his words—then we can talk about a trip to Japan."

"And a move to town?" Patrick prodded.

Bonnie gave him a mock scowl. "Nugget first."

"Fair enough." Patrick picked up another letter. "I'll keep reading."

THE NEXT TUESDAY, Lauren bit into the chocolate chip cookie she'd earned by keeping up with the six octogenarians in yoga class.

Bea was entertaining the group with her description of the new librarian at the Palmer library.

"Honestly, he could be an actor with those eyes. And those muscles." Bea put her hand to her chest and sighed. "Who knew librarians could have muscles? And so helpful. Oh, that reminds me." She reached into a tote bag, pulled out some papers and handed them to Bonnie. "I found this follow-up article written when William Golson died. When Bradley's Heart disappeared, the police interviewed a woman named Margaret Polanski, and the reporter quoted her in this article. Her married name was Smuth. I wondered if you knew about her."

"Margaret Smuth?" Rosemary said. "I know of someone by that name. She lives on the Park Strip in Anchorage. Her garden is one of the highlights on the tour of gardens almost every year. Beautiful flowers, although she spoils the effect somewhat by hollering at anyone who touches a plant."

"Could she be the same person?" Bonnie asked, skimming the article.

"I know lots of Smiths, but very few Smuths," Rosemary pointed out. "If you want, I can get her phone number from the garden tour organizer."

"Let's do that," Bonnie said.

"I'll see if I can reach her." Rosemary grabbed her phone and walked to the other side of the bakery.

"Were you looking up articles in the library to help Bonnie, or just so you could ogle the librarian?" Linda teased Bea.

Bea smirked. "I can multitask."

Bonnie passed the article to Lauren. After reporting William's death, there was a recap of the crime, including a mention of Margaret Polanski Smuth, an employee at the hotel, being questioned by police. When asked for her reaction to Golson's death in prison, she'd been quoted as saying, "Nothing ever did go right for that man."

"The police must have interviewed her for a reason," Bonnie said. "Maybe she knows something."

"But the police questioned her before they knew who took the nugget," Lauren pointed out. "It's not like she was involved in the robbery."

"If she worked at the hotel, she might have known William fairly well," Bonnie said. "It won't hurt to ask, anyway."

"You're right," Lauren said. "It's worth checking out."

"I found something at a garage sale that

you might find useful," Molly said to Bonnie. "I'll show you after calligraphy class."

They continued their conversation, but Lauren had tuned out, reading over the article again, until someone tapped her on the shoulder. "I thought I'd find you ladies here." Crystal stood behind her.

Bea ever-so-casually dropped a napkin over the uneaten half of her bear claw. Alice gave a wry smile. "Busted."

Crystal laughed. "I'm not the sugar police. I just came to find Lauren. Do you have a minute?"

"Sure. Have a seat. Can I get you some coffee or herbal tea or something?"

"No, I only have a few minutes." Crystal perched on the edge of the chair Lauren had pulled out for her. "I just got a call from a friend who's with the Alaska State Fair. One of the exhibitors will be delayed for a week and she's wondering if we could fill in with goat yoga starting weekend after next."

"The state fair? That's huge!"

Crystal laughed. "Not really. But it's a lot of fun. She says there's a grassy area we can use, although we'd need to come up with fencing of some sort. We could do several mini-sessions a day if you think the goats are up to it."

"They'd be fine. We'd have to work around the milking schedule, but the fairgrounds are only fifteen minutes away from the farm, so that's doable."

"So that's a yes?"

"Yes!"

"Okay. I'll send you the details when I have them." Crystal stood. "Talk with you soon. Bye, ladies. Enjoy your sugar."

"Thanks, Crystal." Lauren sipped her tea, wondering if the local hardware store carried any kind of portable fencing panels.

"Goat yoga at the fair. What a good idea," Alice said. "Great exposure. Get your name in front of people so when they see your cheese for sale in stores, they'll remember you."

Lauren smiled, appreciating the natural way Alice had said *when they see your cheese*. Not *if*.

Rosemary returned to the group, carrying her phone. "I called Margaret Smuth. She has a doctor's appointment this afternoon, but she says she'll meet you at eleven thirty. Can you make it?"

"I have Molly's class today," Bonnie said. "Lauren, can you go?"

"Sure." Lauren looked at her watch. "But

I'll need to run home to change out of yoga clothes."

"If I had your figure, I'd never wear anything but yoga pants." Bea glanced down at her own yellow pants. "Oh wait. That is all I wear."

Alice pressed her lips together, suppressing a laugh. "Take Bonnie's car. I'll give her a ride home."

"I'll call Patrick," Bonnie pawed through her purse. "Oh, I forgot my phone again. Molly, could you call him and tell him to be ready to go? He'll want to be in on this interview."

Rosemary, meanwhile, had concluded her phone conversation and jotted down the address. "Here you go."

"Thanks." Lauren typed the address into her own phone. "Does anyone need anything while I'm in Anchorage?"

"My supplier got a new order of jade in for me," Rosemary said. "I was going to pick it up Saturday, but—"

"I'll get it. Just text me the details."

"If you're going downtown—" Bea began.

"Ladies, Lauren needs to run." Bonnie handed over her keys. "Rosemary will text you all our shopping lists, okay?"

"Sounds good. Wish me luck." Lauren hurried to the car in a chorus of well wishes.

At the farm, Patrick was in the middle of mowing the front lawn. He stopped when Lauren drove up. "Where's Gran?"

"Alice is driving her home later. I take it you didn't get a call from Molly?"

"Nope." He pulled out his phone. "It doesn't show a missed call either. It's like a cellular black hole here. What did I miss?"

"We're going to interview a lady in Anchorage who worked at the hotel where Bradley lived. At least I am. You're in the middle of something."

"I can finish later." He followed her into the house. "Who is this lady?"

She filled him in on the way up the stairs. "I'm going to change clothes. We're supposed to be there in an hour."

"Okay. Meet you at the car." Ten minutes later, they were humming down the Glenn Highway. Patrick's phone chimed. "Ah, that must be my missed call from Molly. Bad cell coverage at the farm is one of the reasons I wanted Gran in town."

"Wanted?"

His shoulders twitched in a mini shrug. "I still think she should move, but I feel a lot better knowing that you're there to take care of her."

A happy wave washed over Lauren. The fact that he trusted her with his grandmother said more than any kisses or gestures could have. "I'm glad." Her phone beeped. She checked the texts and smiled.

"What?"

"After the interview, we're supposed to pick up an order of jade for Rosemary and a book for Alice. Molly needs a certain type of ink from a store downtown, Bea wants a new yoga mat and Bonnie wants chocolate-covered strawberries."

"Nothing for Linda?"

"Apparently not. Of course, Linda is the queen of the internet. She probably orders everything directly."

"It sounds like we may be there for a while. Once we finish the interview, we'll have lunch and then we can run all their errands."

The address Rosemary had given Lauren led them to a neat little house a few blocks south of downtown Anchorage. A split rail fence enclosed the front yard, or more accurately, the front garden since every inch of unpaved land was covered with flowers. To the right of the path, some sort of creeping plant with dark leaves carpeted the ground. In the center was a large round bed of blue flowers. A fishing rod arched over the bed, with a hanging basket of salmon-pink begonias dangling from the line above the blue flowers.

"Very clever," Patrick commented.

On the left side of the yard, a maze of stepping-stone paths wove among a cottage garden. Brilliant blue and purple delphiniums towered over pink lilies. Lauren would have liked to stop and examine the gardens more closely, but she didn't want to be late. At exactly eleven twenty-nine, she rang the doorbell.

A frenzy of barking erupted. A minute later, a young woman holding a snarling Chihuahua opened the door. "Hi. You're here to see Aunt Maggie, right? I'm Ava."

"Hi, I'm Lauren and this is Patrick. Margaret Smuth is your aunt?"

"No, she's like my mom's second cousin or something. She's out back. Come on." She led them through an old-fashioned parlor and down a dim hallway that led them into a lean-to greenhouse. The grassy scent of tomato plants hit them as soon as they opened the door.

An older woman stood next to a row of

vines growing up parallel ropes in front of the window, holding a small paintbrush in crooked fingers. Behind her, dozens of tomatoes in various shades of ripeness and many yellow blossoms dotted the plants.

"Those people you said were coming are here," Ava announced.

"I can see that," the woman said dryly. "Give me a minute to finish pollinating this one. I might still get a few more tomatoes."

Ava set the dog down on the floor. He scurried over to sniff Patrick's foot. The woman, presumably Margaret Smuth, tickled a few more blossoms with the paintbrush and turned. The dog had stopped sniffing and seemed to be seriously considering lifting his leg. Patrick gently nudged him away with the edge of his shoe. Mrs. Smuth frowned—Lauren wasn't sure whether it was at Patrick or the dog—and scooped up the Chihuahua. "Okay, that's done. Ava, did you make lemonade like I asked?"

"You didn't say anything about lemonade."

"Water then. Bring it outside." She moved toward the door at the end of the greenhouse. Patrick stepped in to hold the door for her. Instead of thanking him, she snapped. "Hurry up. Don't let the bugs in."

"Yes, ma'am." He allowed Lauren out and

followed quickly, latching the door behind him. They made their way to a patio table and chairs. A prolific mix of vegetables and herbs growing in raised beds filled the backyard.

Ava brought out a tray with a pitcher of ice water, napkins and three glasses. "You left some chickweed in the herb garden," Margaret told her.

"I said I'd finish this afternoon after the doctor's appointment." Ava turned in a huff and disappeared inside.

Margaret scowled in her direction. The dog in her lap looked after Ava with an almost identical expression. Margaret gave a disgusted sigh. "I said she could live with me while she went to college here, but she's supposed to be earning her keep. Look at that herb bed. Disgraceful."

Lauren wasn't sure she could distinguish any weeds among the dozens of different herbs overflowing the bed, but she decided not to comment on that. "Mrs. Smuth. I'm Lauren Shepherd and this is Patrick O'Shea."

"Maggie. Now what's this all about?" She poured water into a glass and took a drink, leaving them to help themselves.

"Well, Mrs.—Maggie, I understand you worked at the hotel at the time the gold nugget, Bradley's Heart was stolen."

"I had nothing to do with that robbery." She punctuated her declaration by thumping the glass down, sloshing water onto the table.

"No, of course not." Lauren used a napkin to wipe up the spill. "We just wondered if you knew William Golson?"

Maggie snorted. "Did I know him? I almost married him."

CHAPTER SIXTEEN

PATRICK AND LAUREN exchanged looks. Lauren's eyes had widened. Were they finally going to get a break? Patrick tried to imagine a younger Maggie as the femme fatale who had lured William off the straight and narrow, but it was hard to picture. Maybe she'd been less abrasive in those days. Lauren leaned closer to Maggie. "You were engaged to William?"

"Well, not officially, but we were getting there. We'd been going out for nine months, and he told me he was saving up. I was hoping for a ring for my birthday at the end of March."

That would have been almost three months before the robbery. "But it didn't work out that way?" Patrick asked.

"Billy broke up with me a week before my birthday, the cheapskate. I still remember that day. He was at the front desk, reading the newspaper. I'd gotten my hair permed that morning, and it looked real nice, if I do say so myself. I came over to show him, but he didn't even look up from the paper. I had to call his name three times."

"Then what happened?" Lauren asked.

"I waited for him to notice my hair, but he didn't say anything." She patted her gray curls. "So I said maybe we should go out somewhere special that night, and he says he's busy. Busy doing what, I ask him. I knew the schedule. He got off at six and it was payday. Then, out of the blue, he says he doesn't think we should see each other anymore." She snapped her fingers. "Just like that."

"So this was all before the robbery," Patrick clarified.

"That's what I'm telling you, and what I told the police. I didn't know anything about that robbery. Me and Billy weren't on speaking terms then. I'd started going out with Jimmy Smuth, and he was a far better catch than Billy ever was."

"Were you working the day of the robbery?" Lauren asked.

"Sure, I was doing my housekeeping, but I never talked to Billy."

"Do you think William knew about the nugget before that day?"

"'Course he did. Mr. Bradley kept it in the

hotel safe. We all knew about it. In fact, Mr. Bradley showed it to me when I brought in some towels one morning. He even let me hold it for a minute. Big ole thing, almost the size of my fist. Heavy. Nice man, Mr. Bradley, but cheap. Never left a tip."

They continued to probe. Maggie's account jibed with what they already knew, but she didn't seem to have any new information. Eventually, they ran out of questions. "Goodbye, then," Lauren told her. "Thanks for talking with us."

"I suppose you can find your own way out," Maggie said. "Tell Ava to get out here and see to that chickweed before it goes to seed."

When Lauren passed on the message in a more tactful form, Ava rolled her eyes. As Lauren and Patrick went out the front door, they could hear her muttering, "Chickweed in the herb bed. Too bad it's not poison ivy. I'd put some in her bed."

Lauren paused in the front yard to admire the flowers. "I never would have guessed someone responsible for such a pretty garden would be so…"

"Ornery?"

"Good description." Lauren started toward the car. "Poor Ava."

"Maybe Maggie's just grouchy because she can't do it herself anymore and Ava's work isn't up to her standards." Patrick opened the car door for Lauren.

"I doubt anyone's would be."

Patrick got into the driver's seat, but he didn't immediately start the car. "Can we assume Maggie wasn't the woman William was trying to impress by stealing the nugget?"

"I feel like we can. She seemed reasonably content with him, at least until he dumped her. Of course, we're only guessing about his motive for the robbery. But the arresting officer did say William mentioned a woman. I just doubt it was Maggie."

"Do you suppose William broke up with Maggie for this other woman?"

Lauren laughed. "If he did, Maggie didn't know about it. She would have definitely mentioned that." Lauren's laugh faded. "I was hoping for more. I'm beginning to think this whole treasure hunt is a total waste of time."

"Hey, don't say that." Patrick put the car into gear. "I'm taking you to Simon's for lunch. You'll feel better after a crab dip sandwich." Lauren smiled at him, but he got the impression it was for his benefit.

They were seated at a table beside the window, overlooking the ocean. Once the server had taken their order, Patrick reached for Lauren's hand.

"Listen. I know you're discouraged, but I haven't given up. It's still possible to find that nugget. And even if we don't, we'll find some way to make this work."

"What do you mean?"

"It will take time, for sure. But I make a decent living and I could probably pick up some side jobs on my two weeks off. Maybe you could get a part-time job, too, and—"

"Why would—"

"I don't want you to go, Lauren. I think I'm—"

"Two crab dip sandwiches and two iced teas." The waiter's interruption couldn't have come at a more awkward time, but maybe it was better this way.

A public restaurant might not be the best place for Patrick to confess he was falling in love with her. Judging by the alarm he saw in Lauren's eyes, she was seeing his sudden declaration as a Free Birdseed sign under a box propped up by a stick with a string.

"Anything else I can get you?" the waiter was asking.

"Everything looks great. Thanks." Lauren

flashed the waiter a smile, but Patrick could see brittleness behind it.

Once the waiter was gone, she turned wary eyes to Patrick, waiting for him to continue. Instead, he reached across the narrow table to smooth a strand of hair away from her face. "We'll talk later. Enjoy your lunch."

"Is THIS THE right title?" Patrick held up the book Alice had requested they look for.

Lauren checked her list. "That's it. Now we just need to find Bonnie's chocolate-covered strawberries, and we're done." And then they'd have an hour's drive back to Palmer, which would be the perfect time for a talk, only Lauren wasn't too sure that was a good idea.

What he'd said in the restaurant, that he would be willing to contribute part of his own money to help her establish the farm, blew her away. But she couldn't let him do that. It was more than enough that he'd spent all this time and energy to help her and Bonnie look for the nugget. But if they didn't find it, what was her next move?

Lauren wanted to stay in Alaska. She loved the farm, she loved Bonnie and she loved—well she was fond of Patrick, but of course, she didn't love him. After seeing her mother fall in love so many times, Lauren wasn't going to put herself in that situation. Sure, she liked him, his sense of humor, his easygoing personality and his generosity. She admired his devotion to his grandmother. And his kisses, well they were in a category all their own. And yes, she missed him when he was gone, and everything seemed better when she was near him, but she...oh. She might be in love with Patrick O'Shea.

No, no, no. That wouldn't do at all. Lauren didn't fall in love because falling in love led only to hurt feelings and recriminations and sudden changes of address. She might be attracted to him, but she was not in love. So there.

Patrick, having paid for the book, joined her at the doorway of the bookstore. "We can get the strawberries at the candy store in the Fifth Avenue Mall."

"Okay." It came out as a whisper.

Patrick shot her a look of concern. "Are you all right? You look a little flushed."

She touched her warm cheek. "I'm fine. It's just hot in here."

"We can stop off at the coffee shop next door and get something cold to drink if you want."

Why did he have to be so nice? "I'm fine.

Let's just get the strawberries and head home. I have lots of work to do this afternoon."

"Are you making soap? I can be your assistant."

"Thanks, but no," she said quickly. "I'm fine alone." But then she remembered the fencing she needed for the fair. "Actually, scratch that. If you aren't in a hurry, I need to stop by one of the home improvement stores in Anchorage and see if they have modular fencing panels."

"Sure, we can do that. What are you fencing?"

She told him about Crystal signing them up to offer goat yoga at the fair.

"The fairgoers will love that. Too bad I'm working next week. Otherwise, I'd help you wrangle the goats."

And he would, too. She knew it was true. Just like she knew he'd help her find the fence panels she needed. Because that's what he did. Was it any wonder she loved him?

Lauren was in deep.

CHAPTER SEVENTEEN

LAUREN SUSPECTED THAT for the rest of her life, the scent of cotton candy and fried food would instantly transport her to the Alaska State Fairgrounds. Over the past few days, in between yoga sessions, Lauren had made the rounds to see the giant vegetables, home-made quilts and best of all, the livestock. She'd loved watching the 4-H contestants showing their goats and sheep. What she wouldn't have given to have been one of those kids, growing up on a farm, raising animals.

She'd even watched some herding demonstrations and found an information booth about livestock guardian dogs. One of the farmers had brought in a Great Pyrenees to guard his sheep and been so impressed he was now breeding them. He had two of the furry white dogs with him, some brochures and some film clips of his dogs with the sheep. Lauren tucked his card into her bag.

Today was their last day of yoga. The original exhibitor would be taking over their spot tomorrow. Lauren wove through the crowds to the grassy area where Bonnie and Crystal sat at a table, selling tickets. Music from the midway, punctuated with shouts and squeals from excited children, carried on the breeze.

Crystal set up her All Sessions Filled Today sign, provoking groans from the people still waiting in line. Lauren toted the bag of alfalfa pellets she'd fetched to a worktable and filled the small treat cups they would give to the goats at the end of the session.

On the hour, Bonnie opened the main gate and instructed everyone to choose a yoga mat from the pile and find a place on the grass. The goats, having learned that yoga mats meant cuddling, climbing and treats, crowded the gate of their small pen, waiting impatiently for the participants to find their places and settle in. Lauren had brought the full dozen kids but left the grown goats back at the farm. The kids were bigger now, eating mostly solid food. It wouldn't be long before they were completely weaned. Chip put her front hooves on the top rail of the iron fence and poked her head between the pickets, watching.

After the last participant filed in, Bonnie closed and latched the main gate of the enclosure Patrick had helped Lauren create before he left for the slope. Lauren wasn't sure she could have done it without him. They'd had to go to three different places in Anchorage to find enough iron fencing panels to enclose the area. Then they'd had to figure out how to anchor them in place. Patrick, using his electrician skills, had set up a supplemental lighting system for evening sessions. It was all working beautifully.

Their relationship seemed to be working beautifully as well, which perversely, had Lauren worried. It felt like anything this good was bound to go wrong, eventually. Patrick must have seen her panic at the restaurant because he'd backed off on the promise of serious conversation, and instead focused on helping her get ready for the fair and reviewing the information they'd gathered about the nugget. Still no breakthroughs, though.

Early Saturday morning, he'd come to the barn where she was milking. "I have to head to the airport now." He'd taken her into his arms, given her a lingering kiss and held her close. If only she could stay there, wrapped in his arms, forever.

But forever was an illusion. If Lauren couldn't afford the equipment Alaska required to certify her dairy, she couldn't make a living here. And chances were that at some point, Patrick would become disillusioned with her and move on. That's how love went. Attraction, connection, enchantment, reality, friction, separation. She'd seen it over and over with her mom and vowed never to fall into that trap herself. And yet here she was.

"I'll see you in two weeks," he'd said. "Take good care of Gran." Then he'd gazed into her eyes and she'd thought for one mad moment he was going to tell her he loved her. And maybe she would have confessed that she loved him, too. Instead, he'd said, "Everything is going to be okay. Trust me on that." Another kiss, a pat for Spritz, and he was gone.

"Lauren!" Bonnie's hiss brought Lauren back to the present. Oops, she'd missed Crystal's cue to let the goats out. She opened the gate, and the kids bounded in among the forty people holding a table pose. Chip led the way, bouncing onto the back of the closest, a young woman with jet-black hair, and then down and onto a middle-aged man who had probably been dragged there by his wife. He grinned, and his wife stopped to snap a picture on her phone before resuming her pose. One of the other kids immediately leaped onto her back. She laughed, and her husband leaned over from his mat to kiss her.

They looked like they might have been married for a while. Lauren watched them for a minute, wondering about the magic glue that kept them together. There was nothing extraordinary about them. He had a round belly and a circle of graying hair surrounding his shiny scalp. Her brown bob framed a pleasant face that had probably never been jaw-droppingly beautiful. But judging from the smiles they shared, they were beautiful to each other.

Crystal moved the group into the child pose. Lauren flitted around, nudging the goats toward the people who hadn't yet had a chance to interact with them. She pried a daisy-embellished flip-flop from Chip's mouth and scooped up its mate. "I'll put these outside, where they'll be safe until you're done," she said, flashing an apologetic smile at the shoe's owner. Chip nuzzled her hand, as if to say she was sorry, and the woman cooed at the goat.

The group moved into downward-facing dog, the goats' favorite pose by far. With forty human mountains to climb, the kids made their selections. Snickerdoodle, one of Spritz's triplets, zeroed in on the tallest mountain at the back near the gate, a young man whose shirt identified him as a member of the university basketball team. She hopped onto his back and climbed higher, perching at the very top. Several people standing nearby snapped pictures. Snickerdoodle bunched her muscles. Lauren saw what she was about to do, but she was too late. Snickerdoodle launched herself off his back, over the fence, and into the fairgrounds.

Lauren dashed for the gate, but by the time she'd reached it Snickerdoodle was nowhere to be seen. Farther down the path, a group of people were pointing and laughing. Lauren headed in that direction, but before she could get close, she got a glimpse of Snickerdoodle slipping between two tents. Lauren squeezed in after her, following the goat around the carousel, past the ring-toss booth, and toward the outdoor stage area where a preteen tap dance group was performing.

Snickerdoodle jumped onto the stage, weaving among the five girls with canes and top hats. They froze momentarily, but at their instructor's call to "keep dancing," they started tapping once again. Snickerdoodle was fascinated with the tap shoes, coming closer to sniff them and then bouncing back. The dancers giggled. Lauren made her way through the chortling crowd until she reached the stage. "Sorry about that. I'll take the goat now."

The dance instructor grinned and held up a hand. "Wait. I want to see what happens next."

Lauren noticed a well-dressed woman carrying a microphone followed by someone with a large video camera working through the crowd. The dancers formed a front-to-back line in order of height, and in time to the music, leaned left or right to appear to the audience one at a time. The shortest girl in front bent forward, leaning on her cane. Snickerdoodle took that as an invitation to jump onto her back. The next girl in line tossed away her cane and picked up the kid without missing a beat. As the girls tapped in a circle, Snickerdoodle looked over the girl's shoulder and let out a bleat. The crowd roared with laughter.

Finally, the routine came to a dramatic end with all the girls holding their canes above their heads. The one who held the goat lifted her up for everyone to see. The audience responded with thunderous applause.

It took several more minutes of adoration before Lauren was able to extract Snickerdoodle from the girls and get her back to the yoga area. Crystal was just bringing the class to a close. Lauren set Snickerdoodle down inside the pen and passed out the treat cups so that whoever wanted could feed the goats and get pictures.

"You were gone awhile. What happened?" Bonnie whispered.

"Long story. But I wouldn't be surprised if Snickerdoodle makes the news tonight."

"SOUNDS LIKE SPRITZ'S escape talents are hereditary." Patrick's voice was hard to hear through the crackling of his cell, but Lauren still loved listening to it. "Other than the impromptu dance recital, did everything go well?"

"It really did. It rained a couple of times, but Crystal went with it anyway and nobody seemed to mind much."

"It always rains during the fair."

"That's what Bonnie told me. Crystal says people have been calling to ask if we're going to offer goat yoga next summer. She's offering to put them on a newsletter mailing list."

"Sounds like you're in demand."

"I guess so." Too bad they couldn't do goat yoga year-round, but with the leaves on the trees already turning yellow and school back in session, the season was over. "Oh, did I tell you Molly found a metal detector at a garage sale?"

"Does it work?"

"It seems to, once we changed the batteries. Bonnie got her engagement ring out of her jewelry box and buried it about six inches deep in the garden."

"Was the metal detector able to find it?"

"Yes, it beeped right away."

"You know, I considered using a metal detector when we checked the walls of the cabin, but then I figured all the nails would be setting it off constantly. But now that I think about it, there aren't that many nails in a log wall. Darn, that would have saved some time."

"Not that much. We'd still have had to go over the chinking, inch by inch. I've been using the detector to sweep the ground near the cabin and the house, but so far all I've discovered were bottle caps and a few coins."

"Anything rare and valuable?" Patrick asked.

"I found a Kennedy half dollar the internet says is worth four dollars. That's about what Molly paid for the metal detector at the garage sale."

"Hey, so that means you've paid back your

investment and everything from here on out is profit."

"I guess so. I'll start sweeping the area around the barn this afternoon."

"Good idea. Are you selling at the Saturday Market this week?"

"God willing and the creeks don't rise."

He laughed. "I can tell you've been spending time with Gran. I'll meet you in Anchorage Saturday."

"I can't wait to see you."

"You either. Take care of Gran for me."

"Will do. Bye-bye." Lauren hung up the phone on the kitchen wall. They hadn't gotten any closer to finding the nugget, and yet somehow the anxiety she'd been feeling was, if not quite gone, at least lighter. Patrick said they'd find a way. Somehow, knowing he was on her side made it seem possible.

It had been drizzling when she took the goats to pasture that morning, which made it a good day to stay indoors and work on soap. Lauren had made a big batch several days ago, so she spent the morning wrapping labels around the bars. Meanwhile, Bonnie put together a big pot of minestrone from their garden vegetables and grilled cheese sandwiches.

Bonnie was wiping down the counter

after lunch when she suddenly paused. "I just thought of something. What did we do with that box of Elsa's letters?"

"Patrick put it back in the attic. Do you want me to get it down?"

"Would you please? I want to check something." There was an undercurrent of excitement in Bonnie's voice.

"What?"

"I'll tell you if I find it."

Lauren smiled. "Okay, if you want to be all mysterious. Let me just load the dishwasher and I'll run up and find it." Lauren was rinsing her bowl when she noticed movement outside the yard. "Oh, shoot. That's Spritz. She must have figured out how to manipulate my new latch." She grabbed her rain jacket from the mudroom, calling to Bonnie, "I'll get that box for you as soon as I get them rounded up."

"Good luck," Bonnie called back.

Lauren flipped up her hood and hurried outside. It was raining steadily now. For once, Spritz didn't run away. Instead she came directly to Lauren, bleating. One of her kids came limping toward them. Lauren hurried to check on Snickerdoodle.

A row of gouges ran over the kid's shoulder. Did he get them crawling under a fence or—Lauren's heart raced as she realized the implications of those parallel wounds.

They didn't look life-threatening. She picked up the kid and carried her to the barn. Spritz followed closely behind. Inside, Lauren locked them in their pen. "I'll be back to treat that wound," she told the goats, "just as soon as I round up the rest of the herd."

She could have sworn Spritz nodded. Lauren closed and latched the barn doors and then ran as fast as her feet would carry her to the pasture. No goats met her at the gate. She slipped inside, calling for them as she walked the fence line. It didn't take long to find the place where the fencing had been pulled loose from its staples and flattened to the ground.

The rain had washed away any tracks, but broken branches and stirred-up mud marked a trail. She followed it to a relatively dry spot under a tree, where goat tracks had been overlaid with another print that confirmed her worst fear. Lauren was no tracking expert, but the broad, almost human-shaped print with five long claw marks was easily recognizable. A bear.

Worse, a streak of red blood was smeared across the white bark of the tree. Was it from the kid she'd put in the barn, or had the bear

gotten to the other goats? She continued to
follow the trail, calling loudly partly to help
the goats locate her and partly because she
didn't want to surprise any bears. It was
probably thirty minutes later when she discovered Biscotti and Chip cowering in an
alder thicket. Both were unhurt, if terrified.
She took them to the barn, and then resumed
her search.

By sunset, she'd recovered all the goats
except poor Pizzelle. She had to assume the
bear had carried him off. Lauren felt like
crying, but instead she washed Snickerdoodle's wounds and used antibiotic ointment
from the first aid kit she'd stashed in the barn
to treat them. Fortunately, they weren't deep
enough to need stitches.

She was almost four hours late for milking. Although neither she nor the goats were
in any mood for it, Lauren knew they would
be more comfortable if she milked them. It
was almost eleven when she finally trudged
to the farmhouse, after having latched the
barn door and barricading it with some leftover fence posts, just in case the bear decided
he wanted seconds.

Frantic barking reached her ears as she
got closer to the house. What in the world
was Wilson so worked up about? Lauren let

herself into the mudroom and shed her rain jacket. Wilson scratched on the other side of the door and whimpered. He'd never done that before. In fact, he seldom left Bonnie's side.

"Bonnie? Sorry I'm so late. I tried to call but I couldn't get a signal." She stepped into the dark kitchen. "You'll never believe what happened. Bonnie?" Maybe she had already gone to bed. But then how did Wilson get out? Bonnie always slept with her door closed.

Lauren started toward Bonnie's bedroom to check on her, but Wilson let out a sharp bark and ran toward the stairs. Lauren followed. A soft moaning sound sent her dashing up the steps. At the end of the hallway the attic ladder had been folded down. A dark shape lay in the hallway at the bottom.

"Bonnie!" Lauren flicked on the hall lights. Bonnie's leg was twisted to one side in an impossible position. A large red lump rose on her forehead.

Another moan, and Bonnie opened her eyes and whispered, "Lauren."

"You'll be okay now. I'm calling an ambulance." Lauren pulled out her phone. No signal. She dropped the useless technology on the floor. "I'm going downstairs to call, but I'll be right back. I won't leave you again. I promise."

CHAPTER EIGHTEEN

PATRICK'S EYES FLEW open as he realized the sound tugging at the corner of his consciousness wasn't his morning alarm. He grabbed his phone and answered, before it woke his roommate. "Hello?" he whispered.

"Patrick, it's Lauren."

"What's wrong?" A glance at his watch confirmed it was a little after three in the morning. He slipped out of his dorm room and into the hallway, closing the door quietly behind him. "Is it Gran?"

"Yes. She's in the Mat-Su hospital."

Patrick swallowed. "What happened? Her heart? A stroke?"

"No." There was a pause. When Lauren resumed talking, her voice quivered. "She was in an accident. She fell."

"Again?" Patrick pushed his hair up off his forehead. "How badly is she hurt?"

"It's pretty serious. A concussion and a broken leg. She fell down a ladder. She's in surgery now for her leg."

Patrick sucked in a deep breath. "I'll be there as soon as I can tomorrow. I'm glad you were there. What was she doing on a ladder, especially in the middle of the night?"

"It wasn't the middle of the night. She fell down the attic ladder. And I—" There was a catch in Lauren's voice as though she was trying not to cry. "I wasn't there. I was with the goats."

"The attic ladder? What was she doing in the attic?"

"I think she was looking for Elsa's letters. She mentioned at lunch that she wanted to see them. I said I'd bring them down for her, but then I saw that Spritz had gotten out—"

"And you went off to take care of the goats, instead." He couldn't really blame her, but why couldn't she have taken five minutes to get the letters so that Gran wouldn't be tempted? And why couldn't Gran just wait until she got back? "How long did she lie there?"

"I don't know." This time there was a full sob in her voice. "The goats were all out. It took the whole rest of the day to round them up. I didn't get back to the house until after eleven. With her concussion, she was too confused to tell us when she fell."

"You left Gran alone from lunchtime until after eleven without even checking in?"

"I tried to call, but my cell wouldn't work. If I'd had any idea—"

"If you'd stopped by the house for five minutes you would have. I trusted you to take care of her."

"I know." He heard her draw in a breath as if she was about to say something, but there was only silence. Patrick was about to check to see if the call had been dropped when she whispered, "Can you give me two weeks?"

"For what?"

"To find a place for the goats and sell the equipment before I go."

"You're leaving?" With Gran in the hospital, she was going to run away? Patrick was shocked. He'd been getting closer to Lauren, even falling for her, and at the first sign of trouble, she was going to disappear? Obviously, Lauren wasn't nearly as committed as he'd believed to either him or Gran. Did he know her at all? "Fine. Two weeks. Text me when Gran's out of surgery, okay? Can you at least do that?"

"Of course."

Patrick ended the call. What was Lauren thinking? Gran had taken her in and treated her like family. She'd even agreed that if

Lauren would help her hunt for Bradley's Heart, she could use the entire finder's fee to finance the equipment she needed for the dairy. And now, at the first whiff of trouble, Lauren was leaving?

He should have headed off this nonsense over the stupid gold nugget. It was the reason Gran had sprained her ankle at the cabin, and it had to be the reason she'd tried to navigate that attic ladder. A woman in her eighties had no business hunting treasure. And Lauren had only encouraged her. He wished Gran had never heard of James Bradley.

And maybe it would have been better if neither of them had ever heard of Lauren Shepherd.

LAUREN HAD KNOWN it was inevitable. Eventually her relationship with Patrick would come to an end. But she'd never foreseen it would happen this way. How long had Bonnie lain there, in pain, while Lauren was out rounding up goats? If Lauren would only have stopped in, even if it was just to say she wouldn't be home for supper, she would have found her sooner.

Part of the reason she hadn't is that she was afraid if she did, Bonnie would insist on helping her round up the goats, and Lauren hadn't wanted to risk having her roaming over the rough ground, especially when there could still be a bear in the area. But that was an excuse. Patrick's last words when he left for work were to ask her to take care of Bonnie, and she hadn't. That was inexcusable.

Spritz nudged Lauren's shoulder, reminding her that it was time to remove the milking machine and bring Biscotti up for her turn. Spritz had produced less milk than usual, but considering the terrors of yesterday, Lauren wasn't surprised. The kids and does milled around the pen in the barn, but their usual playful spirit seemed subdued. She would keep them in the barn for now, until she was sure the bear had moved on. In fact, maybe she should just keep them here until she found another farm for them. She had plenty of hay, after all.

A sob formed in her chest at the idea of selling off her goats and leaving all of this behind, but she pushed it down before it could escape. Right now, she needed to finish the milking and get back to the hospital. She didn't want to leave Bonnie alone for a second longer than she had to.

When Lauren had left the hospital this morning, Bonnie had been sleeping peacefully despite the IV line and monitors and constant whooshing and beeping. The nurse had been waking her every two hours all night to check her concussion, so it was no wonder she was exhausted.

The doctor said she'd come through surgery well, and Bonnie had been alert enough to give Lauren a smile before she nodded off. Lauren wasn't sure if that meant Bonnie wasn't angry with her, or if kindness was simply a reflex for Bonnie. Lauren had texted Patrick, as promised, to give him the surgeon's report.

Laughter drifted out of the open doorway to Bonnie's hospital room when Lauren returned. A young man in scrubs was raising the bed so that she could sit up. Bonnie spotted Lauren, "Oh, there you are, Lauren. Sven here tells me you were by my bed all night. Did you get any sleep at all?"

"A little," Lauren lied. "How are you feeling?"

"Fair to middling." Bonnie waited while the nurse pushed a trolley with a covered plate into place over her bed. "When I woke up, it felt like I was cut wet and baled too soon, but Sven gave me a pill and I'm doing better."

"I'm glad. Patrick texted. He's taking the

next plane he can get out from Deadhorse and should be here this afternoon."

"Oh, he didn't need to leave work to come to me. I'm fine here, with Sven and you to take care of me."

"You know Patrick won't be able to rest until he's seen you with his own eyes."

Bonnie gave an indulgent smile. "That boy."

Sven adjusted the call button to make sure it was within reach. "I'll leave you to eat your breakfast, then. Buzz me if you need me."

"I will. Thanks, Sven." Bonnie took the lid off her plate and looked doubtfully at the overly yellow eggs. "They tell me I came in about midnight and had surgery on my leg."

"You don't remember?"

"The last thing I remember is that Spritz had gotten out again. What happened after that?"

"I was hoping you could tell me. Unfortunately, I wasn't there all day." Lauren explained about the goats.

"Oh, my goodness. A bear got one of your kids? What a shame. I wish you'd had one of those guardian dogs like the one you showed me at the fair. Were the goats all together when you found them?"

"No, they'd scattered all over the farm,

and two had followed the creek almost to town. By the time I got them rounded up and milked, I didn't get home until after eleven. That's when I found you at the bottom of the attic ladder."

"The attic? What was I doing there?"

"Before we saw Spritz outside, you had asked me to get the box with the letters from Elsa." Lauren reached for her hand. "Oh, Bonnie. I'm so sorry I didn't get them for you before I left. And that I didn't check in for so many hours. The thought of you lying there—"

"Now, now. I don't even remember it, so it couldn't have been all that bad. And it's my own fault. I must have gotten impatient. That's always been my weakness. I hate waiting for things. Patrick warned me to stay off ladders and he was right." She winked. "Don't you tell him that, though. Last thing I want to hear is him saying 'I told you so.'"

"I won't tell." Lauren smiled at the woman she'd grown to love.

"Now why did I want Elsa's letters? I wish I could remember." Bonnie took a bit of egg, grimaced and took another bite. "I don't suppose you could smuggle me in a nice cranberry scone?"

"I'll ask Sven if it's okay."

"Nah, in situations like this, it's better to beg forgiveness than ask permission." Bonnie finished her eggs, drank her juice and pushed the tray away. "You're too law-abiding to be a good smuggler. I'll ask Bea."

Lauren laughed. "That reminds me. I should call all the Mat Mates."

"All right, but in the meantime, I'm ready for a nap." Bonnie yawned. "That pill is making me sleepy."

Lauren rolled the food trolley into the hallway and helped Bonnie recline the bed and rearrange the pillows. Within minutes she was asleep.

Lauren studied her beautiful face, especially the deep lines around her eyes earned from decades of smiles and laughter. No one had ever treated her the way Bonnie had, as though she was family. The way families were supposed to treat each other, with kindness, and consideration, and support. The way Bonnie and Patrick treated each other. Leaving them was going to be the hardest thing Lauren had ever done.

She knew Bonnie would protest when she said she was leaving Alaska, but Patrick wanted her gone, and Lauren refused to be a source of friction between Bonnie and her grandson. Besides, how could she stay?

She loved Patrick. It would be agony to see the contempt in those eyes that had looked at her so lovingly before. She couldn't face it, not every time he came to visit his grandmother. For the first time, she understood why her mother had insisted on relocating after every failed relationship.

Lauren sent an email to Marissa, asking if she knew of anyone looking to buy more goats. Then she called Molly to tell her about Bonnie's fall. And finally, Lauren just sat in the chair beside Bonnie's bed, watching her sleep.

Bonnie was still napping when Molly arrived. She whispered to Lauren that she'd called the others, but she'd wanted to see if Bonnie was up to it before the whole group descended on her. Molly looked at the clothes Lauren hadn't bothered to change since chasing the goats through the mud yesterday. "Go home. Take a shower and get some sleep. I'll stay with Bonnie."

"Thanks." Lauren took one last look at Bonnie before passing into the hall and making her way downstairs. She walked into the parking lot, looked around and realized she had no earthly idea where she might have parked. And somehow the thought of looking for her car was more than she could handle in that moment. She leaned on a one-way sign at the edge of the lot, staring into the distance.

Her phone rang. Marissa. No doubt in response to the email she'd sent. Lauren picked up. "Hello."

"Hi, Lauren. I got your message about selling the goats. What's going on?"

"I, uh, I'm moving—" Lauren paused, the combination of exhaustion and emotion somehow rendering her unable to form a cohesive sentence.

"Moving where?"

"Back to Oregon, I guess. Um—"

She must have sounded disoriented because Marissa broke in. "Listen, I'm in Palmer for a meeting. Why don't I come to the farm afterward and we can talk?"

"Wh–when—" Lauren was trying desperately to control her voice, but a sob broke through.

"Lauren? Hey, my meeting's not for another forty minutes. I'll come out to the farm now."

"I'm not at the farm," Lauren managed to say.

"Where are you?"

"Hospital."

"Are you okay?" The growing concern in

Marissa's voice made it even harder for Lauren to stay in control."

"I'm fine. It's Bonnie—"

"The hospital here? In Palmer?"

"Yes."

"Stay right where you are. I'll find you." The call ended.

Lauren stood in the parking lot, looking up at the windows. Which one belonged to Bonnie's room? Lauren's body began to tremble.

A red truck pulled in and parked. Marissa jumped out and hurried toward the front door. Just before she got there, she spotted Lauren and veered over. "What happened to Bonnie?"

"She…" Lauren swallowed. "She fell down the ladder from the attic. Concussion and broken leg. Molly is with her."

"Oh, no. I'm so sorry. Will she be okay?"

"The doctors say so."

"Good." Marissa wrapped her in a comforting hug and then stepped back to look at her. Lauren must have looked as miserable as she felt, because Marissa grasped her hand. "Come with me." Marissa led her across the street to a coffee shop and ordered her to sit. A minute later, she set tea and an oatmeal cookie in front of Lauren. "Eat a few bites. Then we'll talk."

Lauren obediently took a bite from the cookie and a swig of tea. Marissa sipped from her own coffee cup and watched her. After a moment, Marissa smiled. "There. Feeling a little better?"

Lauren nodded. "Thank you."

"Cookies and tea help everything, according to my aunt Becky. Now, tell me what's going on. Maybe I can help. Why should Bonnie's accident mean you need to sell your goats?"

Lauren didn't see how Marissa could possibly help her, but she was being so kind, and Lauren couldn't seem to make sense of it alone. She took a deep breath and started talking and answering Marissa's questions until she'd given Marissa the whole story.

Marissa frowned. "Patrick said you have to leave the farm?"

"I asked for two weeks. If he doesn't want me there—"

"What makes you think he doesn't want you there?"

Lauren shook her head. "You didn't hear him when I called while Bonnie was in surgery. He was angry. It's my fault that Bonnie was hurt."

"Now wait just a minute. How is it your fault?"

"If I hadn't left her alone for so long—"

"Poppycock. I've only met Bonnie twice, and even I can tell she does exactly as she pleases. There's no way this was your fault."

"Patrick doesn't think so."

"Well, then Patrick is an idiot." Marissa stopped to consider. "Of course, most of us are idiots when you wake us up with bad news in the middle of the night. What exactly did he say?"

Lauren tried to recall. "I don't remember exactly. I just know the last thing he said before he left for the slope was to take care of his grandmother. I let him down."

"And you think, because of one mistake—which I must emphasize wasn't your fault anyway—you and Patrick are over? Forgive me, but that doesn't sound like much of a relationship."

Maybe Marissa was right. Maybe what she'd had with Patrick had never been real. But Lauren thought of the way he'd smiled at her. The way they'd worked together. The way she felt when he was nearby. It felt real.

Marissa leaned forward. "You said what happened, and that Patrick is angry with you. But what you haven't told me is what *you* want."

"Me?"

"Yes, you. Do you want to go back to Oregon, or do you want to stay? Do you want it to be over with Patrick, or not?"

"I'm not sure it matters."

"Of course, it matters. You matter. You may not always get what you want, but if you don't know, how can you possibly get there?"

Marissa's watch beeped. She frowned. "I'm sorry, Lauren. I wish I could stay longer, but I have to get to this meeting with Fish and Game." She gave Lauren another quick hug. "Think about it. And don't be so hard on yourself. You're human, my friend, and so is Patrick O'Shea." Marissa grabbed her coffee. "I'll call you this afternoon."

"Thank you, for everything." Lauren nibbled on her cookie and watched Marissa cross the street to her truck. Lauren did feel a little better. Maybe Marissa's aunt's cookie and tea remedy was the reason, but more likely it was the way Marissa had dropped everything to help. *You matter.* It felt good to have a friend.

Lauren finished her cookie and stood up, not so shaky now. She had some decisions to make, but a shower and a change of clothes would help. And there was her truck, tucked into a space on the corner beside a van. She crossed to the parking lot and drove to the farm.

PATRICK, CARRYING AN arrangement of yellow and white flowers he'd picked up in the gift shop, stepped off the elevator and located room 224. The door was open. Gran looked so small, lying in the hospital bed. A plastic cast poked out from under the edge of her bedsheets. Molly sat beside her, reading a book. Lauren was nowhere to be seen.

An ache he'd been carrying inside his chest since their conversation last night expanded into a full-fledged pain. He'd really believed they could make it work, that Lauren was the one. But she wasn't. The kind of woman he wanted to make a life with someday wouldn't be giving up the minute life turned hard. Lauren was leaving him, leaving Gran, leaving Alaska.

He tiptoed into the room and set the flowers on the windowsill. Molly smiled a greeting. Gran opened one eye. "Paddy, boy," she whispered. "You came."

"Of course, I did." He dropped a kiss on Gran's cheek. "That's quite a bump on your noggin. How are you?"

"Not too bad."

"I sent Lauren home to bed," Molly told him, although he hadn't asked. "She was exhausted, poor thing. Spent the whole night here." She stood. "Here, take this seat, Patrick. I'm going to grab a cup of coffee."

Once she was out of the room, Bonnie reached for Patrick's hand. "Paddy, I want you to check on Lauren. Something's wrong. This morning, when she thought I was asleep, she looked so sad. I'm afraid she thinks I'm hurt worse than I am. When you see her, tell her the doctor says I'll probably be home tomorrow. We'll be doing yoga together again before she knows it."

Great. Lauren hadn't told her. Now he had to break the news. "Lauren is selling her goats and leaving Alaska."

"What? Since when?"

"I don't know. Since last night I guess."

"Why? What happened?" Gran eyed him with suspicion. "Did you two have a fight?"

"No. Well, not really, anyway. I was a little upset that she'd left you alone for so long."

"A little upset." Gran huffed. "I imagine she was a little upset when the bear got one of her goats, too."

"What bear?"

"She didn't tell you? A bear knocked down the fence to the goat pasture, got one of the kids, injured another one, and scattered the herd from here to Timbuktu. Took her all day to find them and get them home. Then she comes back and there I am at the bottom of a ladder with a broken leg."

"Oh." Poor Lauren. That was a lot to handle in one day. He wished he'd been there to help.

"So, she's dealing with all that and then you go and give her a hard time for not babysitting me better? I'm not a toddler and I'm not senile. This broken leg is all on me, not her. Besides, if it wasn't for her, I'd still be lying there. You had no business blaming her."

"You're right."

"Of course, I'm right. Now answer me this. Do you want that girl to go away?"

"No." Patrick was clear on that.

"Then tell her so. And apologize while you're at it for leaving your brains in your back pocket."

Patrick nodded slowly. "But it still concerns me that her first response is to run away."

Gran pressed her lips together and shook her head. "Did Lauren ever tell you about her life, growing up?"

"She said she moved a lot. Said her mother was a romance addict."

"Don't you see? That's all Lauren knows. Her mother was so busy chasing rainbows, she never settled down long enough to get the pot of gold. Lauren doesn't understand how love is supposed to work. She's never seen people who fight and make mistakes and then forgive and move forward together. That's her tender spot."

Patrick thought back to that conversation when Lauren said she didn't want to have a relationship with him because when it was over, she'd have to go. He'd assured her it wasn't true. And yet, here she was, offering to leave without ever throwing his words back in his face, because she thought he didn't want her anymore.

"Maybe I'd better go now."

"Go where?" Bea swept into the room, carrying a box from the Salmonberry Bakery.

"Hello, Patrick. You must have been on one of the first planes out this morning." Alice brought an oversize get-well card. Linda followed with a basket of books, Rosemary with a crystal, and Molly brought up the rear, holding her cup of coffee.

Rosemary went to stick a suction cup hook onto the window and hung the crystal from it. Sunlight bounced off it and projected a rainbow on the ceiling. "Where's Lauren?"

"She thinks she's going to sell her goats and move. Patrick is going to apologize now."

All five ladies stopped to stare at him. "Did you hurt that sweet girl's feelings?" Molly demanded.

"I'm afraid so," Patrick admitted.

"Well then, you'd best get moving," Alice told him. "The longer these things fester, the harder the healing."

"Take flowers," Linda advised. "It's hard to stay mad at a man with flowers."

"Although jewelry is nice, too," Bea chimed in. "Sometimes flowers aren't enough. It depends on what you did wrong."

"Ladies, I think Patrick can handle it from here." Gran looked at him. "Don't worry about gifts. Lauren isn't the material type. Just tell her what's in your heart." She grinned. "Although, candy never hurts."

Patrick left Gran in good hands and made his way downstairs to his car, but instead of heading directly to the farm, he decided to stop by a florist, a candy store and a jewelry shop. After all, between the six of them there was close to five hundred years of experience in that hospital room. When it came to repairing relationships, they probably knew what they were talking about.

CHAPTER NINETEEN

THE SHOWER HAD helped, but the nap hadn't materialized. Just thoughts, chasing each other through Lauren's head. Marissa was right. Lauren needed to make up her mind about what she wanted. Marissa had called once her meeting ended, offering to come to the farm, but Lauren assured her that she was okay. She just needed time to think.

Now it was milking time. On the way to the milking stand, Spritz rubbed her head against Lauren's arm as if she knew Lauren needed the extra affection today. Or maybe she needed it herself, after everything that had happened. Either way, Lauren stopped to give the doe a hug.

"I'll miss you so much if I go." And all the other goats, and the farm. And Bonnie. And especially Patrick.

Patrick. The thought of leaving him made her feel as though her heart was cracking into tiny pieces and scattering across the floor of the barn. Even though her body kept going through the normal milking routine, it was as though everything that mattered about her was falling apart.

Was this how love felt? How had her mother gone through this time after time? If she'd ever actually been in love with any of those men, how could she have left them so easily, without leaving her heart behind?

It must have been terrible for Bonnie when her husband died, too, but at least she knew she loved him and that he loved her. They didn't part in a cloud of bad feelings and disappointment. They'd lived happily together for almost fifty years, although...what was it Bonnie said, something about trusting each other to be gentle with the tender spots, and forgiving each other when they weren't? That must mean that they'd had some arguments.

Was that the difference? Trusting each other to forgive and move forward together instead of separating? If she asked, would Patrick forgive her for leaving Bonnie alone for so many hours? Or would he refuse, and grind the shards of her broken heart into dust? Was what they had together worth salvaging?

When Lauren leaned forward to connect the milking machine, the pendant Rosemary had given her swung on its chain. *Insight and communication.* Rosemary had told her she'd need those qualities to find the nugget, but they applied to relationships, too. Maybe even more so.

Lauren finished milking the last goat and put the milk in a circulating water bath to cool quickly while she cleaned the goats' pen, set out hay and made sure their water was fresh. When she reached down to pick up her pitchfork, Chip jumped onto her back.

Lauren laughed, and somehow the laughter broke through her indecision. She thought of all the laughter she'd shared with Patrick. How he'd worked by her side building the fence, searching the cabin, setting up the fencing for the fair, all to help her reach her dream. The way he'd kissed her as though she was the most precious woman in the world. What they had together was worth fighting for.

She bottled the milk and put it in the refrigerator, checked the goats one last time and headed for the house. Wilson greeted her at the door with a bewildered expression, surely wondering where Bonnie was. Lauren fed him and decided to give him a few minutes in the yard while she changed into clothes that didn't smell like goat. Then she would go to the hospital, find Patrick and tell him how she felt. Maybe he would forgive her, maybe not, but she'd never know if she didn't try.

At the end of the hall, the attic ladder was still down. When she went to fold it up, she found Elsa's wooden box lying open, the letters scattered across the floor. Lauren gathered them up. The top letter was the last one. *Meet me at the spot where we declared our love. If you're not there by midnight, I'll know our love is dead and buried there.—B*

Looking at that *B*, with a curving swoop at the beginning, Lauren realized it looked familiar. Could it be? She picked up the letter and hurried to the kitchen, where they'd left the photocopies of the letters from Valdez stacked on the sideboard. She compared the two. Yes!

They weren't completely identical. The *B* in Elsa's letters seemed bolder somehow. Life had stripped some of the arrogance from Billy's handwriting, but both letters were clearly written by the same person. Billy had been in love with Elsa, and never gotten over her. That explained his breakup with Maggie as well. When he was reading the newspaper that day, he must have read about the fire that killed Elsa's husband and children. It must have felt like a second chance for him and Elsa. And when he found out Thomas Bradley would be carrying the nugget with him that day, Billy had been unable to resist the chance to accumulate the wealth he thought would win back the woman he loved.

No wonder when he ran, it was at Elsa's cabin that he chose to hide. A familiar place where he knew his way around. Besides, he'd probably kept track of the family and knew no one was living at the farm then.

Poor Billy. Did Elsa really give up true love to marry into a prosperous family, or was that just what Billy chose to believe? Either way, he was clearly brokenhearted. Lauren read over the letter again, and suddenly it hit her. She knew where Billy had hidden the nugget.

She threw on some clean clothes and galloped down the stairs. When she went to put Wilson back in the house, he whimpered piteously. Oh, what the heck? Lauren grabbed a shopping bag from the peg on the mudroom wall and let Wilson ride along. Once she reached the hospital, she tucked him inside the bag. "Now you'll have to be quiet if we're going to smuggle you past the nurses' station."

Wilson cooperated, and soon they were at

Bonnie's doorway. Sounds of conversation and laughter drifted out. She opened the door and wasn't surprised to see Bonnie's friends all gathered around her bed. But to her disappointment, Patrick wasn't there.

Bonnie, however, had more color in her cheeks and a smile on her face. Lauren slipped closer to where she was sitting up in bed and opened the top of the tote bag. "Someone wanted to make sure you were okay."

"Wilson!" Bonnie lifted the dog onto her lap. Wilson wagged his long body joyfully.

"He was very upset last night," Lauren told her. "He met me at the door and insisted I follow him upstairs."

"He's a regular Lassie," Bonnie said.

The other ladies all looked at each other. "Have you seen Patrick?" Alice asked Lauren.

"I was about to ask you the same thing. Is he missing?"

"I'm sure he'll be along," Molly said, as she typed something into her phone. She gave Lauren a concerned smile. "We're all so sorry to hear about the bear. And then to come home and find Bonnie had fallen from the attic ladder. You had quite a day."

"I wish I could remember why I was in the attic," Bonnie said.

Lauren was dying to tell them all about her discovery, but she didn't feel like it would be fair until Patrick could hear as well. And before she went into that, she needed to set things right with him. Where was he, anyway?

A nurse, a woman this time, knocked on the door and walked in without waiting for permission. Bonnie quickly covered Wilson, but the sheet bobbed back and forth as his tail wagged underneath. The nurse chuckled while she checked Bonnie's monitors. "I overlooked the bakery box and I'm going to pretend those are your fingers wiggling under that sheet, but if any Chippendales dancers show up on my shift, your friends will have to leave."

"Yes, ma'am," Bonnie responded. "We'll try to keep the party under control."

As the nurse reached for the door, Patrick pulled it open from the other side, almost causing a collision. "Oh, sorry."

The nurse waggled her index finger at him. "Just make sure you keep your clothes on."

Bonnie and her friends all burst out laughing, while Patrick just looked confused. After a brief head shake, he crowded into the room, his arms full of chocolates, a small shopping bag and another bouquet of flowers. Lauren felt a sudden jolt of worry that Bonnie had received bad news, and Patrick was trying to make her feel better.

But all the ladies smiled at him the way Bonnie smiled at Wilson when he'd completed a clever trick. "What took you so long?" Alice whispered.

Patrick shrugged and held up the shopping bag. Murmuring his "excuse mes," he made his way toward the bed, but instead of talking to Bonnie, he turned to look at Lauren. Lauren searched his eyes, looking for the blame and anger she'd heard in his voice the night before, but she saw only uncertainty.

"Lauren, I—" He glanced around the room at the six ladies watching their every move, and then back at Lauren. "I wondered if you might take a little walk with me."

"Um—" What if he wanted to get her alone to formally kick her off the farm? But she needed to talk with him, too. She gathered her courage. "Sure." She turned to Bonnie. "I'll be back for Wilson in a little while."

Bonnie smiled at her. "Take your time. I'll be here."

"There's a nice garden south of the main

entrance," Alice whispered to Patrick. He nodded.

Patrick held the door for Lauren, shut it firmly behind him and pressed a hand to Lauren's back to guide her toward the elevator. A tingle of awareness ran up her spine. Would this be the last time she ever felt his touch? On the other hand, the fact that he was touching her at all offered a smidge of encouragement.

In an alcove between two wings of the building, someone had designed a small garden with a few benches, ferns and a tiny pond. Patrick led Lauren there. "Let's sit." She realized that he was still carrying Bonnie's gifts. He must be flustered.

But he sat down beside her and handed her the bouquet. "These are for you."

"You're giving me flowers?" She looked down at the cluster of pink rosebuds. "Why?"

"Linda thought it was a good idea."

"Okay, I'm confused. Linda thinks you need to give me flowers."

"Yes. But Gran said candy." He handed over the chocolates. "And then there's this." He reached in the bag and pulled out a small blue box.

"What is this all about?"

"Open the box."

She pulled open the lid to reveal a silver bracelet. The word *Forever* was worked into the filigree design. "It's beautiful. But I don't understand why you're giving me gifts."

"I'm trying to apologize, and apparently I'm really bad at it. Lauren, I'm so sorry. I lashed out at you about Gran, and it wasn't your fault. Not that it's an excuse for the way I overreacted, but I didn't know about the bear. I'm sorry about the kid you lost."

"Thank you for saying that, but I still should have checked in on Bonnie. I didn't even stop to tell her I wouldn't be home for dinner. If I had known—"

"How could you possibly have known?"

Lauren shrugged. "The very last thing you said to me was to take care of your grandmother."

"And you did." He scooted closer, accidently knocking the chocolates off the bench. He stood and retrieved them, setting them on the bench beside Lauren. "You called the ambulance and you stayed all night with her at the hospital."

"But still—"

"Lauren, will you please quit arguing about this? You are not responsible for Gran's fall. I'm asking you—will you accept my apology for blaming you?"

"Oh, Patrick, of course I will."

"Does that mean you're not leaving?"

"You want me to stay?"

"With my whole heart." He took her hand. "Lauren, I love you. I know life seems to be conspiring against your goat dairy, but if you'll stay—"

"You love me?"

"I do. Is there any chance—"

"I love you, too. Oh, Patrick." She jumped up, dropping the box with the bracelet to the ground. She threw her arms around Patrick's neck, only realizing she still held the bouquet in her hand when she bonked him on the back of the head with it.

Laughing, he took it from her and set it, the bracelet and the candy together on the bench. Then he turned and reached over to cradle her cheek in his hand. He studied her face for a long moment before he wrapped an arm around her waist and pulled her against him.

He brought his face closer. "I love you, Lauren," he whispered against her lips, and then he was kissing her. She closed her eyes, relishing the thrill of his kiss, the warm and wonderful feeling of being in a world that consisted of only the two of them. In that moment, nothing else mattered.

Until the sound of cheering intruded. They looked up, to see Alice, Molly and Bea hanging out the window above them. The ladies waved. Sheepishly, Lauren waved back. "Do you ever get the impression they're always one step ahead?"

"Good thing they're on our side." Patrick chuckled. He gathered up the flowers and boxes. "I'm starting to think I might have gone overboard with the gifts."

"You think?" Lauren smiled. "Not that I don't appreciate them because they're all beautiful, but your words mean more to me than gifts ever could."

"You mean, *I love you*? Those words?"

"Yes, those." Lauren leaned past the flowers to give him another kiss. Funny, a week ago, she'd been convinced that love was a temporary condition, but somehow, hearing Patrick say it now, she knew she could trust him with her heart. Like the bracelet he'd selected, he was talking forever. "I love you, Patrick." She was saying it. Out loud. It felt so good.

Patrick reached for her hand. "I don't know exactly how we're going to manage it, but somehow, we're going to make your dream come true. Because I believe this is where we belong. Together."

"Oh, I almost forgot to tell you. I discovered something about William Golson."

"What?"

"Let's go up to Bonnie's room so I can tell her, too. She started this treasure hunt."

"Okay."

When they walked into Bonnie's room hand in hand, the group applauded. Patrick dropped his armful of gifts onto a chair in the corner of the room.

"Mmm," Bonnie commented. "Good choice on the candies."

Lauren unwrapped the box, opened it and passed it to Bonnie. "Enjoy."

Bonnie selected a chocolate and passed the box to Molly. Patrick slipped an arm around Lauren's waist. "Lauren has something to tell us, about Golson."

All eyes turned her way. What if she was wrong? Lauren cleared her throat. "Well, really it's Bonnie's doing. I found the box with Elsa's letters in the hallway, and I noticed the signature."

"B," Alice said.

Molly gasped. *"B* for *Billy."*

"How could we not have thought of that?" Linda murmured.

Bonnie finished chewing her candy. "Now I remember. I wanted Elsa's letters so I could check the handwriting against Billy's letters to his aunt."

"They match," Lauren affirmed. "And after I reread his last letter to Elsa, I have an idea where he might have hidden the nugget."

"Where?" Bonnie demanded.

Lauren told them. As she explained her reasoning, heads began to nod.

"That makes sense to me," Patrick said.

"What are you waiting for?" Bonnie was almost quivering. "Go dig it up!"

"I thought we might wait until you could come along," Lauren said. "This is really your quest."

"Are you kidding me? The doctor says six to eight weeks in this cast. If I had to wait that long to find out, I might burst."

Patrick checked his watch. "We still have two hours of daylight left.

Go!" Bonnie almost shouted.

Laughing, Patrick grabbed Lauren's hand and maneuvered through the door. "We'll be back," he called.

"I'll be waiting," Bonnie assured him.

THEY RETURNED TO the farm, stopping at the barn to grab two shovels, a flashlight and the metal detector. Spritz bleated when she saw

Patrick, and he stopped to scratch his fingers under her chin.

"Lauren, before we start, I have something to say."

"Okay." She stopped to look at him.

Patrick grasped both of her hands in his and took a moment to appreciate the depth of her green eyes, the curve of her lips. Beautiful. He met her gaze. "I think there's a good chance you've figured it all out, and we'll find the nugget. But I want you to know that whether we do or not, it doesn't matter as far as I'm concerned. I've found my treasure in you, and I'm never letting you go."

She blinked, and her eyes grew shiny. Patrick dropped one hand to reach up and wipe away a stray tear. "Oh, no, no. I didn't mean to make you cry."

"They're happy tears, silly." Lauren smiled, even while more tears escaped from her eyes. "I love you, Patrick."

"I love you, too." He pulled her close and held her. Once the tears had stopped and he'd wiped them away, he leaned down for a gentle kiss, reveling in the sweetness before he drew back and smiled. "Are you ready to hunt?"

She reached for the metal detector. "Let's go find some treasure!"

They made their way down past the cabin to the creek. It took a little while to find the big cottonwood with Elsa's and Billy's initials. Once they did, Lauren turned on the metal detector. "Where do we start?"

"I don't know." Patrick surveyed the twisted old tree. "The roots would make it hard to bury anything right up against the trunk, so maybe start along the dripline and work inward?"

Lauren started walking slowly, scanning the ground as she went. As she reached the edge of the creek, the unit began to beep. She looked at Patrick, her eyes shining with excitement. He grabbed a shovel.

Lauren moved the metal detector back and forth until they'd targeted the place with the strongest signal. Patrick started digging. Almost immediately he hit something solid, but it turned out to be a tree root. Digging carefully around the root, they burrowed further into the ground, only to discover an old rusty can.

"It probably just washed down the river during high water at some point." Patrick tossed the can aside to dispose of later.

Lauren picked up the detector and resumed her search. Patrick gathered a pile of rocks from the edge of the river. "I'll mark the scanned ground behind you as you go, so we'll know we don't miss a spot."

"Good idea." Lauren took another step, and the detector beeped again. Once more, Patrick grabbed the shovel, with perhaps a little less optimism. This time, the "treasure" turned out to be a canning jar ring.

By sunset, they'd recovered a rusty canteen, two soda cans, a women's ring missing its stone, a token for a free drink at a long-defunct bar in Wasilla, a coach's whistle and a mangled pair of wire-rim glasses.

Lauren finished her final sweep up against the trunk of the tree without setting off anything. She leaned the metal detector against the tree and put her hands on her hips while she stretched her back. "I guess I was wrong."

Patrick hated the look of disappointment on her face. "Not necessarily. It could be a little farther from the tree. Or if Billy buried it too close to the water, it could have washed downstream and gotten hung up at the culvert like so many things do. We can come back in the morning and check."

"Okay." She didn't look convinced, but she gathered up the shovels.

Patrick picked up the detector, slung it over his shoulder and turned away from the tree.

The detector beeped once. Both he and Lauren froze. "Did I do that?" Patrick asked.

"I don't know. Hold it up in the air and move it slowly," Lauren advised.

Patrick waved the detector around the air. When he got closer to the trunk, it beeped again. Gradually they were able to pinpoint the location. About two feet above the carved heart, a branch had broken off and rotted away, leaving a hole in the bark.

Patrick reached overhead and tried to poke his fingers into the hole, but he didn't feel anything. "You said Billy was tall?"

"Yes. I saw a picture in a newspaper article, and he was a head higher than the policeman next to him. Thin, with long legs."

"And long arms, probably. I'm going to lift you up to look in the hole. Okay?"

"Okay."

Patrick handed her the flashlight before squatting down and letting her climb onto his knee. He swayed briefly but steadied himself against the tree, so that she could see into the hollow.

Lauren shined the flashlight in and felt around inside. "I feel something. Do you have anything I could use to make the hole bigger?"

Patrick handed her his pocketknife. She

opened it and poked around inside, scraping out some old leaves. "There's some cloth here, rotten." She gasped. "A rock! Oh, Patrick, this might be it! It's kind of wedged. Let me see if I can get the knife blade under it." She fiddled for several minutes while Patrick tried to hold her as steady as possible. Finally, something tumbled out of the tree and onto the ground.

Patrick squatted down again so that Lauren could dismount. She shined the flashlight onto the ground, sweeping back and forth until something reflected. Patrick scooped up the rock and held it out for her to see the heavy object. Two rounded sides and a point on the bottom were the only identification they needed.

They'd found Bradley's Heart.

LAUREN AND PATRICK ignored the look of disapproval the nurse at the desk shot in their direction and tiptoed down the hallway to Bonnie's room. Patrick pulled the door open a crack and Lauren peeked inside. Except for the monitors and the parking lot lights shining through the blinds, the room was dark.

"She may be asleep," Lauren whispered to Patrick. "Maybe we should come back in the morning."

"Don't even think about leaving without talking to me," Bonnie hissed. "Get in here!"

They went inside, shut the door behind them and flipped on some lights. Lauren went to stand beside Bonnie's bed, trying to maintain a poker face. "Where's Wilson?"

"Molly took him home. So tell me what you found."

"Well, it wasn't buried under the tree."

"Darn. I really thought you were onto something," Bonnie told her.

"But—" Lauren couldn't resist a grin "—when we were packing up to go, something on the tree itself tripped the metal detector."

Bonnie's eyes widened. "And?"

"This." Patrick pulled the nugget from his pocket and held it out for Bonnie to see.

The loud whoop Bonnie let out brought a nurse running. Bonnie hid the nugget under her blanket. "Sorry," she whispered to the nurse. "I was momentarily startled."

The nurse turned a stink-eye on Patrick. "It's past ten. Your grandmother needs her rest. Please leave and come back in the morning."

"They'll go soon," Bonnie told her. "They came to give me some good news, and believe me, I'll sleep a lot better now."

At Bonnie's shooing motion, the nurse

backed out of the room. "All right, but keep it down. There are other patients trying to sleep."

As soon as she'd gone, Bonnie put on her glasses and brought the nugget into the light. Patrick stood behind Lauren with his arms around her waist, watching his grandmother.

Bonnie hefted the nugget. "It's so heavy." She brought it close to her face to examine it. "The edges are rounded, not sharp like crystals. It's hard to tell in artificial light, but it looks golden, not brassy." Wonder filled her eyes when she looked up. "This is really it. Bradley's Heart. You've found it."

"*We've* found it." Lauren laid a hand on Bonnie's arm. "It took all of us. If Patrick hadn't arranged to see the letters in Valdez, or you hadn't realized Billy might be Elsa's B, it would never have occurred to me that the tree with their initials would be a hiding place."

"I can't wait to tell the Mat Mates." Bonnie stroked the nugget once more and handed it to Lauren. "Here. Keep it someplace safe. The doctor says he'll release me in the morning. Tomorrow, we'll celebrate."

CHAPTER TWENTY

BONNIE APPEARED CALM and collected, only
the fidgeting of her fingers giving away her
excitement as she waited for her cue. Makeup
covered the lingering traces of the bump on
her forehead, and even with a cast on her leg,
she looked stylish and put together thanks to
Molly's wardrobe assistance.

All it had taken was Alice and Linda putting out a few feelers and reporters from all
over the state had swarmed to Palmer, eager
to cover the feel-good story. Bonnie had been
just as eager to talk with them, except for
Anthony Clark, of course. She'd taken great
joy in turning down his request for an interview. He'd been forced to use a reprint from
the Anchorage newspaper, although, to his
credit, the local editor had run an apology
for his original article on the editorial page.

Various newspapers across the country
had picked up the story over the last two
weeks. Now it was about to go coast-to-
coast. Patrick and Lauren stood behind the

camera operator, watching Bonnie's face on the screen. Bonnie had urged them to join her in the interviews, but fame didn't appeal to either of them. Besides, the journalists wanted Bonnie.

"Five, four, three, two, one."

Bonnie smiled into the camera as the lovely and professional hostess for a national morning show appeared on the split screen with her. "Today we're talking with Bonnie O'Shea from Palmer, Alaska, who recently discovered a historic gold nugget on her goat farm." The picture cut away to a photo of Bradley's Heart, and then back to Bonnie's face. "How are you today, Bonnie?"

"Ever since we found this thing, I've been busy as a watchdog at a mailman convention. And how are you, Marilee?"

The anchor chuckled. "I'm doing well, thanks. So, Bonnie, tell us about this nugget. Where did it come from?"

"Well it all started during the Nome gold rush of 1899."

"Nome. Is that near Palmer where you live?"

Bonnie laughed. "Oh, no, honey. Nome isn't even on the road system. Nome is so far out in the bush, migrating geese have to use GPS to find it. Anyhoo, Mr. Thomas Bradley followed the gold rush to Nome and discovered the nugget on the banks of…" She told the story with flair. The hostess interrupted her with a question or two and then just let her run with it.

"She's a natural," Lauren whispered to Patrick.

"I know." His grin went ear to ear. "I'll bet Marilee's wondering exactly when she lost control of this interview."

"Do I understand correctly that you weren't alone in this treasure hunt?" Marilee prompted Bonnie.

"No indeed," Bonnie replied. "It was a joint effort with my grandson, Patrick and his beautiful girlfriend, Lauren Shepherd. Lauren runs the goat farm and makes these wonderful gourmet goat cheeses which will be available for sale once she gets all the permits and such. You can sign up for her newsletter at NowAndForeverFarm.com."

"Wow, she even worked in an advertisement," Patrick whispered. "I didn't know you had a website and a newsletter."

"I didn't either."

They looked at each other. "Linda!" they whispered in unison.

"What do you plan to do with the nugget?" Marilee asked.

"Well, I'm certainly not going to make the same mistake Thomas Bradley did and carry it around in my pocket." Bonnie laughed. "Actually, we've already turned it over to some experts, and they've validated it's the right nugget. This afternoon, we're all meeting with the Bradley family."

"We thank you for sharing your story with us this morning, Bonnie. Before we go, is there anything you'd like to tell our audience?"

"Don't give up on your dream," Bonnie said. "Sometimes it takes longer than you like, and sometimes the dream changes over time, but if it's what you really want, keep plugging away."

"Good advice, indeed. Goodbye, Bonnie, and thanks again."

"Goodbye, Marilee." Bonnie kept the serene smile on her face until the cameraman announced they were out. "Whew." She reached for a tissue and blotted her forehead. "Those lights are something, aren't they?"

"You did great." Lauren gave Bonnie a hug.

Patrick leaned over to kiss her cheek. "You sure did. Where would the celebrity like to have lunch before this afternoon's press conference?"

Bonnie grinned. "Maybe I should have asked Marilee what TV stars have for lunch. Oh, I know. Let's go to Humpy's for halibut and chips."

All the tables were full at Humpy's, but while they were waiting someone recognized Bonnie from the morning show and asked for her autograph. Someone else, overhearing, asked Bonnie to sign his napkin. A couple who had already grabbed a table invited Bonnie, Lauren and Patrick to sit with them. It turned out they were recreational gold panners and had been following the story in the news. Bonnie propped up her cast on a chair and held court.

The day Bonnie had been released from the hospital, Patrick and Lauren had taken her home to the farm. Meanwhile the Mat Mates had decorated the farmhouse with balloons and streamers intended for golden anniversary parties. They'd spent the whole afternoon eating goodies from the bakery, rehashing the clues, taking pictures and admiring the nugget. The next morning, Bonnie had called the number listed in the reward, and within the hour, an armored car had arrived to transport Bradley's Heart to a safe location.

Life had been a little surreal ever since.

When Patrick and Lauren were repairing the damaged fence in the pasture, they'd spotted someone with a telescopic lens photographing them from the road. Crystal reported people calling her to ask if they would be displaying the famous nugget at goat yoga next summer. Someone had left a message on Bonnie's phone, asking if she was in need of a ghost writer.

With all the hullabaloo, there had hardly been time to draw a breath, much less talk about the future, but Lauren had been having second thoughts about their agreement regarding the reward. Now, before they met the Bradley family, was the time to talk about it. Patrick pulled into the parking lot fifteen minutes before the press conference was scheduled. Lauren cleared her throat. "Before we go inside, could we talk for a minute?"

"Sure, honey, but we don't want to be late. They're giving you the reward money," Bonnie said.

"That's what I want to talk about. We were partners, working together to find the nugget. We should all share equally in the reward. One third each."

Patrick's eyebrows drew together. "One

third isn't enough to equip the dairy to meet state standards."

"Well, no, but it's enough to get started. I can capitalize some of the equipment and then use that as collateral. I can still make it work."

Bonnie shook her head. "Borrowing would put too much pressure on you to make money right away. It's going to take time to find your place in the market. Besides, that was the deal. You get the money and I get to show Anthony Clark he was wrong. We all agreed."

"Well, yeah, but that was when finding the nugget was theoretical. Now we've done it, and we're talking about a lot of money. Bonnie, you broke your leg going after the treasure. You deserve more than a couple of interviews."

"I don't need the money," Bonnie declared. "Tim, bless his heart, made sure I was taken care of. I get a comfortable check every month. Plus, I have a little extra put away in case of emergency."

"I'm doing fine on my salary," Patrick said. "That's why we did all this. So you could start the dairy. It's all yours."

"You're both so generous—" Lauren

fought back a tear "—but no. I can't take advantage of you like that. It doesn't feel right."

Patrick thought for a moment. "Then let's be partners again. We'll put the money into the dairy and own it together. Lauren, you're the manager, so the partnership would pay you a salary. Gran, it's your farm, so the partnership would pay you a lease. And whatever profits are left once we've paid expenses belong to the three of us. We can decide together what to reinvest."

"Brilliant." Bonnie beamed at Patrick. "I knew all that negotiation and diplomacy your father does had to have rubbed off on you. What do you say, Lauren? Can we get in on the ground floor of this operation?"

"You really want to invest your money with me?"

"Absolutely," Patrick told her. "I can't imagine a better investment opportunity. In five years, everybody in the state will be eating your cheese. It's that good."

Their faith in her almost brought fresh tears, but she willed them away. "Then yes, I would love to have you as partners."

"Good." Bonnie looked at her watch. "Now, can we please go inside and accept that check before they change their minds?"

At the press conference, Lauren spotted

Professor Jankowski sitting at the back. She waved, and he smiled and flashed a victory sign. Thomas Bradley's great-granddaughter spoke about how grateful they were to have the nugget back in the family. Bonnie gave a short talk about their search and thanked Professor Jankowski and Debbie Watson for their help. There was a photo op where they brought out the nugget, formally declared it Bradley's Heart and had Bonnie officially hand it over to the family. Then they brought out a giant check for more photos. Finally, they opened the floor for questions.

"What happens now to Bradley's Heart?" one woman asked.

"It will be on permanent loan to the Anchorage museum, just as my great-grandfather intended," Miss Bradley said.

"Were you surprised to get the call that the nugget had been found?"

"Surprised doesn't cover it. We were shocked. After all these years, we'd assumed it must have been melted down long ago."

An older man stood up, and Bonnie scowled. He stepped up to the microphone. "Hello, I'm Anthony Clark from the *Valley Voice*. Many years ago, when I was a freshman reporter, Mrs. O'Shea found what she thought was Bradley's Heart, but turned out to be pyrite. I wrote an article that implied that this gullible lady had been taken in by a hoax. I deliberately embarrassed her. And yet here she is today, returning this valuable piece of Alaskan history so that everyone will be able to see it. She didn't give up, and we're all the richer for it." He cleared his throat. "My question is for Bonnie O'Shea. Will you accept my apology and forgive me for my unprofessional behavior all those years ago?"

Bonnie hesitated, and then she chuckled. "Today is your lucky day, Anthony, because you happened to catch me in a good mood. So, yes, I will accept your apology. Who knows, I might even subscribe to that newspaper of yours." She grinned.

Laughter broke out, and Lauren saw several people jotting notes. After another twenty minutes or so of questions, the reporters filed out, leaving Bonnie, Lauren and Patrick alone with the Bradley family. One of the women who looked to be in her fifties made her way to Bonnie. "Hello, I'm Eunice. I just wanted you to know that my grandfather would have been tickled pink that you were the one who found his nugget and returned it. He always appreciated a woman with spirit."

"Well, I'm glad to hear it, Eunice. But if you want to meet a woman with spirit, let me introduce you to Lauren Shepherd. She's about to launch a business as a cheese maker, using goat's milk from our farm."

"Really? I'm part owner in the Pantry Place in downtown Anchorage, and we're always looking for regional specialties. In fact, we've been discussing expanding the cheese selection." Eunice reached into her purse and pulled out a card. "Once you're up and going, give me a call. We'll set up a taste test."

"I'll do that." Lauren tucked the card into her pocket. "Thank you."

As Eunice walked away, Lauren looked to Bonnie, who squeezed her arm. "See partner? We're on our way."

As soon as they got back to the farm, Lauren changed and started toward the pasture to collect the goats. According to the grapevine via Bea, a black bear, most likely the one who had gotten into Lauren's goats, was spotted breaking into a set of dumpsters close to the elementary school. Fish and Game decided he posed too much of a risk to the students and had relocated him far away, and so Lauren felt safe putting her goats out to pasture again. But now that she had money, her first investment might be one of those livestock guardian dogs.

The goats, standing at the gate, bleated when they saw her. Lauren checked her watch. Yes, she was fifteen minutes late. How did they know that? She snapped a lead onto Spritz's halter, let all the goats out and turned to shut the gate behind her. Suddenly Spritz raised her head, jerked the lead out of Lauren's hand, and galloped toward the barn, with the rest of the heard trailing behind her.

Lauren turned to see Patrick walking toward them. Spritz ran up to him and rubbed her head against his arm. He stopped to give her the attention she craved. Lauren smiled and shook her head. She couldn't really blame the goat. Who wouldn't be in love with Patrick O'Shea?

The other goats crowded around, and Patrick had a pat or word for each of them. Lauren shoved her way through the herd until she was close enough to collect a kiss of her own. "Did you get Bonnie settled?"

"Yes, she's in the kitchen with her leg propped up, going through her email. She's getting congratulations from people she hasn't heard from in years." Patrick took Spritz's lead and started the herd toward the barn.

"I guess you're flying to work tomorrow. Are you driving to Anchorage tonight or early in the morning?" She missed him already.

"Morning, I think. It gives me a little more time with you and Gran."

"I'll take good care of Bonnie while you're gone." Lauren opened the barn doors. "I know I said that last time, but—"

"And you did. And you will. I have no doubt about that." Patrick helped her herd the goats into their pen, but he seemed distracted.

"Is something wrong?" Lauren asked as she took the first goat to the milking stand.

"Not at all. I did want to mention that I called the farm you told me about that had the demonstration at the fair, and they have a six-month old Great Pyrenees that they say is showing good livestock guarding instincts they're willing to sell to you."

"That's great."

"Yeah, it's expensive, but if it can save your herd from bears and wolves, it will be well worth it."

"Our herd."

Patrick grinned. "I like the sound of that, partner." He moved Biscotti into position while Lauren put the milk to cool. Lauren loved that he knew which goat was second in line without asking.

"I'll start looking for equipment and get in touch with the state licensing board this week." Lauren gave a little shiver of happiness. "I can hardly believe this is really happening."

"I know what you mean. When you dug that nugget out of the tree—"

"I still sometimes wonder if I dreamed it."

"But you didn't. I was there."

"You were there." She smiled at him. "Every step of the way."

They finished the milking and got the goats settled for the night. Patrick pushed the barn door closed. Hand in hand, they walked to the farmhouse. When they arrived, Lauren started for the mudroom door. "We're running a little behind today. I'll go warm up the split pea soup you made yesterday."

"Lauren, wait just a minute. I wanted to talk to you about something."

"But Bonnie—"

"Is fine. I told her supper would be a little late today." He grasped Lauren's hand and led her to the front porch. "Here, have a seat."

"So, this is news I need to be sitting down for?" Lauren laughed to cover her nerves.

Patrick chuckled. "I would have liked to do this on a mountaintop, or at a waterfall or something, but since I can never get you too far away from those goats, this will have to do." He dropped to one knee and pulled something from his pocket. "Lauren, will you marry me?"

She gasped. "That's Bonnie's engagement ring!"

"Yes." A flicker of doubt passed over Patrick's face. "If you'd rather pick out one of your own—"

"It means the world to me that you trust me with a family heirloom." Tears gathered in her eyes. "This says that you believe I'll always be a part of your family."

"Well, of course I do."

"You say that with so much confidence." She leaned forward to touch his face. "Oh, Patrick. I never believed that love could really be forever. But now, I do. The way I feel about you, it's not an attraction that flashes hot and burns out. It's something deeper and stronger and..."

"Permanent?"

"Yes. Permanent."

He grinned. "Like now and forever?"

"Now and forever."

"So your answer is..."

"Yes! Yes, I'll marry you. I love you, Patrick." She let him slide the ring onto her finger and then she pulled him to his feet so that she could wrap her arms around his neck and kiss the man she loved. The man she'd love forever.

EPILOGUE

"BUT I LIKE the orange and black ones," Bea
complained when Rosemary rejected the
pansies she'd picked.

Lauren, listening in as she arranged slices
of her latest cheese samples on a tray, tried
to think of a tactful way of saying no to
Bea's offering. But Molly came to the rescue. "They would be fine if Lauren and Patrick were getting married on Halloween. But
they're not."

"Besides, you're not the bride." Alice
dropped a cluster of magenta flowers on the
table in front of Rosemary. "Lauren wants
pressed fireweed for her wedding invitations."

"They'll be just lovely," Linda said. "Especially with Molly's calligraphy."

Rosemary snipped the blossoms from the
stalk and arranged them on blotting paper.
"Fireweed is perfect. It captures summer in
Alaska."

And what a summer it had been. Lauren

thought back to that day when Bonnie had invited her to come and raise goats on her farm in Alaska. She'd almost been afraid to accept, afraid that taking a shortcut to her dream would lead only to disappointment. Instead, her move to Alaska had not only made her dream come true but had given her love and happiness far beyond anything she'd dared to dream.

Bonnie stepped onto the porch, carrying a tray of glasses and a pitcher of lemonade. Lauren hurried to take it from her. "Let me carry that. You're still a little shaky on stairs."

"Thanks." Bonnie relinquished the tray. "I've learned my lesson. From now on, no ladders, and I'll always hold on to the railing."

Lauren carried the tray to the table where Rosemary was making pressed flowers. Bonnie followed. She still limped a bit, but the physical therapist said that was to be expected after several weeks in a cast. If she continued to practice her exercises, she'd soon be good as new.

"Did you hear back yet on the apartment?" Molly asked Bonnie. There was one available at Easy Living, but when Bonnie had applied, she'd been told there were three people on the waiting list ahead of her.

Bonnie grinned. "I just got the word. They all turned it down. I'm in!"

"Woo-hoo!" The ladies crowded around her.

"Let's have a toast," Molly said, passing out glasses of lemonade. "To our newest resident. Bonnie O'Shea."

"To Bonnie." Everyone, including Lauren took a drink.

"And to the best friends in the world," Bonnie answered with a toast of her own. "Lots to do. Patrick might be sorry he was pushing me toward moving when he has to spend his two weeks off carting my furniture over."

"I'm sure he won't mind," Lauren said. "But I'll miss you. I hope this doesn't mean that I'll be seeing less of you all."

"We'll be at yoga every week," Molly said. "And we'll still come out for goat yoga in the summer. You are going to do that, even with the new tasting room and all, right?"

"Absolutely. It will be a big draw. Yoga and cheese tastings afterward, like you and the bakery."

"Maybe we should include something sweet. Cheesecake?" Bonnie suggested.

"I'd stay for cheesecake," Bea agreed.

"We can definitely look into that. Right

now, we're still working on permits to build the kitchen and tasting room, and equipment for the dairy. We can fine tune the menus later."

"Is the permitting process dragging?" Alice asked. "Because I know a few people."

"Any help you can give would be greatly appreciated," Lauren replied. "Here, let me show you the plans." But before she could lead Alice into the house, a bleat sounded at the gate. "Spritz! I thought I'd fixed every possible escape route in the new pasture. Excuse me, Alice. We can talk about this later."

Spritz seemed to be the only goat around, so she'd probably slipped out under a low spot none of the others had discovered yet. Before Lauren could get to her, a familiar jeep turned in and started down the driveway. She made a grab at Spritz, but the goat pirouetted away from her.

Patrick stopped and got out. Lauren ran to him, but the goat got there before her. Patrick laughed and stepped out of the way so he could pull Lauren into his arms. "Good to see you, Spritz, but let me kiss my fiancée first."

The goat let out a bleat, and then as the kiss went on, tossed her head and turned away in a huff. Bonnie and the other ladies laughed.

Patrick broke the kiss, but he kept an arm around Lauren's waist. "Okay, Spritz. Come here. Have you been good while I was gone?" He scratched under the goat's chin.

"Today is the first time she's escaped. She must have seen you coming up the road." Together, the three of them walked to the yard.

Patrick greeted everyone and hugged his grandmother. "Look at you, standing on your own two feet."

Bonnie twirled in a circle. "Isn't it grand?"

"What's all this?" Patrick waved toward the flowers and leaves scattered across the table and the flower press Rosemary was tightening.

"We're pressing fireweed for your wedding invitations," Rosemary answered.

"Will they be ready to mail in two weeks?" Patrick asked. "Because I'm not willing to delay the wedding based on flower drying time."

"They'll be ready," Rosemary assured him. "It sounds like you are, too."

"If it were up to me, we'd already be married. But Lauren has explained that dresses and cakes and such take time. And as far as I'm concerned, whatever Lauren wants, Lauren gets."

"Nice. You should have him put that in as part of your wedding vows," Alice told Lauren.

"I already have everything I could possibly want right here." Lauren put her arms around Patrick. Spritz forced her head in between them. Lauren laughed. "Yes, you're included in that statement."

"Lemonade, Patrick?" Molly offered. "We're celebrating Bonnie's move to the Easy Living Apartments."

"You got in? Good for you." Patrick raised the glass in Bonnie's direction.

Once the flowers were all pressed, Patrick moved the table and fetched the croquet set. The games went on for another couple of hours before Bonnie's friends all headed back to town. Bonnie called Patrick and Lauren into the kitchen. "I know you need to round up the goats for evening milking soon, but before you do, I want to give you something."

"What's that?" Patrick asked.

Bonnie reached behind the corner cabinet and scooted out a large slim paper-wrapped package with an envelope taped to the front.

She handed Lauren the envelope first. "It's for you and Patrick. An early wedding gift."

Lauren opened the envelope and pulled out a document. At first, she wasn't sure what she was seeing, but Patrick did. "A deed. You're deeding us the farm?"

"That's right. And the house, too. It would be yours anyway, once I'm gone, but why wait? It's time for you to build your own lives here, together."

"Wow, Gran, this is more than generous, but—"

"Don't worry about your sister. I'm giving Rowan my one-third share of the dairy just to keep things even. You and Lauren will still have two-thirds, so there shouldn't be any question about who's in charge."

"Wow. Thank you." Patrick hugged his grandmother.

"Oh, Bonnie. I don't know what to say." Lauren stared at her name on the deed until tears made it too blurry to read. "It's too much."

"Nonsense. You've brought life back to this farm. If anyone deserves it, it's you. That's why I had this made." She nudged the package in their direction.

With Patrick's help, Lauren tore the wrapping paper away to reveal a wooden sign painted in a scene much like the one she'd chosen for the soap labels, with a familiar mountain, a tree, and a goat that looked suspiciously like Spritz peering over a fence. Up above, in storybook script, the sign read Now and Forever Farm.

"Just like my story when I was a little girl," Lauren whispered.

"Molly painted it," Bonnie told her. "That's Pioneer Peak in the background."

Lauren placed a hand over her heart. "I love it."

"We'll hang this at the end of the driveway," Patrick said. "So your customers will know they're in the right place."

"Thank you, Bonnie. This is just amazing." Lauren hugged her.

"Dairy farming is hard work," Bonnie warned, "but you're one of the hardest workers I've ever seen. I know you'll be a big success."

"I can hardly believe it's happening. Our goat herd is growing. We're breaking ground soon for the kitchen and tasting room of the cheese-making operation." Lauren turned to smile up at Patrick. "We're going to get married and live here together and our children will grow up here, on the farm. It is like a fairy tale."

"If anyone deserves a happy ending, it's you." He leaned the sign against the wall and they both stepped back several feet to admire it. "Beautiful." Patrick pulled Lauren close and she slid her arms around his waist.

"I love you, Lauren," Patrick whispered as he brushed a quick kiss across her lips. "Now and forever."

* * * * *

For more great romances set in Alaska
from Beth Carpenter,
visit www.Harlequin.com today!

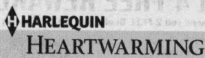

ReaderService.com has a new look!

We have refreshed our website and
we want to share our new look with you.
Head over to ReaderService.com
and check it out!

On ReaderService.com, you can:

- Try 2 free books from any series
- Access risk-free special offers
- View your account history & manage payments
- Browse the latest Bonus Bucks catalog

Don't miss out!

If you want to stay up-to-date on the latest at the Reader Service and enjoy more Harlequin content, make sure you've signed up for our monthly News & Notes email newsletter. Sign up online at ReaderService.com.